THE HORSEPOWER OF THE HOLIDAY

Shiloh Ridge Ranch in Three Rivers, Book 2

LIZ ISAACSON

AEJ
CREATIVE WORKS

ISBN-13: 978-1-953506-24-5

The Glover Family

Welcome to Shiloh Ridge Ranch! The Glover family is BIG, and sometimes it can be hard to keep track of everyone.

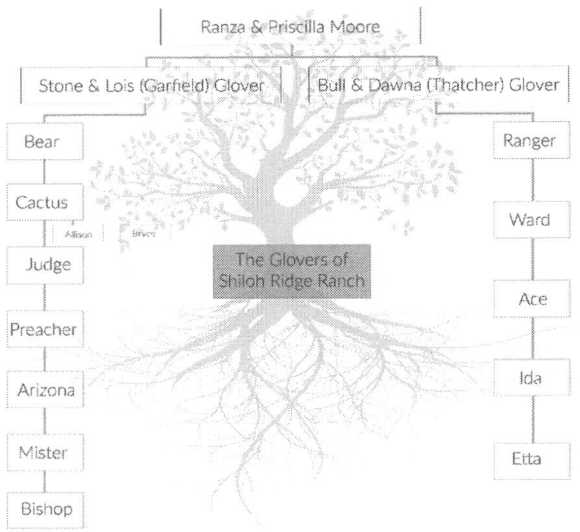

THERE IS A MORE DETAILED GRAPHIC, ON MY website. (But it has spoilers! I made it as the family started to get really big, which happens fairly quickly, actually. It has all the couples (some you won't see for many more books), as well as a lot of the children they have or will have, through about Book 6. It might be easier for you to visualize, though.)

HERE'S HOW THINGS ARE RIGHT NOW:

Lois & Stone (deceased) Glover, 7 children, in age-order:

1. Bear (Sammy, wife / Lincoln, step-son)
2. Cactus (Allison, ex-wife / Bryce, son (deceased))
3. Judge

4. Preacher
5. Arizona
6. Mister
7. Bishop

Dawna & Bull (deceased) Glover, 5 children, in age-order:

1. Ranger
2. Ward
3. Ace
4. Etta
5. Ida

Bull and Stone Glover were brothers, so their children are cousins. Ranger and Bear, for example, are cousins, and each the oldest sibling in their families.

The Glovers know and interact with the Walkers of Seven Sons Ranch. There's a lot of them too! Here's a little cheat sheet for you for the Walkers.

Momma & Daddy: Penny and Gideon Walker

1. Rhett & Evelyn Walker
Son: Conrad
Triplets: Austin, Elaine, and Easton

2. Jeremiah & Whitney Walker
Son: Jonah Jeremiah (JJ)
Daughter: Clara Jean
Son: Jason

3. Liam & Callie Walker
Daughter: Denise
Daughter: Ginger

4. Tripp & Ivory Walker
Son: Oliver
Son: Isaac

5. Wyatt & Marcy Walker
Son: Warren
Son: Cole

Son: Harrison

6. Skyler & Mallery Walker
   Daughter: Camila

7. Micah & Simone Walker
   Son: Travis (Trap)

Chapter One

"Just come on," Ward said, finishing up the dishes. "It'll be fun. It's Winston Lunt, and he's funny."

"Really funny," Ace added, though he didn't look up from his phone.

Ranger Glover looked back and forth between his two brothers, neither of them looking at him. He had enjoyed the comedy of Winston Lunt in the past; he just didn't feel like leaving the house.

He supposed he'd already left the house, as he currently sat at the table in the ranch house down the road from the homestead, where he lived with two of his cousins.

"And he'll only be in town this weekend?" Ranger asked.

"Yes," Ward said. "I *need* to go, Range. Suck it up and get your smile ready." He didn't look over his shoulder this time, and Ranger knew why.

Victoria Smith. The woman had broken up with Ward six days ago, and he'd been moping around the ranch since.

Ranger wasn't sure why. Ward had only been dating her for a couple of months. Maybe only six weeks. No matter what, it wasn't very long, and he honestly hadn't seemed that interested in her.

Ever since Bear had started dating Sammy—and now they were engaged—it was like all the Glovers realized there was a big world out there, with people to find and love.

Ranger knew that, of course. He'd gone out with a few women in the past, but no one really special in a while. Even if he did go to the new comedy club in town, he knew he wouldn't meet anyone who interested him nearly as much as Oakley Hatch did.

And you won't run into her, he told himself. *Or maybe you will.*

Oakley went out a lot. With a lot of different men. At the same time.

She'd wanted to start a relationship with Ranger a month or two ago, but he'd told her no. He still kicked himself for that at least once a day. And at least once a day, he told himself he'd done the right thing. He wasn't going to share his girlfriend with another cowboy. The idea that anyone would do that was ludicrous, in his opinion.

"Fine," he said. "I could use a laugh."

"Yes, you could," Ace said dryly.

"What is that supposed to mean?" Ranger asked, slicing a look at his youngest brother.

"It means you've been pining over that stock car racer," Ace said.

"First off," Ranger said. "I have not been *pining*. And

secondly, she drove in the Formula One circuit, not NASCAR. Two different things, Ace."

"Just the fact that you know that is disturbing," he said with a grin, finally looking up from his phone.

"It's not disturbing," Ward said. "He likes her, Ace. Of course he's going to know things about her."

"Yeah," Ranger said. "Like the three men she's dating right now." He wanted to go back to the east wing at the homestead, change into his gym shorts and a T-shirt, and put something on TV.

Not car racing.

Anything but car racing.

"Are we ready?" Ward asked, joining them at the table. "I can drive, and I'll even buy the first round of sodas."

"You've got a deal," Ace said, standing.

Ranger got to his feet too, and he said nothing as he followed his brothers through the house to the front door. Ward led the way, and Ranger did love and respect his brother. They worked together closely on the ranch finances, and there was nothing better than an afternoon in his office with Ward.

The man loved chocolate licorice—something Ranger loved too—and they'd talk about their dad while they had a little sugar binge before they got down to the decimals and digits.

Ward chatted the whole way to town, and Ranger wondered how he did that. How did he have so much to say, about seemingly everything? Ranger would never know, but he participated enough to keep Ward talking.

He pulled up to a brick building that had seen better

days. Rather, the building had been recently renovated to look old on purpose. The historical society of Three Rivers had preserved the bricks, simply re-cementing them in place. Any new bricks had been purposely made in the same tones and colors, and made to look old so they matched the original ones.

The comedy club was new in town, as were several other shops, restaurants, and venues. Three Rivers had been enjoying a population boom in recent years, and last Ranger had heard, they'd topped twenty-five thousand people over the summer.

He thought that was probably because of tourists, who did come to the quaint Texas town in the Panhandle for great food, good hiking, and plenty of hunting.

Ranger liked to eat, and that was about it.

"There's going to be food here, right?" he asked, getting out and eyeing the entrance. It teemed with people, and the air had a good vibe in it. Ranger started to relax, and it was easier to get through the crowd and inside the club than he'd anticipated.

It was dark inside, with only low lights on every table. Ward stepped up to the bar and ordered sodas for the three of them, and he showed their tickets to a woman who took them to a table on the left side of the stage.

Ranger nodded to a few men he knew, but he stuck close to his brothers. They didn't get to spend a ton of time with just each other, as they all worked the generational family ranch with six of their male cousins.

Ward took a sip of his soda and made a face. "Too much syrup."

"You always forget to say light," Ranger said. He didn't understand syrup in soda anyway. He honestly hardly ever drank the stuff, and he eyed his tall glass of fizzy liquid like it would rot his insides.

Since his embarrassing discussion with Oakley about her dating habits, he'd taken up weight lifting in a more aggressive fashion. He had to have something to occupy his mind, and the upcoming birthing season wasn't enough.

"Welcome, ladies and gentlemen," a man said into the mic, the sound nearly deafening. "If you'll take your seats, we're ready to start the show!"

Most of the crowd cheered and clapped, and Ranger could do the latter easily. He did, glad when the announcer kept talking. "We have a very special guest with us tonight. Straight from the streets of New York, we've got a home-grown, tried-and-true Texan ready to take the stage. Everyone welcome home Winston Lunt!"

The people went nuts, and Ranger decided to really get into the spirit of things, and he whistled through his teeth. Ward grinned at him, but Ace shot him a glare.

"What?" Ranger asked, still clapping. "I'm not the only one who whistled."

"You're always calling too much attention to yourself."

Ranger stared at Ace, but he turned back to the stage. What he'd just said couldn't be further from the truth. Ranger didn't do anything, ever, to call attention to himself.

Winston Lunt came out onto the stage wearing an enormous cowboy hat. He looked ridiculous, and several people were twittering with giggles already.

"Howdy, folks," he said, the words barely comprehensible. "It's good to be back in Texas. Can I get the lights up for a moment?"

The house lights came up, and he held up one hand above his eyes, searching, scanning, scouring. "Nope. I don't see a single man without a cowboy hat."

More laughter.

"Oh, there's one." Winston pointed to a table about halfway back. "Sir, can you stand up and explain yourself? Yes...you...right there...I can *see* you." He made an exaggerated huffing sound. "In the pink shirt.... Yes, you. Stand up so we can—oh."

Ranger grinned from ear to ear, because Winston had not called on a man. But a woman.

"Well, the pink shirt should've given it away, right?" Winston looked like he might throw up, and he paced to the other side of the stage. "Sorry, sir. I mean, ma'am." He placed one flat palm against his forehead, which knocked his cowboy hat off his head.

He was funny, from his jokes to his facial expressions, to his physical stunt humor. Ranger watched as the woman in the pink shirt sat down, and his eyes caught on another woman a table over from her.

His breath caught in his lungs, hooked there by sudden ice. Oakley. She sat with a man on her right and another on her left. Surely she wasn't out with two men at the same time.

Ranger could barely focus after that, and he kept watching her table, eventually learning that the woman across from Oakley was with the guy on her right. Her boyfriend—or more likely, the man she happened to be out with that night—got up and left about halfway through the set, and Ranger never did see him come back.

The show ended, and he stood and cheered along with everyone else. If he stayed over here for a few minutes, pretending to finish his drink and clean up, perhaps Oakley would leave the club first.

He secretly rejoiced when Ace knocked his drink and spilled it, as he took a few minutes to find some napkins and mop up the dark cola. By then, the club was clearing out nicely, and Ranger thought there might be a chance he could get out of there without encountering Oakley. He'd lost track of her since the end of the show, and he refused to look around and try to find her.

"Can you take these to the trash?" Ace asked, shoving the wet napkins into Ranger's hands.

"Gross, no," Ranger said, dropping them on the table.

"It's Haven," he hissed. "Please, help me. Hey, Haven." The last two words were spoken in a much louder voice with plenty of swagger.

"Ace," she said, and she leaned her hip into one of the chairs at their table, her smile pretty and genuine.

Ranger wanted to grumble and roll his eyes. Instead, he picked up the mess of napkins and turned to go throw them away. He suddenly wanted to get out of there.

The trash can sat over by the bathrooms, and he tossed in the wet and sticky napkins before looking at his hands. One glance over his shoulder told him Ace wasn't ready to leave yet. Ranger started walking again, intending to go into the men's room and clean up.

He ran right into a solid body.

He swung his attention forward, automatically reaching out to steady whomever he'd hit. He regretted it the moment his sticky hands touched their arms.

"Sorry," he said, looking down at the woman there.

She had dark trails of mascara running down her face, her tears creating the mess of makeup on her face. It still wasn't hard to tell it was Oakley Hatch.

"Oakley," he said, his heart beating in a strange, syncopated way. "What's wrong?" He glanced over her shoulder to the empty area behind her. "Are you okay?"

Stupid question, he thought as she sniffled.

Her dark eyes flashed with recognition and then what looked dangerously like anger. "Do I look okay to you, Ranger?"

"No," he said quietly. "Sorry. What can I do to help?"

She reached up and wiped her fingers under her eyes, but that honestly didn't do much to help. In fact, it only made the makeup smear further.

He pulled his hands away from her upper arms, both of them sticking for a frightening second before releasing. "Sorry," he said again. "I was carrying these sticky napkins, and I...you're sticky now too."

"Doesn't matter," she said, still glaring up at him. "I'm going to go home and shower this horrific night right down the drain."

"You didn't like the show?" Ranger asked, falling back a step. He didn't dare touch anything in case he couldn't let go of it.

"No," she said. "I didn't like the show." She stepped

around him, obviously headed for the exit. Before she'd taken three steps, she turned back to him. Gone was the anger and frustration in her expression. Now, she wore anxiety tinged with hope. "Could you maybe give me a ride home?"

Ranger's eyebrows went up. "You don't have a ride?"

Oakley's eyes shot fire toward him, but he wasn't sure if it was the good, desirable kind he wanted to get burned by, or the bad, dangerous kind he should run from.

He found himself taking a step forward not back. "I can take you," he said, though Ward had driven. "If you'll tell me the story of why you don't have a ride home."

She looked him up and down, some of her normal confidence returning. "Fine," she said. "I can live with that. I can't live with your sticky hands near me, so you better wash up first."

"Yes, ma'am," Ranger said quietly, tipping his hat and walking away. In the men's room, he texted Ward that they needed to give someone a ride. His brother wanted to know who, but Ranger stuck his hands under the water and started washing so he wouldn't have to answer.

He looked at himself in the mirror, his sky blue eyes also filled with anxiety and hope. "You're in trouble, cowboy," he whispered to his reflection. "You should just drop her off and go home."

No one had said that wasn't the plan, but Ranger was actually hoping this was the second—or was it the third?—chance with Oakley that he'd been praying for.

He closed his eyes so he wasn't looking into his own

eyes, and said, "Dear Lord, if it be Thy will, let this be the second chance I've been praying for."

Then he left the men's room, half expecting Oakley to be gone. She wasn't, but she stood right where he'd left her. Their eyes met, and Ranger couldn't have called down fire from heaven hotter than the current running between him and Oakley.

"Ready?" he asked, and she nodded. He faced the rest of the club, easily finding Ward and Ace. "Okay," he said, putting his hand on the small of her back like it was a natural place for him to touch. It actually felt natural, and Ranger didn't know what that meant.

"I'm with my brothers. Let's go."

Chapter Two

Oakley Hatch could *not* believe her luck. She wasn't sure if it was bad or good that she'd run into Ranger Glover, of all men.

"Oakley," he said in that smooth, rich, bass voice of his. "Have you met my brothers? Ward's next in line behind me. And Ace is the youngest." He indicated each man as he spoke their names.

Ward she knew, as he'd come to the dealership in the past. Ace she didn't, but she managed to shake both of their hands, shreds of her dignity flaking off with every passing moment someone looked at her.

She'd known she had makeup all down her face, because she'd ducked into the ladies' room while Ranger had gone into the men's. She'd cleaned up the best she could, but the evidence of crying and distress still lingered on her face.

"We're just takin' her home?" Ward asked.

"Yes," Ranger said, but Oakley had the distinct impression their conversation was much longer than what had been spoken.

"All right," Ward said. "Ace got Haven's new number, so he's on cloud nine."

Oakley wasn't sure what that meant, and she wanted to trail in the wake of these three cowboy brothers. Maybe she could call a cab, though intellectually, she knew she couldn't. It was too late for the cab service to be running, and Three Rivers wasn't large enough for a sophisticated bus system either. Everyone drove around town, and Oakley considered downloading an app for one of those ride services.

One look at Ranger's strong profile, that delicious jaw, and that oh-so-sexy cowboy hat, and she wouldn't allow anyone else to take her home.

Ward had a big, king-cab truck, and Ranger held the door for her as he helped her into the truck. He went around to the other side and sat on the long bench seat in the back with her. Up front, Ward and Ace started talking about the show that night, but Ranger didn't join in.

About halfway to her house, Ward said, "I don't know where I'm going."

"Oh, right," she said, leaning forward to point. "Up here, turn left. I'm over on Washington Terrace." She sat back, glancing at Ranger. He held up his phone, and she caught the glint of the light in his eyes.

She dug in her purse for her phone and checked her texts, the brightness of the screen burning her eyes. She quickly turned it down and tapped on his name.

Do you have a car I could borrow to get back to the ranch tonight? I'd like to talk to you for a few minutes, and I don't want my brothers to have to wait. We get up early on the ranch, no matter what day of the week it is.

Oakley's pulse pounded in her chest, the reverberations moving up her throat and through the bigger veins in her neck. He'd like to talk to her? About what?

After his rejection a month ago, she'd tried texting him a few times, and he'd never responded. Her old, unanswered texts sat right above his new one, in fact. Her thumb hovered over her keyboard as she contemplated what to do.

Finally, she tapped out *yes* and sent the text. She stuck her phone under her leg and looked out her window. She didn't know what he wanted to talk about, but Oakley sure did like the sound of his voice, and she needed to end this night on a high note.

She continued to direct Ward to her house, and he finally pulled into the driveway of the one that sat at the back of the cul-de-sac. The house hulked in the night, as it was ten times too big for a single person who lived alone. Most men she went out with commented on it, and the one real estate agent she'd been to dinner with had actually looked up how much she'd bought it for, then texted her obnoxious questions about her financial situation.

Needless to say, that relationship had lasted for one dinner and one dinner only.

"Thank you," she said as she opened her own door and got out of the truck. She heard Ranger say something in a low voice, but she couldn't quite catch the words. A conversation ensued, and she closed the door and started toward the garage. The motion-sensor lights kicked on, flooding the driveway with light.

She hadn't even reached the garage yet to tap in the code to lift the door when Ranger got out of the truck. Oakley kept her back to him and continued walking. She started pressing in the code as Ward backed out of her driveway.

The door rumbled up as the truck rumbled off, and Oakley finally turned and looked at Ranger Glover. "What did you want to talk about?"

"Why you didn't have a ride home."

The man knew how to go right for the jugular, that was for sure. He tucked his hands in his jacket pockets, and it should've been illegal to sell him that leather jacket. He'd cause traffic accidents if he walked down the street looking so good, with broad shoulders and tight, strong muscles everywhere she looked.

"Do you want to come in?" she asked. "It's kind of a long story, and I'm going to need caffeine if I'm to tell it."

"Coffee sounds great," he said, a small smile riding on his mouth.

"Great," she said. "You can make it then. I'm terrible at it, and the last thing I need to do is poison you tonight." She stepped into the garage as he chuckled. Oakley paused, because his light laughter was one of the most magical sounds she'd ever heard. At that moment, she realized her crush on this man was wide and deep, and Oakley wasn't even sure how it had happened.

She managed to reach the entrance to the house at the

back of the garage, and he reached past her to hold the door while she went in. She hadn't been lying about the coffee, and if he asked how she found the time to keep her house so clean after a long day at the dealership, six days a week, she'd have to admit to having a cleaning service.

Nothing wrong with that, she told herself as she stepped into the mudroom and hung up her jacket. He copied her, and she finally eased out of the way when he tucked those hands back into his pockets.

He went first down the hall and into the kitchen, which was more of a cave than a comfortable place to be. Sure, it had high-end appliances—a fridge she could see into without even opening the door—and plenty of upgrades in the quartz countertops, the cherry-wood cabinets, and the matching, coordinating art on the walls.

Ranger started opening cabinets, and it only took him three tries to find the coffee. Oakley sighed and retreated to the couch. He finished getting the coffee started and came to sit with her in the living room off the kitchen.

This room had no TV, and she wanted to keep it that way. She liked the quiet sometimes, as the dealership was never truly quiet. The race track hadn't been either. Oakley craved silence, but one look at Ranger, and she started spilling her guts.

"I was at the club with Dave Pratchett," she said. "He picked me up, but he had to work late, so we didn't get dinner." Her stomach growled as if it just now remembered she hadn't eaten since lunch. "Only a few minutes into the show, he got a text and said he had to go make a phone call." Oakley shrugged, though her shoulders barely moved against the cushy couch. "I get it. I run a business too."

Ranger said nothing, but he also didn't look away from her. Oakley didn't know what to do with the silent, brooding type. Her nerves screamed at her, and she pressed her fingertips together.

"He left, and he never came back. It was over an hour, and I decided to call him." She shook her head. "He didn't answer, but not ten seconds later, I got a text back from him. It wasn't the one I wanted."

"What did he say?"

"He said I was 'fun and all,' but that he didn't think we should see each other anymore." Desperation and tears built up inside her again, and Oakley determined not to hold them in as long as she had last time.

"That was that?" Ranger asked. "He didn't come back to take you home?"

She shook her head. "I texted that I didn't want to break up and could we please talk about it?" With some of her last remaining energy, she leaned forward and handed Ranger her phone. "He sent me that."

Ranger took the phone, a quizzical look in his eye. He swiped on her phone, and she knew the moment he saw what she'd seen. His eyes rounded, and he looked up.

Oakley's stomach had dropped out of her body, and she'd been so angry that tears had pressed into her eyes. So angry and so betrayed.

Dave had sent her a picture of him with another woman. He'd said he'd left the club, because he wanted to go out with Terelyn and not her.

Oakley had been broken up with before—heck, the man still holding her phone had ended things between them before they'd even really gotten started. But to see Dave with another woman and know that he'd left her sitting in the comedy club all alone, with no ride home, it was as if a dam had broken.

She'd felt betrayed and lonely at the same time.

She'd realized what she'd been asking the men she'd been out with that year to do. Share her. Allow her to go out with whoever she wanted, their feelings notwithstanding.

"So I needed a ride home," she said, taking back her phone.

He studied the floor for a moment and then met her eyes. "Who are you seeing now?" he asked.

"No one, anymore," she said. "I was...." She cleared her throat. "I did what you suggested, Ranger. I decided to try dating one man at a time."

If he was surprised, he didn't show it. "And?"

"And...." How much did she lay on the line? How brave could she be? How forthcoming and straight-forward without coming across as too confident or intimidating? "And honestly?"

"I would prefer honesty, yes," he said, focusing back on the floor again.

"I only want to go out with you," she said. "But you aren't asking. I texted you a few times, and you didn't respond. I figured I might as well start somewhere."

"Well, Dave Pratchett was a bad choice," Ranger said, a chuckle coming from his mouth.

Oakley scoffed as the tension in the room broke up a little. "Yeah, no joke."

Several seconds passed where the only thing that happened was the scent of freshly brewed coffee filling the air. Ranger finally lifted his head and met her gaze again, head-on. Strong. If anyone was exuding confidence and making her feel intimidated, it was him.

She sure did like that about him.

"Oakley?" he asked. "Would you like to go to dinner with me?"

Oakley blinked as her pulse skyrocketed. "Yes," she managed to say. "Yes, I would."

"Tomorrow night?" he asked.

"Sure," she said.

He nodded and stood up. "Okay, great. I know where you live now, and I'll have my brother follow me down in my truck so I can return your car." He moved into the kitchen as easily as if he'd lived in this house his whole life. Oakley twisted as she watched him fix himself a cup of coffee.

He took one sip and called back to her, "Do you want some coffee, Oakley?"

"Yes, please," she said. Was he really going to stay for coffee? What else did he want to talk about?

He brought her a purple mug, a bowl of sugar, and the carton of cream. "I don't know what you like," he said.

"Just sugar," she said, picking up the spoon and adding three healthy teaspoons of the sweet stuff to her coffee. She took a sip and groaned. "I don't know how you do this. It's so much better than how I make it."

He simply smiled, and when he took a seat this time, it was on the couch next to her. He lifted his arm, and she curled into his side, the motions so natural for both of them, Oakley felt like they'd sat together on the couch like this countless times before.

Ranger took another sip of his coffee and said, "Tell me why you came to Three Rivers."

"Okay," she said, drawing in a deep breath. "If you must know, it was on this dating app I was using in Florida. That's where I lived when I trained for the racecar stuff."

"Mm."

"Anyway, the dating app had a Top Ten Cities to Fall in Love in Texas list, and Three Rivers was on it."

"What number?" he asked.

"Two," she said.

"What was number one?"

"Austin," she said. "But I dislike Austin, so I packed up and I came north."

Ranger leaned forward and put his mug on the coffee table in front of him. "You've been here a couple of years. Do you still think Three Rivers is one of the best places to fall in love?"

"Oh, it's so overrated," she said, her voice snappy but with an edge too. "I've been out with dozens of men, and I haven't found a single one to love."

"Maybe you haven't been out with the right one," he said quietly.

"Obviously." She needed to keep this conversation light and flirty. Otherwise, she might fall too fast for him, and she knew what happened with fast falls. They hurt people. Hearts got broken and unkind words got exchanged.

After another several seconds of peaceful silence, Ranger groaned as he got to his feet. "You done?" He reached for her coffee cup, and she let him take it though she'd only had a few swallows.

"Let me get you the keys to my truck," she said, getting up and following him into the kitchen. She pulled out a drawer and handed him a fob. "It's easy. Push on the gas." She grinned at him, but the spark in his eyes was borne from something besides playful banter and innocent flirting.

"Well, that's what I'm hopin' to do tomorrow night," he said. "See you then." He bent down and swept his lips across her forehead, put the truck keys in his pocket, and walked out of her house.

She stood in the kitchen for several long seconds, wondering if she ever had to wash her forehead again. She didn't see why she should. That part of her body didn't get very dirty....

It amazed her that she'd gone from a sobbing mess in the bathroom to having the man of her dreams—who'd already rejected her once—ask her to dinner. A squeal started in her stomach, but Oakley silenced it.

"Don't freak out," she said to herself. "This is the first step, and it's going to take a lot to keep and hold the interest of a man like Ranger." She continued to coach herself as she went down the hallway to her master suite.

"Get it together. You can do this."

Ranger was a man among men, and Oakley knew she'd

need her every wit, her every charm, and her every ounce of patience to win him over.

Oh, and the cutest dress for tomorrow night's date with the dreamy cowboy she'd been crushing on for months now.

She faced her closet, her determination the strongest it had ever been. "The very cutest dress."

Chapter Three

Ranger yawned as he logged onto the backend of the app he'd spent the better part of the last three years building. He'd been up far too long at Oakley's, and it had taken forty minutes to get back to the ranch.

Even then, he'd been too keyed up to go straight to sleep. He'd gone over and over the things Oakley had said, and he needed somewhere amazing to take her to dinner that night.

Lucky for him, he had all the data he needed right at his fingertips.

The site loaded, and he leaned forward, suddenly awake. "What in the world?"

The spike on the bar graph was unbelievable. Ranger glanced at the metrics on the side, his mouth dropping open. "Bishop," he said in the next moment. "Ward."

He jumped up from his desk, knowing neither of them

would have heard him. Ward didn't even live in this house, and Bishop often got up before everyone else. He'd be moving downstairs so Bear could live in the suite upstairs once he and Sammy got married.

Ranger had not told Bear about Two Cents, the recommendation app he'd built for Three Rivers. Everything from the best restaurants for a first date to the best activities to do in the summer, for Thanksgiving, and the month of April.

He'd collected data upon data through surveys and polls, all of which were done anonymously and posted on the town website. Besides Bishop and Ward, only Frank Russo knew about the recommendation app that had gotten over five thousand downloads literally overnight.

"Bishop," Ranger called as he went thundering down the stairs, his phone gripped in his hand. "Bishop?" He hurried through the foyer, where the angel tree stood, and into the kitchen. Bear sat at the table, a cup of coffee in front of him. His eyes were glued to his phone, and he didn't even look up as Ranger entered.

"Is Bishop around?"

"Haven't seen him," Bear said, his voice almost a monotone.

"Texting Sammy?" Ranger asked, going to the kitchen window and looking outside. He quickly pulled out his phone and called Bishop, who answered after the second ring.

"What's up, Range?"

"Five thousand downloads," Ranger said. "Fifty-two hundred actually, and counting."

"What are you talkin' about?" Bishop asked.

Ranger turned around, but Bear didn't even know he was there. Still, Ranger left the kitchen before speaking again. "Of Two Cents, Bishop. Overnight. People are downloading it."

"You're kidding."

"I'm not. I just looked at it." He took the steps two at a time back to his office. "Why do you think they're downloading it?"

"Someone must've blown it up," Bishop said. "Have you checked social media?"

"Not yet." Ranger jogged back to his desk and sat down. His heartbeat sprinted in his chest, and he quickly opened another tab and navigated to his social media.

Click, click, click.

Ranger sucked in a breath. "Someone put it on the Three Rivers community page," he said, his voice awed. "It has over a thousand comments, and three thousand likes."

"Who?" Bishop asked. "Who posted it?"

"Oh, well, this makes perfect sense now," Ranger said, frowning at the screen. "If he knew who owned the app, Kyle Morris wouldn't have given it such a high recommendation."

"I'm coming in."

"No," Ranger said, looking up from his computer. "If you come in, Bear will think something is up. I don't want him to know."

"Why not?" Bishop asked, a familiar question for Ranger. He didn't want anyone to know about the app, because who was he to tell people what to do for their first dates? He hadn't been on a good one in years.

Ward had told him the collective voice of the men and women who'd answered his poll were the ones making the recommendations. He'd just compiled all of their opinions into one convenient place for people to access it.

"I just don't," Ranger said. "Remember when Bear bought that whole food truck after the tornadoes? He hated that publicity. I'd hate this."

"Okay," Bishop said. "I just think you should take credit for it."

"I do take credit for it," Ranger said. "I don't need my name known for that to happen." His identity hid behind a company name, and that was fine with him.

"Read me some of the comments," Bishop said.

Ranger blinked, trying to wrap his head around this new development. He leaned toward the computer screen. "Guess I know where my boyfriend is taking me tonight for a romantic date."

"That would be Mulligan's," Bishop said. "Right?"

"It's still in first place," Ranger said. "Oh, wow."

"What?"

"Mulligan's commented. They said, honored to be number one for the most romantic date in Three Rivers." He clicked on their name, which took him to their page. "They posted it on their page and told people to download the app to know all the hottest spots to visit when in Three Rivers, Texas."

He leaned away from the computer, already overwhelmed. "I can't believe this."

"The city has it on their website too," Bishop said, his voice farther away than before. He must've put Ranger on speaker so he could use the Internet on his phone. "That's where Kyle got it. He says so in some of the responses to comments."

"I didn't think Frank was going to put it up."

"He obviously did."

"Obviously." Ranger ran his hand through his hair. "This is incredible." He clicked back over to the app dashboard and yelped.

"What?" Bishop asked. "I really could come in. Bear wouldn't even know. I'd just run straight up to my room."

"We're up to eighty-six hundred downloads."

Bishop whistled, and Ranger couldn't agree more. Three thousand downloads in ten minutes?

The town of Three Rivers had been growing in the past few years—maybe a decade—and their population had just hit twenty-five thousand. But with the number of children in town, as well as the older generation who didn't use apps like this, Ranger had set a goal for ten thousand downloads in the first year.

He didn't even know when Frank had put the app on the website, and Ranger needed to call him and find out. "I'm gonna call Frank."

"Keep me posted."

Ranger said he would, and he quickly put out a call to Frank. The man didn't answer, so Ranger texted him. *When did you put Two Cents on the city website?*

In a meeting, came back almost instantly. *Call you after*.

Then Frank said, *Yesterday morning. Why?*

It's at almost ten thousand downloads this morning, Ranger sent him. Thirty seconds later, his phone rang. Frank's name sat on the screen.

"Hey," Ranger said.

"Almost ten thousand in one day?"

"Yes," Ranger said, refreshing the dashboard again. "This is insane. Someone posted it on the community page, and the individual restaurants and businesses are spreading the word on their social media too."

He went back to the original post and saw Wilde & Organic—best organic grocery store in Three Rivers—had shared the app on their page. Satisfaction filled him every time he saw the logo he and Ward had worked on and then hired out so it would be as professional as possible.

Two pennies sat on a blue and white checkered background, with the name of the app across it all. Two Cents.

The description of the app told everyone exactly what they were getting. *A cowboy's two cents for the best places to visit, the best activities, and the best restaurants in Three Rivers, Texas. Wow your next date with the very best in the Texas Panhandle.*

He'd originally thought he'd market it to men as a way they could get good recommendations to plan excellent dates for the women they liked. The concept had expanded past that now, and Ranger should probably update the description. It wasn't about wowing his next date. It was about recommending—giving his two cents—all of the things Three Rivers had to offer, from grocery stores to where to find the freshest chocolate licorice.

That honor belonged to Theurer's Corner Store, and Ranger's mouth watered for the stuff.

"This is great," Frank said.

"I didn't know it was going up."

"I thought it was working well," Frank said. "You said if it was working well, to put it up."

"Yeah," Ranger said. "Well, thank you, Frank. I better go. Sorry to pull you from your meeting."

"Please," he said. "You did me a favor."

Ranger laughed with his friend, hung up, and continued to click around on social media, finding all the businesses who'd linked to and recommended his app.

Our two cents? the botanical gardens had posted. *Get the app Two Cents to experience the best of Three Rivers.*

People were listening too. The buzz around Two Cents filled Ranger with a sense of life he'd been missing the past few years.

"Holy cow," he whispered when he saw Mack's Motor Sports had posted about it too. *Number one place to buy your next car or truck!* they boasted on their social media page. He clicked on the website link, though he wasn't going to shop for the two trucks he needed via their site.

The Two Cents logo sat at the top of their screen, and they encouraged people in Three Rivers and the surrounding towns to download it.

"I can't believe this," he said. His phone buzzed, and he glanced at it. Oakley's name sat there, and he swiped to get to the text. *Have you heard of that new app? Two Cents. It has great suggestions for restaurants.*

Ranger almost scoffed at the message. He quickly tapped out a response, because if he didn't get dressed and get downstairs, Bear would start to bellow about where he was and what he was doing.

Pretty sure Mulligan's is going to be full for a while.

Right?

We could try Dutch Baby. That's number two.

Not a fan of eggs, Oakley sent back, and Ranger just stared at the text.

Really? he asked. *Other things I should know you're not a fan of? Allergies?*

Nothing else, she said. *Number three is Pizza Pipeline, and I gotta say, that doesn't seem that romantic.*

Ranger shook his head, surprised that someone who went out as much as Oakley didn't know about the shaded gardens behind the restaurant. The manager threaded lights through the trees, and she kept the tables back there clean.

You've got to tap on the name, he said. *It gives you more info.*

Has someone been using this app? she asked, sending a winking smiley face with it.

"You could say that," Ranger muttered to himself.

"Ranger?" Bear called, and Ranger turned off the monitor so he'd stop looking at it.

"Coming," he called. He dashed into his bedroom and switched his gym shorts for a pair of jeans. He grabbed the nearest shirt and pulled it over his head. He took his socks downstairs, as they kept their boots by the back door to avoid tracking various substances through the house.

"Hey," he said breathlessly as he entered the kitchen. "Sorry. I was out late last night."

"Yeah, how was the comedy club?"

"Great," Ranger said, pouring coffee into a thermos he'd take with him. "I ran into Oakley afterward, and we went back to her place."

Bear came toward him quickly. "I'm sorry. What did you say?"

"She was a sobbing mess," Ranger said, telling the rest of the story quickly. "We're going to dinner tonight."

"You should get this new app I just heard about," Bear said. "Two Cents. It recommends the best of the best in Three Rivers, including things like where to buy your date the best flowers and what not to do on the first date."

Ranger snorted. "What does that one say?"

Bear swiped and read aloud. "Number one: Don't talk about marriage."

"Given," Ranger said.

"Two: Don't go on and on about superhero movies."

"I gotta say, these seem like common sense things." He looked at Bear and stirred sugar into his thermos.

"A little," Bear said. "Three: If you find yourself starting sentences with 'My last girlfriend,' stop." He looked at Ranger. "I'm pretty sure I've done that."

Ranger burst out laughing, glad when Bear did too. Since he'd started dating Sammy, he'd really turned into a gummy bear like Zona had said. "I've probably done everything on that list," Ranger said. "Wait. That would require me to go on first dates, which I don't do." He grinned as he sipped his coffee.

"You're going tonight," Bear said. "Did she stop dating multiple people?"

"Yes," Ranger said. He'd finally talked to Ward and Bear a couple of days ago and told them everything that had happened at the dealership with Oakley.

"I already called Mulligan's," Bear said. "They're full."

"Yeah?" he asked as if he didn't know. "Is that in your app?"

"Yep."

"I was just going to take her for pizza. Something easy. Casual."

"That's actually number three, so you'll probably be good."

Ranger just nodded, using all of his energy to keep his smile to himself. The coffee had started to get his energy buzzing, and he set the thermos in the sink. "Ready?"

Bear pocketed his phone. "Yes. Let's get these fields put to sleep once and for all."

THAT EVENING, RANGER ADJUSTED THE COLLAR OF HIS shirt as he walked toward Oakley's front door. He hadn't entered the house through this entrance last night, and her double-wide doors looked like a giant mouth, waiting to devour him whole.

He hadn't been this nervous in a long, long time, and he wondered what that meant. He'd liked Oakley for months now, and she seemed to like him. They kept coming back to each other, anyway.

Ranger climbed the steps, mentally checking all the pieces. Clean clothes. Check. Cowboy hat. Check. Flowers. Check. Cologne. Check.

The guys on the radio this afternoon had been talking about Two Cents, and Ranger could still hear what they'd said. *The quality of dating all over town is about to get kicked up several notches.*

They were right, as Ranger would've never stopped to buy flowers for this date. He'd seen it on his own app, and he'd stopped by the florist to find they were practically sold out of everything. Thus, Ranger carried a handful of wildflowers he didn't know the names of, and he almost tossed them into her bushes so she wouldn't know he'd used his own app in anticipation of this date.

He crushed the stems as he reached with his other hand to ring the bell. He stood there feeling like a dunce, waiting. Oakley's neighbors had probably seen so many men make this pilgrimage, and Ranger suddenly wanted to go home.

The door opened, and Oakley stepped forward and put her hand on one hip as she cocked it.

With the sight of her, Ranger couldn't breathe. She wore a denim dress that had been glued to her body, swelling and dipping with all of her curves. A wide, bright pink belt circled her waist, and around her shoulders sat what could only be described as a furry, pink jacket.

"Wow," he said, scanning her down to her toenails, which had been painted pink as well. His eyes moved up every inch of her to that gorgeous hair he wanted to run his fingers through. Every dark strand fell in the exact right way, and Ranger knew she was way out of his league.

Beyond. Way beyond.

He pushed the thought away and dropped the flowers in favor of taking her straight into his arms. "You look *amazing*," he said. "Thank you for agreeing to go out with me."

She giggled as she lifted her hands to his shoulders. Little pops and zings raced through Ranger at the nearness of her. He'd stifled his feelings for her for so long, he now felt them racing forward and zooming around.

"Thank you for asking," she said, her smile infectious.

He wanted to kiss her so badly. She revved him up in the best way possible, and Ranger swallowed before asking, "Have you kissed a lot of men on these steps?"

"A few," she said, her smile slipping. "But not usually before the date."

"Maybe it's time to change things up," he said, honestly unsure of where the words had come from. He pressed his lips to the corner of her eye, and then to her cheek. "What do you think?"

"About?" Her voice had turned as quiet and throaty as his.

"Me kissing you right now."

Oakley's grip on his right shoulder intensified, and her other hand moved to the back of his neck. "Okay," she said.

Ranger didn't hesitate. He touched his mouth to hers, expecting sparks and getting fireworks. He wanted to stomp on the accelerator and kiss her like he'd never kissed a woman before.

Instead, he forced himself to go slow. He took his time, and that was just as passionate as fast would've been.

Wow, was all he could think as he kissed the woman he'd been thinking about for months. *Just...wow.*

Chapter Four

Oakley tried to stay inside her own mind so she could memorize the way Ranger smelled. The gentle yet insistent stroke of his mouth against hers. The warmth of his hands on her waist and moving up her back.

He broke the kiss, and Oakley pulled in a long breath. Ranger was absolutely everything in a man she'd always wanted. He pushed his fingers through her hair and said, "Wow, Oakley."

She opened her eyes and met his, which were bright blue pools of desire. For some reason, that made her cool down a little bit. She knew she was pretty. She knew she could turn heads and get dates.

She'd been in Three Rivers for almost two years, and she'd been out with dozens of men. Most not more than a few times, but a handful. None of them ever stuck around either, because they just liked the way she looked and that she had a lot of money.

Ranger cleared his throat and stepped back, his own expression cooling slightly. "Sorry. I probably shouldn't have done that."

Oakley fell back a couple of steps, which took some serious calf muscle because of the wedges she wore, and picked up her handbag. "Why's that?"

"I don't normally do that," he said, reaching up and rubbing the back of his neck. His fingers trailed along his collar as if he needed to loosen it. Those beautiful eyes flitted all over to different items on her porch. "I'll, uh, I think we should probably get to know each other better before we do that again."

Oakley walked toward him, and he lowered his hand back to his side. He was always so perfectly collected. Sure, he was exhibiting a little bit of nerves, but nothing like some of the men who'd come to pick her up for dinner. "It's okay, Ranger."

"No," he said. "I hope I didn't imply that I'm only interested in you because you're beautiful."

Her eyes widened. "Do you always just say what's on your mind?"

"No," he said again. He relaxed, though his eyes shot a decent level of sparks at her. "If you asked the other boys at Shiloh Ridge, they'd say I'm the quiet one."

"Quiet," she said, slipping her arm through his and turning him to face the steps. "Yeah, I can see that."

"What about you?" he asked. "What do your friends say about you?"

"Oh, uh." Oakley waved her hand through the air as

they descended the steps. How could she answer that? *I don't have friends.*

That wouldn't work, though if Ranger stuck around for any amount of time at all, he'd realize the truthfulness of that statement. Making friends was easy for Oakley. Keeping them was so much work.

"They'd say I'm really good at drawing lines."

"Drawing lines?" Ranger opened her door for her and looked at her. "Explain that one." He put a smile with the sentence, and Oakley's pulse shot to the back of her throat.

"I'm the boss at work," she said. "A friend when we're not at work. I know when to have fun, but I know when to rein it in and get down to business too. There are lines, and I'm really good at drawing them." She stepped past him and climbed into his truck, wondering where she'd put the line for him.

She'd let him kiss her on the first date, and that meant his line was a lot closer to her than many others had ever been. Her nerves pealed out a warning to her. "If you get close to this man, you'll have to tell him about Roberto."

Oakley had not told anyone in Three Rivers—heck, in the whole state of Texas—about Roberto. Just thinking she'd have to tell some of her secrets made her want to rush back inside, remove all of her makeup, and crawl into bed.

She held her spot in his truck, noting the scent of leather and horses and something citrusy that tried to cover all that up. The truck bore a certain amount of dirt, which she liked. It meant he used the truck and didn't worry that he was a cowboy living in Texas when it came to cleanliness.

There was no trash, though, and the little tree trying to fight off the masculine scents meant he tried to keep his vehicle presentable.

He opened the door and climbed into the truck in a graceful move that defied his height. "Ready?" He glanced at her as he pressed a button to start the truck.

Oakley nodded, determined to see this date through to its conclusion. She'd see how she felt at the end of the evening, though deep down, she knew she'd want to go out with Ranger again. She'd want to see him every morning, every afternoon, and every evening.

He'd said that to her once, and she snuck a look at him out of the corner of her eye as he backed out of her driveway.

"Where are we going?" she asked.

"Did you tap on Pizza Pipeline in that app?" He looked at her and draped one hand over the steering wheel while the other rested on the armrest.

"I got distracted," she said.

"I'm glad." He chuckled. "I guess you'll see why it's number three on the list."

She pulled her phone out of her handbag and lifted it up. "I can check."

"Maybe it could be a surprise," he said quickly, his voice louder.

Oakley turned toward him, her hand pausing as it hovered over the screen. "Oh, someone wants to be romantic."

"Did you read the description of that app when you downloaded it?"

"No," she said.

"If you can do that without checking out the notes on Pizza Pipeline, you might want to." He grinned at her, his teeth white and straight, and that mouth doing plenty of distracting for Oakley. He ducked his head and chuckled again, and Oakley gave herself a little shake.

She cleared her throat and tapped to open Two Cents. Three lines sat at the top of the screen, and she tapped there. She tapped on About this App, and read the description.

A cowboy's two cents for the best places to visit, the best activities, and the best restaurants in Three Rivers, Texas. Wow your next date with the very best in the Texas Panhandle.

"Wow your next date," she said.

"I think a man made that app."

"Seems obvious." She re-read the description while he said, "For other cowboys in Three Rivers. So yeah, I checked out the app." He shrugged. "A man does like to have a plan for the woman he's going out with."

Oakley adjusted herself and crossed her legs, which was quite difficult in the denim dress she'd shimmied into. She thought for a moment about how she didn't have a girlfriend to text to see if that was the dress she should wear or not, but she pushed that thought away quickly.

"Is that why there were wildflowers all over my porch?" she asked, teasing him.

"Uh." Ranger made a right turn and glanced at her. "I got distracted by that furry jacket."

Oakley burst out laughing, though she did reach to adjust her jacket. "This is not fur, I'll have you know."

"Yeah? Well, it's not leather."

"Would you like it to be leather?" She reached over and touched his dark leather jacket. "It's too hot for leather." Maybe she meant to say he was hotter in leather, but she was glad she didn't. She knew how to flirt with a man, and she knew she didn't want to do that with Ranger. If she wanted him to respect her, she had to act like more than a flirty schoolgirl.

She *was* more than that, and she was more than a pretty face with a big bank account.

Ranger made another turn and went past the statue of the pioneer woman looking east.

"You'll have to tell me the story of that statue," she said. "I've heard different versions."

He turned into the parking lot at the pizza parlor. "If you'd like." He turned off the ignition and got out of the truck. "Give me a sec."

He rounded the truck to open her door, taking off his hat and putting it back on again as he did. Oakley recognized nerves when she saw them, and she found Ranger adorable. She would never tell him that though, because he was by far the most masculine man she'd ever been out with. He likely wouldn't appreciate it.

He opened her door and extended his hand toward her. She put hers in his and scooted to the edge of the seat. She really should've thought through her wardrobe choices. Her skirt hitched higher up on her legs, and she quickly pulled it down once her feet hit solid ground.

She smoothed back her hair, wishing she'd worn it up like she usually did at work. She settled the "furry jacket" over her shoulders and looked up at Ranger, who'd seen her do all of that. She supposed she had a few nerves running through her too.

"Ready to see why a pizza joint is number three in most romantic places to take your date."

He gestured for her to go first, and he quickly fell into step beside her. He did not touch her, and she found herself wishing he would. He held the door for her, and he approached the hostess station.

"Two please," he said. "Is the garden available?"

"Sure thing, honey," the woman there said, her eyes flowing down to Ranger's cowboy boots and back to his face. "Follow me, cowboy."

Oakley knew flirting, and she knew women, and this one wanted Ranger to notice her. The man didn't even seem to realize the sandy-haired woman was a woman, and he once again indicated that Oakley should go first.

She followed the woman with way too much swagger in her hips to a side door that led out of the building. It wasn't particularly hot in Texas in mid-November, but Oakley didn't think she'd want to eat in a garden in the summer.

She'd only taken two steps outside before she recalled her thought. "Oh, my goodness," she said. She tried to take in everything at once, but that was impossible. Potted plants stood guard next to the doorway. A black wrought-iron fence sat to her left, in the direction of the street, but she'd never be able to get into the garden that way. Vines and flowers grew through the breaks in the fence, with those top spikes poking through in an almost gothic way.

"This is incredible," she said.

"I think so too." Ranger nudged her to keep moving, and her eyes swept along the hedge that ran parallel to the building. Tables sat next to the hedge, and under an awning that connected the building to poles running up through the hedge.

There was not a spot of sunshine back here, and quaint lampposts had been set up, with vines and flowers twined around them. Oakley imagined it as a place the fairies would come for tea parties, and she turned to Ranger, feeling a glow of happiness she hadn't in a while.

"This is a thousand times better than eating inside with those yellow walls."

He chuckled, his eyes bright too. "I'm glad you like it." He waited for her to sit at the table the hostess had given them, and then he removed his leather jacket and sat across from her, a sigh coming from his mouth.

"I meant to tell you that you look great tonight," she said. "I like the color red on you. Looks good with your hair and eyes." She told herself to stop talking and pick up the menu. She liked pizza as much as the next person, but she honestly hadn't dined here that much. If she'd known about this garden, she would've.

"I wonder how many other hidden gems this town has," she said.

"You're not going to let me plan any dates, are you?"

"I can't make suggestions?" she teased.

"Only about the pizza," he said, picking up his menu,

but his eyes still stuck on hers. She held the gaze, because men usually broke before she did. Ranger did not, and Oakley finally nodded with a light laugh and picked up her menu.

"What's good here?"

"Everything's good here," he said, looking up when a waitress approached.

"Drinks?" she asked. "Appetizers?"

"We want the cheese braids for sure," Ranger said. "And I want that orange-mango concoction you guys have."

"With alcohol or virgin?" she asked.

"Virgin," he said, looking at Oakley. "They have great frozen smoothies here."

"I'll take one with strawberry," Oakley said. "Do you have something like that?"

"We have strawberry lime rickey," she said. "It's phenomenal."

"I've had that one too," Ranger said. "She's not wrong."

"Then I want that," Oakley said. "And I don't know what a cheese braid is, but it sounds fantastic."

The waitress smiled and left them, and Oakley looked at Ranger. This was honestly one of the better starts to a date she'd had in a long time. Maybe in her entire time in Three Rivers.

"Cheese braid?" she asked.

"Imagine the best bread you've ever eaten," he said, his eyes bright. The man certainly loved food, and that made Oakley happy. "Then add a lot of butter, a lot of garlic, and a lot of cheese." He grinned and added, "Mmm-hmm. It's the best thing I've ever tasted."

"Wow," Oakley said, giggling. "The best thing you've *ever* tasted?"

His eyes dropped to her mouth, and when his gaze came back to hers, he simply nodded. Oakley did too, because while teasing Ranger would be fun, she wanted a more serious relationship with him too.

"All right," she said. "We better get serious about this menu, because I can't just eat bread, cheese, and butter for dinner."

"Sure you can," Ranger said. "I do it all the time."

She laughed fully then and shook her head. "All right, cowboy. Since you want to be in charge of the dates, you order for us. I eat plenty of meat, so that's not an issue."

Ranger focused on his menu and said, "You got it, sweetheart."

"Then you have to tell me two truths and a lie about yourself, and I'll see if I can guess which is which."

He looked up at her, a sparkle in those baby blues. Several seconds passed while he obviously tried to figure out if she was being serious. "You've got yourself a deal," he finally said, and Oakley hoped she could get herself a second date with this charming, handsome cowboy.

Chapter Five

Ranger grabbed his keys from the bowl in the kitchen and immediately turned around to leave the homestead again.

"Where you off to?" Bear asked. He got up from the table where he'd just finished a couple of pieces of leftover pizza. They'd had a lot of it last week when they'd decorated the angel tree, and Ranger had brought home more last night.

"Mack's," he said, pausing. "I'm going to get those two trucks."

"Mm hm." Bear put his plate in the sink and glanced at where Ace sat at the table still. "I think you're goin' to see Oakley."

"Oh, that's for certain," Ace said without looking up. "You should be grateful you didn't have to work with him this morning. It was Oakley this and Oakley that and did you know Oakley once lived in Spain?" Ace glanced up then, plenty of good-natured teasing on his face.

Ranger opened his mouth to deny it but found he couldn't. Not really. He'd maybe said a few things to his brother about his date. "You asked," Ranger said, glancing to the door as Ward walked through it. This was shaping up to be a right old family reunion. He didn't have a timetable to get down to the car dealership. He'd just rather spend his afternoon with Oakley than his brothers and cousins, especially if they were going to tease him.

"I did ask," Ace said, passing his phone to Ward, who looked at it. "Tell me what that means."

Bear nodded to Ace, and Ranger suppressed his sigh as he stuffed his keys in his pocket. "You're going to need someone to go with you if you're getting two trucks."

"I was thinking I'd just call Ward when the deals were almost done, and he'd come down with a couple of people."

"I volunteer Judge," Bear said. "He's driving Mister crazy, and I think we're going to need to do something to separate them."

Ranger nodded as he waked over to the table where Ward stood reading Ace's phone. The youngest of his brothers sat at the table, tension in every muscle in his face.

Ward frowned and handed the phone to Ranger. "Honestly, Ace?"

"He wants you to be honest," Bear said. He'd obviously already told Ace what he thought, and Ace was gathering more opinions.

Ranger half-expected him to take the phone before he

could read it, but Ace just let him scan the texts. Lindsay Forsythe had been texting him a lot lately. Ranger knew he'd been out with the woman several times in the past few months. Ace had mentioned her plenty of times, and he'd used the word *girlfriend*.

These texts didn't read like she wanted to be his girlfriend, and that perhaps she'd never viewed herself that way.

"She's putting you in the friend zone," Ward said. "I'm old, and I can tell that."

"He's too close to the situation," Bear said. "Be nice to him."

"I *am* being nice to him," Ward said, looking at Bear. "Look who's talking."

Bear ducked his head. "I just know how this feels."

Ranger put the phone on the table. "I'm sorry, Ace, but I agree with Ward. She's leading you on to boot."

"She is?"

"Ace," Bear said. "She said she'd let you know for Friday night...on Friday. She's waiting to see if something better comes up."

Ace stood, a sigh leaking from his mouth. Instead of looking at his phone again, he shoved it in his pocket. "I guess."

"You're supposed to just sit around and wait for her to decide if she'll go out with you?" Ward asked. "Ace, she should be so excited to see you again, she can't even wait until Friday."

"It's only Monday," he said. "Lots of people don't know their schedules for Friday yet."

"I know I'm going to see Sammy," Bear said.

"You're engaged," Ace said with a glare. "Completely different."

"I asked Sabrina Hendrick to dinner for Friday," Ward said. "At church yesterday. She said yes."

Ranger swung his eyes to his brother. "What in the world?" he asked at the same time Bear said, "Ward, you devil. I asked you if you asked her out and you said no."

Ace even exclaimed, "You did? For real?"

Ward rolled his eyes. "This is why I didn't say anything." He moved away from the group. "Is there any pizza left?"

"Some," Bear said, tracking him with his eyes.

"He's probably just doing what the rest of us are," Ace said. "Tryin' to live up to Bear."

"Come on," Bear said. "No one's ever done that."

Ranger smiled at his cousin. He sure had tried to emulate Bear in a lot of ways. No, the man wasn't perfect, but he did have a lot of admirable qualities.

"You did say someone needed to get married and start having babies," Ranger said. "I think every one of us heard that down deep in our souls."

"You?" Bear asked, his eyebrows going right up under his cowboy hat.

"Of course me," Ranger said, puffing out his chest. "You think I don't want a wife and family? We built this house specifically so we could have those things in the future." He gestured to the house with both hands. "It's done now. It's time."

"You think you and Oakley...."

Ranger turned and started toward the front door. "I've been out with her once, guys. It's way too soon to know that or even be thinking about it." He waved over his shoulder. "I'm going down to buy the trucks. Ward, I'll call you later."

"All right," he called to him, and Ranger continued out the front door while Bear said something else to Ace about Haven. Ranger got behind the wheel of his truck and glanced to the passenger seat, where Oakley had ridden last night.

He'd walked her to the door, but he hadn't kissed her. He'd meant what he'd said about getting to know her before he did that again. He wanted to be the Texas gentleman she deserved, and the moment he'd pulled away and looked into her eyes, he'd realized that kissing her so early had been a mistake, almost like the Lord Himself had whispered it in his ear.

Ranger took a moment to get the radio on and to the station he liked. He'd turned it off after driving Oakley home, because he'd just needed the silence to think in. He adjusted the air conditioning too, and his phone rang before he'd even put the truck in gear.

"Ace," he said. "I'm still in the driveway. What do you need?"

"Did you really tell Oakley you wouldn't go out with her if she was seeing other people?"

Ward, Ranger thought. "Who told you that?"

"Bear."

Ward was better at keeping secrets than Bear, though Ranger considered his cousin very good at knowing when to say something and when not to. He must have felt like he should in this instance.

"Yes," Ranger said. "That's true."

"That she was interested and wanted to go out with you, and you said no."

"Yes."

"Do you regret that?"

"No," Ranger said, confused now. "She ended things with everyone and started dating one man at a time. I guess that man is me now. Why would I regret that?"

Ace sighed and said, "I don't know."

"Listen," Ranger said, putting the truck in gear and backing up. "No one can tell you what to do here. I know that's what you want. Bear doesn't really get how you feel about Lindsay. I don't. Ward doesn't. We're all spectators here. We don't know what your relationship with her has been like. Only you know that. Either she's for you, or she's not. If she is, the Lord will bring you back together again. If she's not...well, He'll tell you that too."

Ace increased the volume and length of his sigh. "Okay, *Dad*."

Ranger frowned, because he didn't want to act like Ace's dad. "Sorry, Ace," he said. "I know you don't like the answer of 'go pray about it.'"

"No, I don't," Ace said, his voice more animated with anger now.

"I'm sorry," Ranger said. "You'll figure it out." Religion, and his feelings for Lindsay, and what he should do about her. "You're smart and capable, and you'll figure out what to do here."

Several beats of silence came through the line. Ranger passed beneath the arch that welcomed people to Shiloh Ridge Ranch and said, "I'm coming up on Dead Horse Point. I'm going to lose you for a few seconds."

"I'll let you go," Ace said quietly. "Thanks, Range."

"Yep."

The call ended, and Ranger stewed over Ace and Ward the rest of the way to Mack's Motor Sports. He pulled into the parking lot and saw no less than three salesmen eyeing his truck. He stayed inside and closed his eyes real quick. "Lord," he prayed. "Send clarity of mind to Ace when it comes to Lindsay. He's a good man and a good brother, and he wants to do the right thing."

Ranger believed that with his whole heart. "Bless Ward with whatever he needs to be happy too. I'm not sure what it is, and I don't think Ward does either."

He opened his eyes. "Amen," he said, and he got out of the truck, ready for a long afternoon at the dealership.

Heath approached, and Ranger smiled and shook his hand. "I'm lookin' for Oakley," he said. "I've been working with her about a couple of trucks."

"Let me get her for you," Heath said. He'd taken Ranger to meet with Oakley before, so he didn't seem too surprised by Ranger's request. He went with him into the showroom, where Oakley came around the counter in the corner the moment she spotted Ranger.

She wore a smile that stretched from ear to ear, and Ranger imagined a scene where she giggled as she ran to him and he swept her into his arms as they both laughed.

She did seem excited to see him, but she didn't run. She

wasn't wearing the pencil skirt or heels from the last time he'd come here to see her, but a pair of blue jeans and a pale pink T-shirt with a sunset on it. Her dark hair was secured in a ponytail, and it contained a remnant of the curl he'd seen last night.

"Hey," she said, glancing at another woman who held something out for her. Oakley took the pen and signed whatever the woman wanted, and she moved back over to her desk. "You're here about those trucks, aren't you?"

"Yep."

She looked at Heath, who smiled at both of them. "Thanks, Heath. I've got him." She grinned at Ranger, and goldarn if his heart didn't skip a whole bunch of beats. Her mouth moved as she said something else, but all Ranger could hear was *I've got him.*

She sure did, her fingers right around his heart.

"Come on, now," she said. "I won't bite." She turned and walked away from him. Ranger glanced at Heath, and then he made to follow Oakley. He'd missed what she'd said, and she was heading for the exit from the showroom.

"Two trucks," he blurted as he followed her outside. "Big engines. We use 'em for hauling and pulling posts and towing."

"Right," Oakley said. She let him catch up to her, and Ranger exercised all of his self-control to keep his hands to himself. He'd done it last night too, so he knew he could. He relied on that knowledge as they walked toward a row of the tall trucks.

"F-450?" she asked. "Four-wheel drive capability?"

Ranger actually loved talking trucks, and he went over

the specs he wanted. "We do fifth-wheel towing when we go long distances," he said. "Definitely four-wheel drive. Sometimes it snows here, and we live up in the hills."

She nodded and started tapping on a tablet he hadn't seen her pick up. "Color?"

"Don't care."

"Leather interior?"

"Something that'll clean," he said. "Cargo is somewhat important. If we don't have to tow a trailer around the ranch that's better. We do almost everything from horseback. No ATVs, no helicopters. Just us and the animals." He gestured to the huge Ram 3500 in front of him. "And trucks, I suppose."

"You only work from horseback?"

"Mostly," he said, glancing at her. "We use tractors, obviously. We're not out there plowing with a blade behind a horse."

She grinned at him. "That's what I was envisioning."

"I could tell." He moved toward the dark blue truck. "I'm sure this is fine." They'd had Ram's before, and they were good trucks.

"Do they need to be the same truck?"

"No," Ranger said. "It just makes maintenance easier. We try to do all of that ourselves too."

"These will come with warranties." She circled the truck. "I've got four of these in stock, but not two the same color."

"Color isn't important," he said, though he preferred a darker vehicle.

She continued to show him a couple of other makes

and models, but he settled on the Ram 3500, and after twenty minutes he said, "I want the blue one and the tan one."

"I'll get them started for you," she said as they walked back to the showroom. "You know, I could show you some ATVs if you think you might be interested. They're really nice nowadays, especially for smaller jobs on the ranch. We sell a ton of them to farmers and ranchers."

She looked at him with questions in her eyes, and Ranger would like to spend a few more minutes with her, so he shrugged.

"Sure," he said. "Show me what you've got."

"They're easy to maintain too. Easy to ride. Gets you there quicker...." Oakley veered to the right and took him down the side of the building. "These even have tow capacity. They're great for moving rocks, dirt, poles, equipment, anything you want really." She bent over and touched the back of one. "Most don't come with a hitch; it's an additional add-on, but they're not expensive."

She went over the different styles, and Ranger found himself asking real, genuine questions. He had not spoken with Bear specifically about buying ATVs for the ranch, and somewhere in the back of his mind, he knew his cousin would not be happy if Ranger showed up with the quads.

At the same time, Oakley was building a very good case for why ranches used all-terrain vehicles. Life on the ranch did seem like it would be easier if they had a couple of those.

"All right," he finally said. "You sold me on these too. I

want the ones we saw back there with the towing capacity."

Her smile lit up his whole world. "Great. I'll put that in for you. You want the hitching system?"

"Yes, ma'am."

"That's a day in the shop," she said, studying her tablet. "Looks like we can get you in on Thursday for that install." She looked up. "Does that work? You could come pick them up in the afternoon."

"Sure, Thursday works," he said, glancing left and right. They seemed to be the only ones in the near vicinity. "Does dinner work for you tonight?"

She smiled as she tapped on her tablet to schedule the time in the shop. "Dinner would be great," she said. "We don't have to go out every night, though, Ranger." She looked up at him, a measure of seriousness entering her gaze. "Really, I'm not high-maintenance like that."

"Do you cook?" he asked, taking a step closer to her. "Seems like you said you couldn't even make coffee, so...."

"I do not cook, no." She emitted a light laugh that made Ranger smile.

"I do," he said. "Not much, but you don't get to be forty without knowing how to put a meal together. Once my momma had three boys in a row, she made us all learn."

Oakley gazed up at him. "You have sisters, too, right?"

"Yes," he said. "Two of 'em. They live here in town, though, not up at the ranch. The rest of the family—besides Momma—live up there."

"Where does your mom live?"

"Nestled Oak," he said. "It's an assisted living facility.

She's fine; she's mobile and all that. She just has a few health problems and wanted to be closer to town. She doesn't want to cook or take care of a yard. All that." He put a smile on his face and reminded himself that he should go see his momma after he finished here at Mack's.

"You're forty?" she asked.

"Yes, ma'am." They'd had a great conversation last night, but age hadn't been part of it. His family had, though mostly his brothers and cousins and life on the ranch. He'd asked her a little about her days in the Formula One circuit, but she'd been vague and moved the conversation back to him, then onto pets.

"I'm thirty-three," she said. "I can see you dying to know." She bumped him with her hip. "Come on, Ranger. Let's go get started on your financing."

"Oh, uh." He went with her but kept his eyes on the ground. "No financing. We'll pay with cash."

"Cash?" Her voice sounded like she'd inhaled helium. "For two trucks and two ATVs?"

"Yes, ma'am."

"Ranger, with taxes, titles, fees...that's over a hundred and thirty thousand dollars."

"Yeah," he said. "Do you take checks?"

Chapter Six

Oakley could not get Ranger out of her head. She didn't really want him to go, but she did want to think about something else for five minutes. Anything else.

He'd literally written a check to Mack's Motor Sports for one hundred and thirty-two thousand dollars and some change. Just signed his name on the line like it was nothing.

"And you thought you had a lot of money," she muttered to herself.

She hadn't left Mack's yet, because Ranger said he'd get his brothers to help him get the trucks he'd just bought up to the ranch, and then come right back down for dinner with her. He'd suggested while they were waiting for the trucks to be washed and detailed that they could go to the grocery store together, get some ingredients, and he'd make dinner at her place.

She'd immediately texted Susie to see if she could run

by and make sure the kitchen was ready to cook in, and her housekeeper was so amazing that she'd said yes.

He'd left twenty minutes ago with Ward and Ace, the same two men she'd met the other night at the comedy club. She's met another cousin, Judge, who'd brought them all down, and the four of them had each gotten behind the wheel of a different truck and rumbled away.

Oakley had immediately retreated to her office, where she'd closed the door. No one would bother her without knocking or texting first, and she suddenly found she needed a distraction. Vanessa was her dealership manager, but Oakley wouldn't classify them as friends. They were co-workers at best, and she'd never ask Vanessa for advice about a man she was dating.

"Are you dating?" she wondered. She'd been out with him once, and he was coming over tonight. Just because the dates were back-to-back didn't make them a couple. She'd gone out with other men in rapid succession in the beginning.

"Dear Lord," she said, her voice pitching up as she looked at the ceiling. She couldn't continue, because a ball of emotion choked in her throat. She had so much she wanted to say. So much to ask for. So much to be grateful for.

She sat at her desk and closed her eyes. She couldn't speak, but she believed the Lord would accept a prayer she thought. *I don't want to hurt Ranger. He seems like such a great guy, and I like him a lot. Do I like him too much already? How will he take the news about Roberto? About my father? What if I tell him, and he doesn't want to be with me anymore? Have I lost all hope of a life of happiness?*

Tears filled her eyes, and while Oakley fought desperately against them, they won. Every time, they won.

Water tracked down her right cheek, and she quickly wiped it away. She opened her eyes, but they burned, and she hurried to close them again. She lay her head in her hands, and let her mind wander now that she'd opened the door on all the things she was afraid of.

One step at a time.

The thought came to her, and Oakley took a long, deep drag of air into her lungs. She imagined all of the tightness in her shoulders releasing as she blew it out. She lifted her arms high above her head and pressed her palms together, trying to make the halves of her brain fire in sync with one another.

She stretched to the right first, and then the left. She stood and circled her arms up and then down in front of her, once again pressing her palms together. She breathed in, and then out, her mind finally settling.

Opening her eyes, she could suddenly see the next step she needed to take with Ranger. Just one, and after she took that one, she had full faith that light would be shed on what she'd need to do next.

Tonight, she wouldn't skirt the topic of her racecar driving or her family, both things Ranger had asked about last night. He'd let her dodge the questions, though, probably because he was a gentleman and wanted the first date to go well.

Sighing, she pulled out her phone and sat down again.

"Let's see what Two Cents says about a second date," she muttered. There wasn't much, though she supposed Ranger could've picked any of the restaurants or activities on the first date list.

Making dinner at the woman's house wasn't anywhere on either of those. She saw something labeled *Three Rivers at Thanksgiving*, and she tapped on that. The holiday was next week, and she wasn't sure what Ranger would be doing.

"Sure you do," she muttered. "He's got a ranch full of people, his family, and a ton of work to keep him busy." Even on Thanksgiving.

The app opened to another menu, this one with activities, recipes, and restaurants. She tapped on the one at the top and learned she could go to a cider tasting at the mill just northeast of town. She'd had no idea she could do that, and it suddenly sounded like the perfect Saturday afternoon date with Ranger at her side.

He'd hold her hand and they'd walk among the apple trees.... Oakley sighed, everything in her fantasies made of emerald green grass and the bluest sky God could paint over the earth.

The recipes ranged from pies to potatoes to puddings. Oakley didn't understand recipes, and she navigated out of that arena quickly. The restaurants listed were actually open on Thanksgiving, and that was what she'd done last year. She'd attended a group lunch at The Pork and Barrell, which served exclusively Thanksgiving dinner from eleven a.m. to seven p.m. The group had consisted of people from her church, and as far as Thanksgivings went, it wasn't bad.

The first Thanksgiving she'd been in Three Rivers, she'd spent alone in her giant house with The General, her grumpy cat that had eaten more of the sliced turkey breast she'd bought than she had.

Maybe this year, she'd get a seat at the Glover's table. She wondered what that would be like, and an image of a long, wooden table entered her mind. Flowers and greenery sat down the middle of it, with a cowboy boot shaped vase with wildflowers spilling from the top.

A cattle skull took the prime spot in the middle, and it was Bohemian and rustic and Texan all at the same time.

The food would be hot and plentiful, and the company loud but fun.

Oakley sighed, because she'd never been part of a family like that. She'd never *be* part of a family like that.

Someone knocked on her door, and she looked up from the app. "Yes," she said. "Come in."

Ranger entered, and he came toward her with strong steps. "Trucks delivered. Ward really liked the one he drove." He beamed at her and sat in the chair opposite her. "I gotta say, Oakley, that was one of the least painful experiences buying a car I've ever had." He grinned at her. "No wonder you're number one on that Two Cents app."

"Yeah," she said, glad her phone had turned off because it had been idle. "Should we go?"

"Are you done here?"

"Yes," she said. "I've got Heath and Heather closing tonight."

"Heath and Heather," he said, standing up. "That's almost the same name."

"I think they might be secretly dating," Oakley said with a smile. "I haven't asked them, but I see the way they look at each other." She stood too and came around her desk, her eyes never leaving his. "What are you going to make for dinner?"

"I was thinking something easy," he said. "Have you ever had those ready-to-go meals from Wilde & Organic?"

"Can't say I have." She looked up into his eyes, her hand automatically moving that way. Ranger opened his mouth to respond but froze when her fingertips ran down the side of his face, where his beard was.

Oakley wasn't sure what she was doing. She seemed to exist outside of her mental capacity to tell herself to stop touching him. She brushed her fingers along his eyebrow. "If we have kids, do you think they'd have eyes like yours? Or like mine?"

Ranger pulled in a tight breath, his dazzling blue eyes widening.

"It's just...." Oakley felt herself falling into a giant hole she'd have to dig herself out of. "I've never seen a man with such dark hair, but such light blue eyes."

"Sure you have," Ranger said, the words grinding through his throat. "You've met Bear."

Oakley smiled at him. "Is it your momma or your daddy who's dark?"

"Daddy," Ranger said. "Momma has the blue eyes." He cleared his throat and backed up, meeting the desk behind him. "I'm hoping we can make a stop on the way to Wilde & Organic."

"Okay," Oakley said. "Where?"

"To see my mother," he said. "I don't get down here to see her as often as I should, and I'd like to stop by tonight."

Oakley nodded, though she wasn't sure what he was saying. "All right. I can wait in the truck."

"You don't need to do that," he said. "You can come in. If you want." He shrugged like he didn't mind one way or the other, but surely he did.

Oakley stepped over to the coat rack and plucked her purse from it. "Okay," she said, facing him again. "How will you introduce me?"

Ranger didn't move, and those eyes devoured her from the shadows created by his hat. "I'll say, 'Mother, this is my new girlfriend, Oakley Hatch. She owns the number one car dealership in Three Rivers.'"

So many things he'd said in one sentence made Oakley start to fall for him. Mother. The bit about her dealership being number one. The word *girlfriend.*

"Would that be okay with you?" he asked.

She smiled and said, "That sounds perfect."

He dropped his chin and said, "Great. I'm ready, but I can wait if you need a minute."

"I don't need a minute." Oakley slipped her arm through his, smiling at him. "I hope this doesn't sound terrible, but I'd kind of like to keep...us on the down-low here where I work."

"Sure, no problem." Ranger stepped away from her as he went toward the door. He did open it for her, and Oakley gave him what she hoped was a coy, flirty smile as she stepped into the hallway. He followed her, and once they got outside, she said, "I'll meet you at Nestled Oaks?"

"Sure," he said, something she'd heard him say a lot. She navigated herself to the assisted living center and parked next to Ranger's truck. He didn't drive one of the new ones back down from the ranch, and he got out of his personal vehicle.

Oakley scrambled to get out of hers, suddenly wishing she wasn't wearing dirty jeans and a pathetic T-shirt to meet his mother. He hadn't said anything about her clothes, and he still wore his blue jeans and a long-sleeved shirt in brown, black, and white plaid.

"Where do you get your shirts?" she asked as she joined him on the sidewalk. She ran her fingers up his buttons to his collar before she dropped her hand.

"Oh, uh." He looked down as if he'd just realized he was wearing a shirt at all. "The Boot Barn? Online. I order them online." He looked up at her, a flicker of nervousness in his gaze.

"Really? They fit?"

He looked back at his shirt. "I think so?"

Oakley laughed, and Ranger met her eyes again, clearly perplexed. She took his hand, sobering as he continued to gaze into her eyes. "Is this okay here?" she asked.

"If it's okay with you," he said.

"It is." She faced the entrance to the care center, but Ranger took the first step.

He nodded to the woman sitting at the front desk, and Oakley recognized her. She'd come into the dealership and bought a minivan several weeks ago. "Evening, Ranger," she drawled, her eyes moving to Oakley. Her smile widened. "Heya, Oakley."

"Hello," she said, her hand tightening in Ranger's. She hoped that was code for, *Help me with this woman's name.*

"Evening, Cheryl," Ranger said, glancing at Oakley. "She hasn't gone to dinner yet, has she?"

"She ordered dinner up to her room tonight," Cheryl said, taking the pen he'd used to sign in. She gave Ranger a bright smile like his mother ordering dinner to her room was normal.

"Thanks." Ranger tipped his hat at her and moved toward a huge staircase that went up. "Stairs or elevator?"

"All of those?"

He chuckled and said, "Elevator it is." He took her behind the steps and pushed the button. "You should know it's faster to climb."

"Yeah, but then I'll be sweaty to meet your mother." She smoothed down the front of her T-shirt. "I'm already wearing the ugliest clothes I own, so I need everything else I can get."

"Those are the ugliest clothes you own?" Ranger scanned her down to her cowgirl boots. "I think you look fine."

"Yeah," Oakley said with a scoff. "And what woman wants to look *fine* when she's going to meet her boyfriend's mother?" She shook her head, looking up to see where the elevator was. Floor three and moving real slow. "By the way, if I just look fine, don't say anything at all. Women don't want to hear they look fine."

"Noted." He reached out and pressed the up button again. "What other adjectives are off-limits for how you look?"

"Decent," she said. "Good isn't all that great. Cute is definitely out."

"Why is cute out? Cute is good, right?"

"And good isn't all that great," she said, grinning at him as the elevator finally dinged.

"I thought women liked to be cute." He got on the elevator, her right at his side. He pushed the three, and Oakley was relieved she hadn't opted for the stairs.

"No," she said. "Teenagers and college students like to be cute. I'm neither." She really didn't want to fish for compliments.

Ranger narrowed his eyes at her, his chin dropped toward her slightly. But he said nothing.

"What?" she finally asked.

"Just looking," he said, glancing up at the numbers above the door. "You're right. Cute isn't good enough for you."

Oakley basked in the deep, throaty quality of his voice, and a certain measure of warmth moved through her.

"Here we are," he said as the car came to a stop. He led her down the hall about halfway and knocked on a door with 3417 on the front of it. "Mother?" he called as he leaned closer to the seam where the door closed. "It's Ranger. Can I come in?"

Oakley didn't hear anything, but Ranger must've, because he twisted the knob and opened the door. He entered first, and Oakley held back. She hadn't met a man's mother in years, and she had no idea how to act. She didn't know what kind of condition she'd be in, and she didn't even know the woman's name.

This is our second date, she thought as Ranger released her hand and said, “Hey, Momma. You look good tonight.” He crossed through the simple kitchenette just inside the door to a couch. He bent down and hugged his mother, a laugh coming from his mouth.

She said something to him in a weathered voice, the love on her face as she hugged her son pure and full of joy. Oakley sighed and pressed one hand to her heart as she watched them. If she thought Ranger was sexy in a leather jacket, that belt buckle, and that cowboy hat, watching his kind heart and love for his mother was one of the best things he could’ve done to elevate him in her eyes.

He straightened and turned back to her, reaching toward her though he was paces away. She walked forward, very aware of how *fine* she looked. She slicked her hands down the front of her jeans and went to his side.

“Mother,” he said, putting his arm around her waist. “This is Oakley Hatch.” He didn’t use the word *girlfriend*, and Oakley’s confidence took a dive. “We just started dating.” He smiled at her and bent his head to press a kiss to her cheekbone.

“Nice to meet you, ma’am,” Oakley said.

“Oakley,” he said. “This is my mother, Dawna.”

Oakley took her hand between both of hers and squeezed. Her skin felt papery and powdery, and Oakley loved her instantly.

“Lovely to meet you too, Oakley,” Dawna said with a smile. “She’s beautiful, Ranger.” She switched her gaze to her son. “You two make a handsome couple.”

“Okay, Mother.” Ranger chuckled and indicated the love

seat. Oakley sat down, and Ranger took the space beside her, taking her hand into his. Their eyes met briefly, but there was plenty of time for a quick conversation with him.

He was asking how the introduction had gone, and Oakley assured him it was fine. He turned back to his mother. "How was bridge this morning, Mother?"

"Oh, that Mary Ellen. She cheated through the whole thing." She waved her hand and scoffed.

"You still won, I bet."

Dawna slid her gaze toward Ranger. She bobbled her head a little, one shoulder lifting up slightly. Ranger burst out laughing and bent his head toward Oakley. "Mother is a champion bridge player."

"Is that right?" Oakley asked, looking from him to her. "Tell me more about that."

"Here we go," Ranger muttered, leaning back into the couch.

His mother's blue eyes lit up, and she said, "My daddy taught me to play bridge in the evenings."

Oakley's heart squeezed, but she kept the smile on her face. Dawna continued to talk about how she'd learned and that she'd won her first championship when she was only fourteen.

"Do you play bridge?" Oakley asked Ranger, who raised his eyebrows.

"No, ma'am."

"I taught the girls," Dawna said. "Bull kept the boys so busy on the ranch."

"Mother," Ranger said as he scooted to the edge of the

couch. "I'm starving, and I promised to make dinner for Oakley. We have to go, okay?" He stood up and kissed both of her cheeks before he pressed his forehead to hers. "I love you, Mother. I'll come again real soon."

"Oh, okay, baby," she said. She struggled to get up, and Ranger held tightly to her upper arm as she did. "I'll walk you out." She limped slightly at first, and Ranger did not let go of her.

At the door, she hugged him again, and he said he'd bring her some of Bishop's pecan pie. He stepped back, and Oakley, who'd trailed along like a puppy, stepped into his mother's arms.

"Thank you for having us," Oakley said.

"You keep him if you can," Dawna said, her voice a whisper. "You seem like a nice woman, and he needs someone like you."

Surprise filled her, but Dawna was so warm and so soft. She smelled like peaches and strawberries and baby powder. She held Oakley with a surprising amount of strength, and Oakley hadn't been hugged by her mother in decades, so she clung to her too.

She'd had no idea how good it felt to be held by a parent, as she hadn't had such a luxury for so long. Far too long.

Tears filled her eyes at the same time horror started to rear up. She couldn't cry over this. Ranger would have questions, and Oakley wouldn't be able to shrug them off.

You already decided to take the first step, she told herself as Dawna's grip on her shoulders lessened. Oakley stepped back and smiled at the woman, hardly able to see through the water in her eyes.

"Oh, baby." Dawna reached up and touched Oakley's hair. "You come see me anytime now, y'hear?"

"Yes, ma'am." Oakley's voice pinched in her throat, and she fell back to Ranger's side. He peered at her, concern and shock in his eyes.

"Go on now," his mother said. "My dinner will be here any minute." She opened the door, and Oakley stepped through it first. She walked fast as Ranger said something behind her. She reached up and wiped her face quickly, glad she hadn't worn much makeup that day. The last thing she needed was a repeat of the mascara tears from the comedy club.

She tapped the down button for the elevator and looked up at the numbers as Ranger came around the corner. His eyes searched hers, and Oakley felt everything crumbling again.

So he wouldn't see the tears spill down her face, she lunged at him and wrapped her arms around him tightly.

"Okay," he said, holding her in place right against his chest. "All right." He hummed, the vibrations and sound way down in his chest where Oakley had buried her face.

How in the world could she explain things to him? Maybe he could just hold her forever, and she wouldn't have to.

The elevator bell dinged, and Ranger eased her back so they could get on. She did, once again turning her face away from him and wiping her eyes.

"Do you want to ride with me?" he asked, not quite the

question Oakley had been expecting. “You don’t have to tell me what’s goin’ on if you don’t want to.”

She nodded, trying to push out her sadness and loneliness and gather together her courage. She liked this man, and she trusted him. She could tell him.

She could.

Chapter Seven

Ranger kept the radio low as he pulled out of the parking lot and onto the road that led to Wilde & Organic. His stomach tightened, partly from hunger but mostly because Oakley had started crying for some reason he didn't know.

She kept her gaze on her hands in her lap, the seconds ticking by. She finally lifted her head and said, "I haven't spoken to my mother in twenty-three years."

Shock moved through Ranger again, and his fingers tightened on the steering wheel. He couldn't think of a single reason why he wouldn't speak to his family members, but he knew there were plenty of people who didn't.

"I'm sorry," he said. "Did she pass away?"

"No," Oakley said. "She lives in Italy."

"Wow," Ranger said. He and Oakley really were from two different worlds. "Italy. That's...is that why you don't talk to her?"

"She left my father when I was ten," Oakley said, her head drooping again as she picked at her fingernails. "I chose to stay with him. He was a professional racecar driver, and I wanted to be one too." Her voice pitched up, and Ranger couldn't stand watching her in so much turmoil.

He reached across the console and took one of her hands into his. "Hey, it's okay," he said. "You don't have to tell me."

"I want to tell you."

"You're upset," he said, lifting her hand to his lips. "I don't like seeing you upset." He looked at her, and the charge between them struck him like lightning to the heart. They simply looked at each other, the moment silent but incredibly powerful.

"I haven't had anyone care about me the way you do in a very long time," she said, her voice breaking again. "I'm sorry. I'm not going to cry all night." She gently removed her hand from his. "I'm not. I'm not usually such a bawl baby."

"You're not a baby," he said quietly. He focused on the road, trying to search through his own emotions. He couldn't imagine a life without his mother and father, the ranch, his siblings, and all of his cousins.

Oakley had no one.

"I was a sobbing mess just two nights ago," she said. "And I'm doing it again."

"I don't mind," he said.

"I've never told anyone about my mother," she said.

"No one?"

"No one."

He looked at her again, and the raw vulnerability on her face made Ranger fall a little more in love with her. She was usually so strong and so confident. He found that sexy and desirable, but he sure did like this softer and more subdued version of Oakley Hatch too. Then *he* could be the strong one.

Ranger didn't need to be the strong one all the time, but everyone wanted to feel needed and necessary. Everyone wanted to help someone else. He did, at least.

She drew in a long breath, and Ranger did too. "I just got emotional from that hug. It sure was nice to hug your mother." She shook her head and wiped her eyes again. "I miss that, and I didn't know how much until that moment. It just sort of hit me." She glanced at him. "I'm sorry."

"Please don't apologize," he said. "I love a good hug from my mother, and I can't imagine not having one." His own throat closed, as his mother was older, with health problems. He didn't know how much longer he'd get to hug her, and he cleared his throat. "I lost my father about five years ago. I miss him, probably in a lot of the same ways you miss your mom."

"Probably." Oakley kept her head up now. "I don't talk to my dad either. We...had a falling out a few years ago—five or six—and we went our separate ways."

Ranger wanted to know more about that, but the night already felt so heavy. He didn't like that, though he did appreciate the things she was sharing with him.

She exhaled heavily. "What? No questions?"

"No questions," he confirmed. "You can tell me what you want, when you want."

"Thank you, Ranger." She put her hand back in his, and Ranger quickly adjusted his left hand on the wheel.

They arrived at Wilde & Organic, and he pulled into a parking space without other vehicles around. He took the truck out of gear and faced her. "I'll just run in real fast, okay? Or do you want to come?"

She leaned her head back against the rest there and tilted it toward him. A smile crept across her face, and she was the most beautiful woman in Ranger's world. "You're an amazing man, Ranger," she said.

He smiled too, just something small, though his blood definitely ran faster and hotter through him with the compliment. "I think you're pretty amazing too," he said. He dropped his eyes to their joined hands. Hers were lighter and smaller than his, but they fit together so well. "What's your favorite ice cream?" he asked.

"Ice cream?"

"We'll eat it first," he said. "Doesn't tonight feel like a dessert-first thing?"

Her smile widened, making her downright angelic. "Yes," she said. "Yes, cowboy. It does."

He grinned at her too, the mood in his truck lightening. "Tell me what to get, sweetheart." He reached over and brushed a piece of hair back. "Whatever you want. Well, whatever Wilde & Organic has." He found himself thinking he'd go to any end of the earth to get her what she wanted, and he needed to box those feelings and examine them later.

"Mint chocolate chip," she said. "And as many brownies as you can find."

"Brownies and mint ice cream," he said. "Comin' right up." He reluctantly withdrew his hand from hers and slid from the truck. As he strode toward the grocery store, he once again found himself in very deep water when it came to Oakley.

At the comedy club, he'd warned himself to be careful. Now, he just wanted to keep swimming around and see where he ended up.

"I'M DEFINITELY GOING TO BE GETTING MORE OF THESE ready-made meals," Oakley said, swiping up the last bit of noodles and sauce from her plate. "That was really good." She smiled at Ranger, and he got up to pick up her plate.

"I'm glad you liked it." He'd slid everything he'd bought at the grocery store into the oven when they'd arrived at Oakley's, and even he couldn't ruin spaghetti and meatballs, garlic bread, and a bagged salad.

They'd enjoyed their desserts while everything heated, and Ranger also liked the homemade, organic, ready-to-eat meals.

He put the dishes in the sink and started rinsing them. He loaded them in her dishwasher while she brought over their dessert dishes, and Ranger had a flash of what a real life with her would look like.

Maybe not in a house this big, and Ranger's insecurities

fired through him. "You should come up to the ranch," he said.

"Yeah? What would we do up there?"

He handed her a bowl to put in the dishwasher. "I could just show you...the horses." He pressed his eyes closed. A moment later, he started laughing. "Wow," he said among the chuckles. "That was really lame."

Oakley giggled and nudged him with her hip. "I don't have anywhere to go for Thanksgiving."

Ranger should've put those dots together already. "You do now," he said.

"And I'd love to come see the horses," she said. "Your ranch. Where you're going to house those *really* nice trucks you bought today."

He sensed her questions about his money, but he wasn't sure he needed to say much more. He'd written a check for all the vehicles he'd bought that day. When she saw the homestead, she'd see the wealth at Shiloh Ridge.

He thought of the other houses and barns they had on the expansive property, and a sigh moved through his body. He didn't let it out of his mouth, though, because he should share personal things with her. She'd told him something very hard for her tonight.

"Now, when you come to Shiloh Ridge," he said. "You're going to see a lot of amazing things. *Amazing*, Oakley." He turned off the water and faced her, leaning his hip into the counter where he'd been working. "Bear and I run the ranch together. I work with Ward on the financial side. Each of us has something to do that's integral and important. Without any one of us, things fall apart."

"I can imagine," she said. "I have a zillion little pieces at the dealership too."

"Yeah, like that," he said. "You have that great big beautiful showroom and loads of expensive vehicles." He cleared his throat as she closed the dishwasher. She faced him too, and Ranger's desire to take her into his arms and kiss her intensified.

"At the ranch, we have a lot of stuff like that. Big buildings and barns. We're starting a major renovation in our main cowboy cabins and the Ranch House. We have something like eight houses there, and more cowboy cabins, and the homestead is this massive building we just finished, and—"

"You're rich," she said, cutting him off. A grin accompanied her words. "I gathered that from the check you wrote this afternoon."

"Yeah," Ranger said with a chuckle. "I just—it seemed like you wanted to know how rich."

"I do," she said, her eyes wide and interested. She leaned a little closer to him, her voice a whisper when she added, "I have a lot of money too."

"How much?" he asked, breathing in the floral and clean scent of her skin.

"You first," she whispered.

"Personally, or on the ranch?" He kept his voice low too.

"Let's start with personal."

"Eight or nine billion," he said, his throat closing on the words. "Give or take a little bit."

Her eyes rounded even more, and the smile slipped

from her face. "That's personal?"

"Yes, ma'am."

"And on the ranch?" Her voice squeaked, and she straightened.

"More than that," he said, though he knew the exact figure. "My daddy and my uncle bought the ranch adjacent to ours, found oil, and sold it for a lot of money. My father had an incredible mind and a real knack for knowing what to invest in. He took that money and increased it five times over in only a few years."

Ranger stepped away from the sink. "The ranch has something close to fifty billion dollars at its disposal."

"So the trucks were nothing."

"Our motto is reuse, repair, and recycle," he said. "It took me months to admit I couldn't fix those blasted trucks, and that I simply had to replace."

Oakley followed him into the living room, where they sat on the couch together. Ranger put his arm around her as she cuddled into his chest, her legs tucked underneath her. She didn't ask him any more questions about his money, and Ranger exhaled a sigh of relief.

"I only have a few hundred million," she whispered, a laugh following that.

Ranger closed his eyes and smiled. "How ever will you survive?" he teased.

"It's hard," she said with plenty of flirtation in her voice too. "Somehow, I manage."

They laughed together, and Ranger let himself fall further in love with her. He fell and fell and fell, and by the time he left her house and dropped her at her truck in the parking lot at the care facility, Ranger was fairly certain he was all the way in love with Oakley Hatch.

"Ridiculous," he muttered to himself as he drove back to Shiloh Ridge. "Who falls in love after two dates?"

"You can't bring them here," Bear said, his voice made of pure growl.

"They're dead useful," Ranger said. "I could move all of that sawdust we got delivered this morning in an hour instead of three." He looked at Bear and prayed that he'd have an open mind.

"We don't need them," Bear said, turning his back on Ranger and pulling a mug from the cupboard.

"But what if we do?" Ranger said. "Have you ever stopped to think why we don't use motorized vehicles? We have trucks."

"Yes. Use one of those expensive trucks you just bought to move the sawdust." Bear turned from the coffee maker, his face arranged in full grizzly mode.

"We needed those trucks," Ranger said, drawing himself to his full height. Bear may have half an inch on him. Maybe. He owned half of this ranch too. "We can't move our horses or haul anything without a blasted truck." He could adopt a foul temper for this discussion too, though it didn't really fit his personality.

He'd never much cared if he had to shovel sawdust into the back of a truck or a wheelbarrow before. But now, it was like his eyes had been opened to the efficiency an ATV could provide.

"You should've talked to me about this before you bought them," Bear said. "And Ward. Everyone. You can't just change how we do things here singlehandedly." He took a sip of his coffee when in the past he might've thrown the mug—coffee and all—at the wall and stormed out.

"You're right," Ranger said, realizing his mistake. "Can I get it on the agenda for this week's meeting?" He and Bear chatted every morning and evening about official ranch business, but they weren't official meetings. "I can make sure Ward's there, and Cactus, as they get to have deciding votes on important things. You seem to think this is one of those things."

"This *is* one of those things," Bear growled. He shook his head as he brushed by Ranger and stepped over to the microwave to pull out the scrambled egg bowl he'd put inside several minutes ago. "Get it on the agenda. Send a poll in an email. Make sure Cactus and Ward can attend on Friday morning."

"Yes, sir," Ranger said, and he wasn't trying to be disrespectful. "They're done Thursday, though...."

"Find somewhere else to store them until we can decide as a family." Bear stirred his sausage and eggs.

Ranger sighed, but he suddenly had a reason to call Oakley. *You don't need a reason to call her*, he told himself. "You're really someone different, Bear."

Bear looked at him, his bright eyes firing plenty of fire at Ranger. "It's a good thing, right?"

"A very good thing." Ranger smiled at him. "Okay, I'm headed over to the south stables. I've got three farriers coming this morning."

"We're demo-ing the cabins on Saturday," Bear called after him. "You got the memo?"

"Yes," he called back.

"You're different too, you know," Bear said right as Ranger closed the front door. Part of him wanted to go back and ask him what he meant. The other part didn't want to know, and a truck came rumbling down the lane and past the homestead, the familiar horseshoe logo on the side. The farriers were here, which meant a personal conversation with Bear had to be put on hold.

Chapter Eight

Bishop Glover leaned against the post holding up the side deck, having positioned himself in a spot where no one would see him unless they leaned over the railing above or came down the steep side of the lawn on the north side of the homestead. No one would do either, though at least three of his brothers or cousins were inside, eating lunch.

Where he should be.

He'd heard them laughing a minute ago, though he wasn't sure who was there. He couldn't go inside and get something to eat until this text was sent.

"You've put it off for long enough," he muttered, his fingers flying over the screen now. His stomach barked at him to eat something, and soon, so he kept texting.

Hey Charlotte. I can't meet up on Friday. I've got way too much going on at the ranch.

That wasn't really the message he wanted to send.

He sent it anyway, a frown pulling down his eyebrows. It was the same negativity that had been lashing him for days now.

That's okay, Charlotte sent back almost instantly.

"Of course it is," he said, looking up. He'd tethered Marigold only a few paces away, and she snacked on the grass in the lawn. Bear wouldn't be happy about that, but she'd only be there for a few minutes.

He'd told himself that if Charlotte acted upset that they couldn't get together on Friday, he'd reconsider his decision to end things with her. All things. Everything.

She hadn't acted upset.

"Maybe she'll suggest another day," he said, returning his attention to his phone. She didn't. And didn't. And didn't.

Bishop had to accept the truth, as hard as it was. He pictured the beautiful blonde in his mind, and his determination wavered. Something Ace had said that morning rammed its way into his head. *There are a lot of blondes in the world, Bish. Find a different one.*

He couldn't find a different one if he was so whipped with this one.

I don't think we should see each other anymore, he typed out. *I'm sorry, but it's not working for me.*

His thumb hovered over the arrow that would send the message to Charlotte, and he gritted his teeth and tapped it.

The message swirled and then the word *sent* popped up next to it. A moment later, that changed to read, and Bishop's pulse pounded in his chest. Would she call? If she called, he'd reconsider.

She didn't call. She didn't even text back.

Bishop took a deep breath and looked up again, facing the world as a newly single cowboy again. "Three Rivers is wide open," he told himself.

His phone chimed, and he practically dropped it he tried to lift it so fast. It wasn't Charlotte, but his cousin Ida.

We're still on for tonight, right?

Yes, Bishop sent back, a smile touching his mouth. *Can you bring up that sourdough bread from Heidi's so I can experiment with the stuffing?*

And while you're there, he continued. *I'll take a pumpkin soufflé.*

Oh, jeez, Ida said, the exact answer Bishop had expected from her. Ida and Etta were twins, and they were only six months younger than him. He'd grown up with them on the ranch, and they were some of his very best friends. Perhaps they knew some blonde women, as they lived in town while Bishop usually only saw men on the ranch.

I'm your courier now?

He laughed, his fingers flying. *I think more of a DinnerDasher.*

I will die before I work for DinnerDash.

I'll tip you.

Okay, this is getting worse. See you at six.

Bishop laughed, glad his cousin had been able to cheer him up, whether she knew it or not.

He went around to the steps that led to the deck and

up them. Through the sliding glass door, he found Judge had been to town, and he'd brought back huge quantities of barbecued chicken, potato chips, and lemonade.

"There you are," Ace said, looking over and catching Bishop's eye. He jumped up from the table where he'd been sitting. "So, how did it go?"

"It went," Bishop said, glancing around at the crowd in the house. He'd severely underestimated how many men had come to eat lunch today. Almost everyone was there, besides Cactus—of course—and Mister.

Zona laughed at something Ward said, and Bishop realized Bear wasn't there either. He'd probably gone down to town too, to see Sammy. Bishop really wanted someone to go visit in town, but he pushed the feelings away. He was the youngest brother or cousin, and he had plenty of time to find his soulmate.

"What did she say?" Ace pressed.

"Nothing," Bishop said, finally meeting his cousin's eye. "That's the problem, Ace. She said nothing." He pressed his phone to Ace's chest, who covered it with both hands. "I'm going to get something to eat. Save me that seat beside you."

"Will do."

Bishop didn't really want to discuss the situation to death. He felt like he and Ace already had. He just wanted chicken and chips and some good conversation that didn't include Charlotte's name.

THAT NIGHT, BISHOP SET THE BOWL OF M&MS ON THE table and looked at Bear and Sammy. "Don't touch those. They're for my meeting." He turned away from them and nearly ran into Lincoln, who carried the other bowl of snacks, this one almost overflowing with potato chips.

"Those are Cousin Etta's favorite," he said as a few fell to the floor. "Best not to lose any."

"I'll get 'em," the little boy said. Bishop sure did like it when Sammy and Lincoln came to the homestead, and he couldn't wait to have children of his own.

Bishop had just set the bottled water Ida would like and the bottled sweet tea Etta preferred on the table when the front door opened and one of the twins said, "Hellooo! We're here."

"In the kitchen," he yelled, though they knew where to come. The three of them had been planning and orchestrating Thanksgiving dinner for the past four years. Since their mother had gotten too sick to manage it, even with Mother's help.

Mother had said that first year that she sure did like just enjoying the turkey and mashed potatoes, and Bishop, Etta, and Ida had been doing all the cooking since.

His cousins entered the kitchen, one beside the other. They wore matching outfits—black leggings, and the ugliest Christmas sweaters Bishop had ever seen, along with wide smiles.

"Well?" Etta asked. "What do you think?"

Bishop burst out laughing. Lincoln scurried over to the twins, and they both gave him a hug.

"I think you've lost your minds," he said, taking a spot

at the table. Etta and Ida joined him, both of them talking over one another, as they were wont to do. Sometimes they finished each other's sentences too.

They'd lived together in a townhouse in Three Rivers for a few years, but they'd each gotten their own place a couple of years ago when Etta had started dating Larry Banks with some measure of seriousness. That relationship had ended after a six-month engagement where a wedding date still hadn't been agreed upon.

Etta had been a shell of her former self for about a year, and she was just now starting to return to the fun-loving woman who loved corny jokes and eating nachos for every meal. Bishop gave her a hug as she sat beside him. "How's Charlotte?" she asked. "Are you coming to town this weekend?"

He sometimes slept in her spare bedroom if he was in town too late and didn't think it safe to drive through the pitch darkness back to the ranch.

Before he could answer, Ida plunked a white pastry bag in front of him. "Your soufflé, your highness."

"Thanks, Ida." He grinned at her, and got to his feet to give her a hug too. "I'm going to make that stuffing tomorrow and test it on the boys here."

"Good idea. I think it has too much sage."

"I like sage." Bishop sat down and opened his binder. "But I'll make a note of it." He flipped to the recipes section and did just that before looking up at her again. "What?"

Both Etta and Ida were watching him, and neither of them had opened their binders yet.

"Sit," he said. "Snack. Settle in. We've got a lot to do tonight."

"Are you coming to town this weekend?" Etta asked again, opening her binder slowly.

"Yes," Bishop said, lowering his gaze back to his binder. He had a shopping list already started, and he whipped it out of the front pocket of his binder. "I'm planning to spend a couple of hours at Wilde & Organic."

"He didn't answer about Charlotte," Ida said.

"I noticed," Etta said. "I suppose I won't expect him on Friday night."

"Maybe he'll still want us to go shopping with him."

"*He's* sitting right here," Bishop said, his pulse hopping through his chest. He knew what they were doing, and as they continued to quip back and forth, he just smiled and let them.

They finally both turned their eyes on him again, and while his were definitely a couple of shades darker, their blue eyes sparkled at him with plenty of knowledge.

"All right, all right," he said. "I'm assuming you've spoken to Ace." He looked down the table to Bear, who had been absent at lunchtime. Lincoln climbed onto the bench next to him, and Bishop grinned at the little boy and his ham sandwich.

"I did," Ida said.

"Then you already know I broke up with Charlotte." He looked up to find both Bear and Sammy listening now. "That's right. I broke up with her."

Sammy got up and came toward them, sandwiching

Lincoln between her and Bishop. "I'm sorry, Bishop. That had to have been very hard."

"It was," he admitted, hating that he had to do such things in front of Bear. He wanted to be strong for Bear. He wanted to be the brother Bear could count on for anything, despite his being the youngest.

Bear just looked at him, his eyes curious. He simply reached up and touched the brim of his hat, and Bishop took that to mean, *Good for you, Bish. You deserve better.*

"I deserve better," Bishop said out loud. "She didn't care at all." He shrugged like he didn't care, though a sting still lived within his chest. He drew in a deep breath and looked from Sammy to his cousins. "Therefore, if any of you know any blonde women looking for a cowboy who knows how to use that Two Cents app, you give them my number."

Etta reached over and patted his forearm. "Sorry, Bish."

"Yeah, me too," Ida said. "I should've gotten *two* soufflés. Ace texted too late, or I would have."

"How about I come down on Friday and we go to that Turkey Trot?" he asked. "I was planning to take Charlotte. Maybe there'd be someone else there for me." He met Etta's eye. "And someone for you, Etta. I know you've been looking for a nice guy."

She snorted and shook her head. "You think nice guys go to the Turkey Trot?"

"I mean...." Bishop swung his attention to Ida, as she usually clued him into what he should say. She was shaking her head, her eyes lit with laughter she was trying to hold back. "No?" he guessed.

"No is right," Etta said. "You know who goes to the Turkey Trot, Bishop?"

"No, ma'am," he said, grinning at Ida first. He swung his attention to Etta. "Who?"

"Losers," Etta said, the word exploding out of her mouth. "That's who, Bishop. Men who live in their mother's basements, without jobs and without any tint to their skin."

"Oh, boy," Bishop said, rolling his eyes. "Have some candy, Etta."

She kept talking right over him about the quality of men at the Turkey Trot—"and probably the women too," she ended with. She clucked her tongue. "No, Bishop. No Turkey Trot."

"Fine," he said, grinning at her. "It's rated number three on Two Cents, though, so maybe there will be a different caliber of men there." He raised his eyebrows and shrugged one shoulder. "That's all I'm saying."

"What's number three on Two Cents?" someone asked, and Bishop looked up to find Ranger standing there, a beautiful brunette at his side.

Bishop froze, as he didn't have a single thought in his head at that moment.

"I forgot you guys were meeting tonight." Ranger looked nervous as he glanced at his sisters and back to Bishop. Down to Bear. Back to Bishop. "Uh, I invited Oakley to see the ranch."

"It's fine," Bishop said as his cousins got to their feet. Sammy did as well, and Bishop got up but went in the opposite direction—toward Bear—as the women descended on Ranger and Oakley.

He raised his hand when Ranger said his name during the introductions, and Bear did the same. "He looks good with her."

"They do look good together," Bear said under his breath. "We should stop staring. He's turning purple."

"Right." Bishop moved back down the table. "Come on, ladies. Come *on*. We have so much to do, and we've wasted so much time chit-chatting about my pathetic love life that we're twenty minutes behind."

He met Ranger's gaze as Etta and Ida resumed their seats at the table. His gratitude streamed from him, and Bishop added, "There's plenty of candy in the bags over there. Sweet tea in the fridge."

"Butterscotch for the horses?"

"In the cupboards in the stable," Bishop said. "Ward refilled them last week." To his surprise, Grizzly down the table didn't say anything about not feeding their horses candy, and Bishop knew that had a lot to do with Sammy, who'd also retaken her seat across from her fiancé.

"All right." He took a deep breath. "Let's start with the menu. What was a hit last year, and what we need to remove from the offering." He looked at Etta. "I believe you had those notes." He took out his soufflé while she reached for a handful of potato chips.

"Yes," she said, crunching her way through one chip. "The cranberry mint sauce was a disaster...." She continued to review her notes, and Bishop pushed all thoughts out of his head about meeting a new woman.

Perhaps he just needed some time to reset. Then he'd start petitioning the Lord to send him inspiration as to where he should be and when so he could meet the right woman for him.

That finally decided, he was able to focus properly on the most important meeting he attended each year.

Chapter Nine

"That was so much fun," Ranger said, swinging himself off the quad. He took his helmet off as Oakley did, and she looked at him as he strode toward her. "Incredible." He wore a look of wonder and pure joy on his face, and he laughed as he jogged the last few steps to her and swept her into his arms.

She squealed and laughed as he spun her around, both of them laughing. Oakley held onto his shoulders, the muscles beneath that stylish blue and purple and brown plaid shirt bunching as he lifted her.

"Thanks for letting me store these here," he said, his smile so brilliant. "That Bear can be two-hundred-twenty pounds of attitude." He set her on her feet, and they laughed again.

"Sort of like someone else I know," she teased, feeling herself fall for him another degree. It was so easy being with him, and the only other man she'd ever felt like this with was Roberto.

"Hey now," he said. "I take offense to that."

"Yeah? Why's that?"

"I'm barely tipping two hundred," he said. "You just called me fat."

She pealed out another round of laughter, tipping her head back and enjoying the happiness as it filled her from top to bottom.

"Thank you for taking me," he said, lowering his forehead to meet hers. "I had so much fun."

"I'm glad." She swayed with him, the moment turning serious. She thought he'd finally kiss her again, but a familiar *whoop-whoop!* of a police siren sounded behind her. Ranger lifted his head to look over her shoulder, and she twisted in his arms.

"What did we do?" he asked, releasing her and stepping around her to take care of the situation. A tall, broad-shouldered man got out on the driver's side, and a woman not much bigger than Oakley did on the passenger side. She swept the front yard and cul-de-sac like there would be a massive threat behind one of these suburban fences.

Oakley edged forward while Ranger covered the distance to the car. She'd been out with two policemen in Three Rivers, but not this guy. If she wasn't head over heels for Ranger, she might flirt with him to get out of whatever ticket he was about to give them.

She joined Ranger, who reached forward and shook the man's hand. "This here's Brady Burton," he said.

"Pleasure, ma'am," he said, tipping his hat. "Uh, I caught you guys speeding back there, Ranger."

"For serious?" Ranger asked, glancing at his partner. "Howdy, Shayla."

"Ranger." She nodded at Oakley too, her mouth turning up in a smile.

"Couldn't have been that fast," Oakley said. "He was behind me, and I was going thirty."

"Which is too fast, ma'am," Brady said. "These also don't have plates, and to drive them on roads, they need to be licensed."

"I just bought 'em today," Ranger said. "Well, Monday, but they were in the shop gettin' the hitches until today. Oakley was just showing me the trails that go up into the hills."

"Mm hm."

Ranger reached up and ran one dirty hand through his hair. "Okay, so speeding? Is that it?"

"You can prove you bought 'em on Monday?"

"We put in the paperwork through Mack's," Oakley said, pulling her phone out of the side pocket of her leggings. "I can call my manager and get you the applications for the plates."

"Give me a second," Ranger said, turning toward her for a moment. He wore mischief on his face, and Oakley adored it.

She held up her hand as if in surrender and turned her attention to Shayla. She'd never been great at relating to women, but she'd given her number to Ranger's sisters, and they'd been texting up a storm over the past twenty-four hours. In fact, the three of them were getting together for lunch tomorrow, something Oakley had literally never done with girlfriends.

She was as excited as she was scared. They hadn't asked her not to tell Ranger, but she hadn't mentioned it to him yet. He'd come down from the ranch to pick up the ATVs, and she'd suggested they take them for an inaugural ride.

The next thing she knew, he'd traded his cowboy hat for a helmet and was handling the ATV as if he'd ridden one every day of his life. She lived closer to the trails than the dealership was, and he'd needed to use the bathroom and get a drink.

She did too, but she clenched everything tight as she met Shayla's eyes. "Do you like being a cop?" she asked.

"Yes, ma'am," Shayla said with a smile. She cut a glance at Brady. "He's going to get out of that ticket."

"Yeah?" Oakley looked at the two men, both of whom had their backs to the women. "How do you know?"

"He's Ranger Glover," Shayla said. "And Brady's had a crush on those twin sisters of his for a while now."

"You think Ranger knows that?"

"He'd have to be dead not to," Shayla said. "Those Glovers are tight, and Brady's asked Ida out before." She looked at Oakley again. "I guess I'm assuming Ranger knows."

"He probably does," Oakley said. "His family is tight." She'd loved the tour of the ranch last night. She'd stood in the living room of his three-bedroom wing of the house, marveling at the built-in cabinets, the high-end flooring even in a kitchenette, and the attention to detail that was displayed everywhere.

He'd asked her if she could stand to live with such a small kitchen, and she'd said she never cooked anyway. "Still," he said. "This whole wing is barely the size of your kitchen."

"It is not," she said, laughing. "Don't be ridiculous."

"Admit it—your house is huge."

"It's too big for me," she'd admitted. "This place is great, Ranger. Really." She'd smiled at him, and she'd thought she'd get her second kiss then too. But he'd pulled in a breath and ducked his head.

"Is it weird we're talking about stuff like this so soon?"

Oakley didn't think it was weird. Surprising, especially for her, yes. But not weird. Nothing with Ranger felt unnatural.

"I don't think so," she'd said. "So Bear and Sammy will live across the hall?"

"That's right," he said. "They're getting married in March. I think we're going to mix things up at our next meeting. Mister and Judge live together right now, and they don't get along. Since Bishop's gonna have to move anyway, I think we're going to put him in the Ranch House, and move Mister over here."

Oakley had nodded and asked about the names in their family. Ranger had started to explain, but he didn't get far—certainly not to what his real name was—before they'd gone outside and been distracted by a flurry of cowboys on horseback, driving a group of cattle back to the corral they'd escaped from.

He hadn't come back to it as he'd showed her the barns, the stables, the horses, and a couple of the other houses on the ranch.

He'd been right. Shiloh Ridge Ranch was an immaculate piece of land that seemed to ooze wealth from the dirt itself.

"Are you still having that sale on scooters?" Shayla asked, and Oakley blinked out of her memories from last night.

"Yes, ma'am," she said as Ranger turned toward her, a wide smile on his face. He clapped Brady on the shoulder, and they shook hands again. "It goes through next weekend. You come on by, and ask for me, and I'll get you the best deal."

Shayla smiled. "Thanks. I'll bring my boyfriend with me." She stepped closer and lowered her voice. "Not all men are as observant as Ranger. I've mentioned the scooter about ten times, and I still don't have one."

Oakley giggled with her and said, "I'll be sure to play up how romantic they can be. You can put two people on them, you know."

"I did know that." Shayla grinned at her and waved as she walked back to the passenger side. "Burton? No ticket?" she barked.

He grumbled something as Ranger came to Oakley's side. He put his arm around her and they both lifted their hands in farewell to the cops.

"How'd you get out of that?" Oakley asked, her mouth barely moving out of the smile she'd formed on her face.

"I gave him Ida's number," Ranger said with a chuckle.

"Now I have to call her before he does, or I'll be dead by nightfall." He pulled out his phone. "I also got the name and number of his very blonde sister, so this was a win for me all around."

He stepped away from her as the police cruiser left and Oakley's brain caught up to what he'd said. "His blonde sister?"

"For Bishop," he said, pulling his phone down from his mouth. "I've got to use the bathroom. I'll be right back to help you with these."

She watched him go, not surprised by the false note of joviality in his voice when he said, "Ida, my dear sister," just before the door closed behind him.

She shook her head and wiped down the helmets before bagging them. If these were her machines, she'd spray the dust off them and let them dry in the sun before containing them in the garage.

She looked at her expansive garage, thrilled Ranger had asked her to store his ATVs here. He'd called her Wednesday morning to ask, and they'd talked for forty-five minutes before she'd had to get in the shower, and he'd had to get to work or risk "Bear's wrath."

After hooking up the hose and attaching it to the sink in the garage, she sprayed down the ATVs. Ranger had not returned, and Oakley left the machines where they were so she didn't have to lean into the wet seats and add water to the dust all over her clothes.

She had to get back to work tonight, and they could take these on paved roads, so she went inside to change her clothes.

She nearly collided with Ranger, who was on his way out. "Sorry," he said, grabbing onto her. "Sorry. Whoa, you okay?"

Oakley relied on his strength to keep her from falling, and she found her footing. "Yeah." She grinned up at him, a thrill running up her back and down her leg, originating from where he touched her hip. "I need to change, and we can go. I have to get back to work."

"Okay." He stepped back and allowed her to squeeze by him.

"How did Ida take it?"

"She wasn't thrilled," he said.

"I'll talk to her at lunch tomorrow," Oakley said.

"Lunch tomorrow?" Ranger's voice sounded far away as she moved through the kitchen and left him behind. She crossed through the living room and toward the master bedroom, his footsteps behind her. "You're going to lunch with her tomorrow?"

"Yes," Oakley called over her shoulder as she went into the bedroom. "You can stand just inside the door there. I'll stay in the closet." She ducked inside and stripped off her dust-laden leggings. "Your sisters have been texting me all day. Last night too, before I'd even left the ranch."

"Why?" he asked.

"Because they're nice?" Oakley wasn't sure why either, but she didn't want to say so.

"I can talk to them," he said.

Oakley stepped into a fresh pair of jeans and switched her T-shirt for another one. She was just pulling it over the waistband of her jeans when she stepped out into the bedroom and found Ranger with his back pressed against the wall, right inside the doorway.

He was the most adorable man she'd ever met, and she grinned at him as she took her hair out and shook her head to get all the loose dirt out.

"You don't need to talk to them," she said, straightening and gathering her hair back into a ponytail. "I like them."

He frowned. "What if *I* don't like them talking to you?"

She cocked her head, trying to find a reason for that. "Why wouldn't you like that?"

Ranger sighed, plenty of darkness on his face. "No reason. Come on. We better get you back." He ducked out of the bedroom, and Oakley hurried to get her boots from the closet and follow him.

He'd gone all the way to the garage, and she stepped to his side, saying, "Ranger, if you don't want me to be friends with them, that's fine."

"No, you can," he said.

"Good," she said. "Because I like them, and I have no friends."

Ranger turned and looked at her, his eyes inquisitive. "You have no friends?"

"No," she said honestly. "Who would I be friends with? Women treat me like I'm going to steal their boyfriends, and men are only interested because I'm pretty."

"Oakley." Ranger shook his head. "That's not true."

"Oh, it's true," she said. "Very few people actually stick around to get to know the woman underneath the confidence and the makeup." She reached up and ran her hands through his hair, enjoying the way he closed his eyes and seemed to enjoy it.

She sure did.

"You're one of the few, Ranger Glover."

"There have been others, though," he said, opening his eyes.

"A few," she said, not wanting to talk about this at all right now.

"The last woman Etta and Ida befriended dropped me after six months of pretty serious dating," he said. "I know it's not the same at all, and they weren't the reason she broke up with me. It just...feels oddly similar."

"What was her name?"

"Leslie." He cleared his throat. "You? Who was the last serious boyfriend you were with?"

Oakley's mind screamed one word at her, and she couldn't see straight. Thankfully, her phone rang, and Vanessa's name sat there. "It's Vanessa," she said, showing it to him so he'd know she wasn't making that up. "Hey, Nessa," she said. "What's up?"

"Where are you? Mister Cleaveland is here, and he says you had an appointment at five?"

Oakley's stomach dropped to the soles of her boots. "Dang it. I'll be there in ten. Offer him a drink and something to eat from our client fridge."

"Okay," Vanessa said in a low voice. "Hurry. He doesn't look happy."

"Ten minutes," Oakley said again, and she hung up. "I have to go, Ranger. I have a client I'm late for."

"Let's ride."

On the way back to Mack's Motor Sports, Oakley couldn't help letting Roberto out of the carefully crafted box she'd made for him. He'd been a beautiful man, and Oakley had imagined a beautiful life with him.

His face morphed and changed as the wind pushed into her face. By the time she dismounted from the ATV and called to Tyler to help Ranger get his quads loaded in the back of his truck, Ranger's face had replaced Roberto's completely.

Do I dare ask for a second chance at that life full of happiness? she wondered as she dashed inside. *Didn't I already blow my chance?*

She wasn't sure where the word had come from, but a resounding *no* had entered her mind. *Okay, then*, she thought, changing it to a prayer a moment later. *Lord, if possible, I'd like another shot at a life full of love and happiness. With the husband and the kids and a cat and a dog. Horses, too. And a really loud family with this amazing homestead on this beautiful piece of Texas land....*

She entered her office, where Mister Cleaveland sat. He rose and faced her, a frown filling his whole face.

And a little help with this sale, please, she concluded just before she said, "Karl, my goodness, look at your beard." She laughed and crossed the room like she'd arrived at the precise moment she should have. "I bet Karen *really* likes that."

"I'M JUST SAYING SHE'S IN THE CLEAR," IDA SAID, glaring at her twin sister. "That's all."

Oakley stirred her drink and watched them. They were so much fun. Where Ranger was quiet, they were loud. Where he was serious, they were playful. Where he was reserved, they were wild.

They'd called him the business in the front, and they were the party in the back. Oakley thought that was the most apt way to describe his twin sisters, and she'd enjoyed herself at lunch immensely.

"So he didn't have the meeting this morning?" she asked. He hadn't texted her to ask if she could keep the quads longer. She could, of course. Especially if he'd come ride them with her again.

When she'd gotten home last night after closing at Mack's, his ATVs had been in her closed garage and one of those ready-to-eat meals from Wilde & Organic had been sitting on her kitchen counter.

She'd texted him for a while, and he'd said he was meeting in the morning with the family about introducing ATVs to the ranch.

"Ward had a meeting with the construction manager this morning," Etta said. "So no, there was no meeting. And anyway, it's not your fault Ranger bought two ATVs."

"It's not?" Oakley asked. "It kinda feels like it is. He mentioned you guys did everything from horseback, but I don't know. I thought he'd like them."

"He likes them," Ida said. "It's Bear, Cactus, and Ward you're going to have to win over."

"And Judge," Etta added. "He's very traditional."

"Zona too." Ida shook her head. "I'm glad we just do the outreach programs. Can you imagine living up there full-time?"

"It wouldn't be terrible," Etta said. "I love the ranch."

"I do too," Ida said. "Maybe we should have Bish build us a house up there. Start dating one of the full-time cowboys." She wore a sparkle in her eyes.

"Aren't you dating a cop?" Oakley asked, making her voice as casual as possible.

"What?" Etta asked.

Ida's eyes widened, and she looked from Oakley to Etta and back. "How did you know that?"

"Ranger mentioned that there was a cop friend of his that had a crush on you." Oakley stirred her drink and glanced at Etta. "I guess I just assumed you were dating him."

"You're dating a cop?" Etta practically shrieked. "Who is it?"

"Brady Burton," Oakley said while Ida sputtered. "Right?"

"No," Ida finally spat out. "We're not dating. He called last night and asked me to—" She cleared her throat.

"To what?" Etta asked, leaning almost all the way across the table.

Oakley sure did love these two. They were like the siblings she'd never had but always wanted.

"The, uh, Turkey Trot," Ida said, clearing her throat again.

"Oh, Dear Lord," Etta said, falling back to her seat, her eyes wider than a dinner plate. "*Please* tell me she said no."

She looked up at the ceiling as if really petitioning the Lord.

Ida raised her chin, her eyes shooting fire at her twin. “In fact, I said yes. We’re going out tonight. Dinner and dancing.”

Etta brought her eyes back to Ida’s. She started a slow shake of her head, and Ida rolled her eyes and then her whole upper body. “What are you and Ranger doing tonight?”

“You know what?” Oakley lifted her drink to her lips. “I’m not sure. He’s very mysterious when it comes to what he’s planning for our dates.”

“Mysterious, sure,” Ida said, snorting. “I think that’s him not having a plan, Oakley.”

Oakley looked at her in surprise. “He always has a plan.”

“Yeah, he probably looks at that Two Cents app at the stoplight down the street from your house.” Etta raised one eyebrow as if to say, *I know my brother, and that’s what he’s doing.*

Oakley smiled and shook her head. “Either way, we have a great time when we’re together.”

“Tell us more about our dear, romantic brother,” Ida said. “Then maybe Etta will see that not every date has to be made of magic and unicorns.”

Oakley laughed as she fished an ice cube from her nearly empty glass. “Nope,” she said. “No details about Ranger.” She looked between Etta and Ida. “He wasn’t too keen on me having lunch with you two, and I really like you. If he finds out I was gossiping about him, I'm afraid we won't be able to have lunch again."

"Aw," Ida said, reaching across the table to cover Oakley's hand with hers. "You'll have to listen to me talk about Brady for hours."

Oakley laughed with her, noting that Etta did not join in. "I can handle that," Oakley promised. She glanced at Etta. "And you know, Etta, I work with ninety-five percent men. I'm sure I could find you someone to dazzle at the Turkey Trot."

"I would rather eat garbage," Etta said, picking up her purse. She stood and looked at Ida and Oakley. "But I suppose another venue would work...with the right man." She walked away. "I'll pay and be right back."

"Okay, that gives me sixty seconds," Ida said. "First off, Etta is super Texas proper. She wants a man to open her door for her and bring roses—red roses—and who always looks like a million bucks. She says she's not picky, but she so is. She wants tall, dark, handsome. Full beard, full head of hair. Tan, muscular, with the biggest belt buckle you can find."

"Wow," Oakley said, feeling like she should be taking notes.

"Yeah." Ida glanced in the direction her twin had gone. "And I've been holding this in for an hour, but oh my goodness, Brady Burton is amazingly good-looking." She fanned herself and grinned at Oakley. "I don't care if it's the Turkey Trot, if he'll hold me with those strong hands...." She glowed she was so giddy. "Mm-hmm."

Oakley laughed again, and since she'd never had a lot of

girlfriends—or any, really—she suddenly knew what she'd been missing for all these years. She loved Ranger's sisters, and once lunch ended, and she went back to work, she started thinking that perhaps she'd already fallen in love with Ranger too.

If he'd just kiss her again, then she'd know for sure.

Chapter Ten

"Ranger!" Lincoln called, already running toward where Ranger stood with a whole crew of cowboys. Ranger grinned, took a couple of steps forward, and scooped the little boy into his arms.

"Howdy, partner," he said while Lincoln pressed his cowboy hat back onto his head. "You here to help this morning?"

"Yep." Lincoln grinned at him. "Bear said he'd even let me use the tools."

"I see." Ranger looked to his cousin, who was approaching the group much slower. "We're not tellin' your mom, are we?"

"Shh," Lincoln said. "No."

Ranger grinned as he put Link down, and the two of them blended into the crowd as Ward stepped forward with the construction manager they'd hired to help with the cabin remodel.

"All right," Ward said. "The plan is to get everything out of all five cabins in the next few hours. Everything. Carpet. Cabinets. Appliances. We want to salvage anything we can. The cabinets are going in the barns and stables under Bishop's direction."

Ranger looked at his youngest cousin. He raised his hand as if anyone there didn't know who he was. He was a good, hard worker, and Ranger would miss living with him in the homestead. He cooked almost every night, and Ranger saw a lot of trips to the Ranch Home in his future, as neither he nor Bear did much in the kitchen if they didn't have to.

Being able to and wanting to were two different things. He reminded himself that Judge was a decent cook, and none of them would starve before turning back to Ward, who'd moved on to talking about preserving the appliances, as they were going to needy families in town.

"The cowboys have cleaned out their personal effects, so we're taking down blinds, anything on the walls, everything in the bathroom." He glanced around at the group assembled there. All twelve Glovers had come, even Etta and Ida, and Shiloh Ridge employed six full-time cowboys. They hired on seasonally too, if they needed it, but Ranger didn't see any of those men there that morning.

"There's eighteen of us," Ward said. "Let's do three in each cabin, with Bishop, myself, and Cactus stepping in to help where needed. Cactus will help me with the appliances and Bishop with the cabinetry. Questions?"

No one had any, and Ward didn't split the group.

People had others they naturally gravitated to, and Ranger took a step toward Bear, bringing Link with him.

"I don't think he counted me, Bear," Link said, looking up at the man who would be his father soon. "Should I go ask him?"

"You come with me, son," Bear said, smiling at him. "I'm sure Ward just didn't look low enough." He took Link's hand, and Ranger's heart swelled with love for both of them.

"I'm with you two," Ranger said. "Ace, you come with us too."

"All righty," his brother said, and the three of them started toward a cabin that hadn't been claimed yet. Inside, the air smelled like sausage and dirt, and Ranger's nose wrinkled up in distaste.

The carpet had been flattened by years of cowboy boots walking on it, and when he'd sat in the meeting and said things weren't that bad out here, he'd been wrong. Dead wrong. "Wow," he said.

"I had no idea things were like this," Bear said, reaching for the ugliest set of curtains Ranger had ever seen. Their eyes met, and Ranger's jaw tightened.

"We're not letting things get like this again," he said. "Deal?"

"Deal."

With that, they got to work. Bear directed Link, and he let him use a hammer to loosen a curtain rod, and then to smash in the remaining legs on the dining room table that were already wobbly and broken.

Embarrassment accompanied Ranger, and he felt like

he should seek out the men who lived here and apologize. Christmas was almost upon them, and perhaps he and Bear should give a bonus this year.

He and Bear approached the kitchen cabinets together, and Ranger asked, "What do you think about offering a holiday bonus this year?"

"I think if we have the money, we should," Bear said. "It's been a hard year for people."

"I agree." He reached up to hold the bank of cabinetry while Bear used the drill to remove the screws holding it to the wall. "I'll put it on our agenda for our next meeting. Whenever that will be."

"It can be when it needs to be," Bear said, glancing at him. "Just get Cactus and Ward there, and we're good."

Ranger nodded, grunting as the weight of the cabinets landed on his shoulders. "Okay, that's down," he said, his voice tight. He hefted the cabinets up higher and hurried toward the back door.

Outside, someone had laid a tarp on the ground, and nothing sat on it yet. Ranger assumed it was for the appliances and cabinets, as those were the two items they wanted to preserve.

He groaned as he bent to put the cabinets on the tarp, and he got out of the way mighty fast when he heard Bear huffing and puffing. He turned to find him carrying a bank of cabinetry too, and he deposited his next to Ranger's.

They both took a moment to catch a few extra breaths, and they went inside to do it all again.

Ace was still fiddling with the countertop, trying to get it off the short length of cabinets that made an island between the back wall and the living area of the cabin. Ranger picked up the drill this time, and Bear shouldered the weight of the cabinets.

"Pull that cord closer for me, would you, Link?" Ranger asked. Lincoln hopped up from where he'd been helping Ace and did what Ranger asked.

A terrible screeching sound filled the cabin as the drill tried to get the screw out of the wood and it slipped. "Let me see," Bear said, and Ranger handed him the drill.

They started to switch places, and before Ranger could get squarely beneath the cabinets, they started to fall from the wall.

"Move," Bear bellowed, and Ranger's first instinct was to curl into himself. That, or throw out both hands to hold the cabinets where they were supposed to be.

He turned toward the cabinets instead of away from them, his foot catching on Link's leg. "Lincoln," he said, throwing his arms up.

"Move, Link," Bear said again, and he turned his back to the cabinets as if he could hold them the way Atlas did the weight of the world. He hunkered over Lincoln, who was a wisp of a boy at best.

Ranger's muscles groaned. The cabinets slid to the right. He said something as the weight disappeared from his hands and arms, but he wasn't sure what.

An awful clattering sound filled the cabin, and dust exploded into the air. A cry immediately followed, and Ranger turned to see who'd been hurt.

His heart pounding, he took the few steps to Lincoln,

whose ankle was stuck under the cabinets that had slid across Bear's back and to the ground.

"Pull him out," Bear said, his voice full of panic. "I'll lift it. One. Two. Three." He growled like a grizzly as he lifted the cabinet, and Ranger slid Lincoln out of the way. The child cried, and Ranger gathered him into his lap and chest.

"It's okay, Link," he said. "Shh." His heartbeat pounded through his veins.

"Do I need to call the ambulance?" Ace asked.

Bear bellowed as he shoved the cabinet out the back door and turned back to Ranger, Ace, and Lincoln, his chest heaving. "Let me see." He arrived and knelt down, looking up to Lincoln's face. "Link, talk to me and tell me how bad it hurts."

"Breathe," Ranger said, and Lincoln took a big breath. "Tell us on a scale of one to ten. How bad is it?"

"Five or six," Link said in his tinny, childlike voice. "Is it broken, Bear?"

"I'm going to touch it now, okay?" Bear watched Lincoln for a moment, and Link nodded. Bear did, and Link flinched. Slowly and surely, Bear was able to bend Link's ankle forward and backward, around and around.

"It's not broken, baby." Bear took Lincoln from Ranger and held him, saying, "You can cry again, okay? Just cry for a minute."

Lincoln did, and Bear closed his eyes, pure agony radiating across his face.

"I'll get a towel, and we'll clean up the blood," Ranger

said, getting to his feet. "Ace, run to the house and get some painkillers."

"I have some in my truck," Bear said. "Middle console."

"Be right back." Ace jogged out the front door, and Ranger wetted a towel, wringing it out, and hurrying over to Link.

"I'm going to wipe off the blood, buddy," he said.

Bear continued to stroke Lincoln's hair as Ranger cleaned up his ankle and leg.

"It's not bad," Ranger said. "A pretty big scrape, but it doesn't even need stitches."

"My momma's gonna find out," Lincoln said, sitting up. He looked at Bear with wide eyes, and then switched his gaze to Ranger. "Then she won't let me come to the ranch anymore."

"You weren't doing anything wrong, Link," Bear said. "Come on, stand up. Hold onto Ranger. Let's see how you do with some weight on it."

Ranger steadied Link with both hands until he was up and on his uninjured leg. He put weight on his ankle gingerly, then a little bit more. He watched the ground, finally taking a step with it. He looked up at Ranger with hope in his expression. "It's not bad."

"Pills," Ace said, entering the cabin at a jog. "Take these, Link." He joined them and helped Lincoln over to the sink to get a drink to swallow the painkillers.

Lincoln wiped his mouth and faced the three of them. "We don't have to tell my mom."

"Lincoln," Bear said. "Yes, we do. I'm going to call her right now, in fact."

"No." Lincoln shot forward, nearly tripping over the cord on the drill. "I'm fine, Bear. Honest." He wiped his eyes again. "I just cried for a minute, and I'm okay. I won't cry again." His bottom lip shook, and Ranger wanted to wrap him inside the safety of his arms and tell him to cry all he wanted to.

Bear bent down so his eyes were the same level as Lincoln's. "You can cry all you want, buddy. That was scary. I felt like crying too." He smiled at Link, and it did wobble slightly. "I love you, and I don't want you to get hurt. But we have to tell your mom. She's your *mother*. She gets to know everything." He raised his eyebrows. "Okay?"

"Yeah, okay," Lincoln said.

"Okay," Bear said, straightening. "Now, grab your cowboy hat and put it back on. Let's take a break and go call her." He waited for Link to get his hat, and then he took the child's hand and said, "I'll be back in a minute, boys."

"Good luck," Ranger said. Once they were gone, he looked at Ace. "I love that boy too."

"As do I." Ace sighed. "I don't think I've ever realized how much I want a son until that very moment. Bear's so good with him." He looked at Ranger with uncertainty in his eyes. "Do you think we'll know how to be dads when it's our turn?"

"I hope so," Ranger said. "Bear is amazing with Lincoln. Maybe we can just watch him." He'd lived a lot of his life watching Bear and trying to do what he did.

"Let's get this done," Ace said. "I can't get this counter off, so I say we move on to the appliances."

"Let's do it." Ranger kept working, and after several minutes, Bear and Lincoln returned. They got their cabin cleaned out, and they walked over to the stables to help Bishop install the cabinets in their new home.

"Sammy's here," Bear said as his phone rang. "Link, she's gonna wanna see you." He paused next to Ranger, who was holding a handful of new screws for Bishop. "She'll want to talk to me alone after that, so when I send Link back in, will you watch him?"

"Of course." Ranger watched Bear wait for Lincoln, and they walked toward the big doors at the end of the building.

"Done," Bishop said, easing out of the cabinet. "Hand me that door, would you?"

Ranger did what he said, one eye always on the door down the aisle. Lincoln came in after only a few minutes, and he wasn't limping or crying. "Okay?" Ranger asked.

Lincoln shrugged. "I guess? She didn't say I couldn't come out here anymore."

"That's good," Ranger said, watching the closed doors again.

"Screw," Bishop said, and Ranger handed one to Link and nodded to Bishop's palm. Lincoln put the screw there, and the drill buzzed again as Bishop put on the cabinet doors. He stood up with a groan. "I'm getting too old for this." He grinned at Ranger. "We're done here."

"Thank heaven," Ranger said. "I'm starving and surprisingly sweaty."

Bishop removed his hat and wiped his brow. "It's warm today. No discernible breeze."

Ranger's phone rang, and he pulled it out of his pocket. The name Don Travers sat on the screen, and Ranger's chest squeezed tight, tighter. "I have to take this," he said, walking away. "Hey, Don."

"Ranger," his financial advisor said, practically yelling his name. "I have some news for Shiloh Ridge. Is Bear nearby? Can I get you both on the line?"

"He's around," Ranger said. "Let me get him. Give me a second." He continued toward the doors, but he didn't want to interrupt Bear and Sammy. The window was open, and Ranger blinked, remembering how the whole family had eavesdropped on the two of them as they'd made up a few weeks ago.

He paused and leaned closer to the window.

Sammy said, "Don't say that, Bear. It's ridiculous. I'd rather have Lincoln up here, getting dirty and yes, hurt on the ranch, than sitting on my momma's couch playing video games."

"I know how stressed you get," Bear said. "He didn't want to tell you, but I can't—I can't do that."

"You did the right thing—well, until the part where you said you'd understand if I didn't want to let him come back up here." She sighed, and she sounded frustrated. "I don't want a martyr Bear or a growly Bear. I want the strong, capable Bear who took care of my son today."

"Okay," Bear said.

"You would kill Lincoln if you told him he couldn't come up here. He loves this ranch. He loves you. I love you, and I love this ranch, and the only way I'm not coming back here is if you tell me to go and never return."

Her footsteps crunched on the gravel outside. "Is that what you want?"

"Of course not," Bear said. "I'm just not sure I deserve you."

"Come on, Bear." She exhaled heavily. "I don't want this self-deprecating Bear either. Where's the Bear who prayed with me when I was afraid? Where's the man who told me we can do anything if we cling to each other and the Lord?"

She blew out her breath. "Where is my strong, sexy Bear?"

He growled, and she giggled, and Ranger grew uncomfortable listening to them. He stepped away from the window and called, "I'll be right back," though no one had said anything to him.

Three seconds later, he opened the door and stepped outside, finding Bear holding Sammy in his arms. At least they weren't kissing.

"Sorry to interrupt," he said. "Don's on the line. He wants to talk to both of us."

"Put him on speaker." Bear released his fiancée, and Ranger joined them, tapping the speaker button.

"All right, Don. I've got Bear with me." His stomach swooped and then felt like he'd swallowed cement and it had hardened in only a second.

"Good news, my friends," Don said, his Southern accent so thick that every vowel sounded like it had an H behind it. "I've just gotten some news about the Netways stock."

Ranger met Bear's eye. "Go on," he said.

"News on the street is they're going to split on Monday

morning. Now, y'all have some choices here. Splitting means you'll own twice as much, but the price is going to be so low at that time, that you'll be basically committing to waiting another decade to sell. Which is fine, y'all are in this for the long haul, I know that."

He took a breath and started again. Ranger's head started to pound, and he needed some of those painkillers from Bear's truck. "If you sell now, we can take your sixty-thousand-dollar investment and cash out with two hundred and eighty-seven thousand."

Bear whistled as Ranger's eyebrows went up. *There are the Christmas bonuses*, he thought.

"I can reinvest the original sixty in something else if you want," Don said. "Maybe that company Ranger sent over earlier this week."

Fear ran through Ranger, and he avoided Bear's gaze, which was suddenly heavy and focused only on him.

"What was it, Ranger? Dura...globe? Dual...something?"

"Nothing," Ranger said. "That was a personal investment, Don." He cleared his throat.

"Anyway," Don said as if Ranger hadn't even spoken. "I just need to know if you want to sell. If I put in the transaction today, it'll go through the second the market opens on Monday, and even if they do split, they'll have to wait until all transactions are complete."

Bear looked at Ranger, curiosity in his eyes, as well as several questions.

"It could be the Christmas bonuses," Ranger said.

Bear nodded, but he still didn't speak.

"We could choose another smaller company like that to invest in," Ranger offered.

"Yep," Bear said.

Ranger nodded and gestured to the phone. "Give the man the word."

"I'm waiting for you to say yes," Bear said.

Ranger smiled and shook his head. "We want to sell it, Don. Make it happen."

"Yes, sir," Don said with a laugh. "Now, let's talk about DualBreak. Do you want the sixty-thousand there?"

Ranger jabbed at the speaker icon and lifted the phone to his ear. "We're gonna have to meet to talk about where we want to reinvest the sixty," he said. He turned away from Bear and Sammy. "The DualBreak is a personal investment for just me, Don."

He'd growled the words, and he didn't care. He could be a bear if he had to be.

"Right, right," Don said.

"That should be done already," Ranger said. "You sent me the docs on Thursday."

"Right, right," Don said. "My mistake."

Ranger breathed in through his nose and pressed his eyes closed. "We'll be in touch with a new investment. Let me know what you need from me for the sale."

"Will do." The call ended, and Ranger lowered his phone from his ear. He tuned back to Bear and Sammy, and they hadn't moved.

"We should go see what Bishop—"

"What's DualBreak?" Bear asked. He bent his head

toward Sammy and nearly whispered, "Could you give me a minute with him, love?"

"She doesn't have to leave," Ranger said over Sammy's, "Sure thing."

She froze again, and Ranger rolled his neck out. "She can stay. You're going to marry her, and you'll just tell her later anyway." Ranger sighed and took a few steps away and then paced back.

He pinned Sammy with a look. "You should know this man does *not* have a Bear box he puts things in and keeps them secure."

"Bear box," she said with a grin. "That's funny."

"Ha ha," Bear said dryly. "Heard that one before, Ranger Rick."

Sammy burst out laughing then, but Ranger settled his weight on one hip and glared at his cousin with everything he had.

"Ranger Rick," Sammy said. "Is your real name Rick?"

"Richard," Bear said, throwing a hard smile at Ranger. "Start talking."

"I didn't tell you, because I...don't know. I just wanted this to be my thing for a while."

Bear folded his arms, softening a little bit.

Ranger wiped a hand down his face, his distress becoming too much for him. *It's just an app*, he told himself. *Not a big deal.*

"I wanted to invest in DualBreak, which is a worldwide app hosting company out of Austin, because I'm interested in apps."

"Apps?" Bear repeated.

"Yeah," Ranger said, looking at his phone and tapping to the Two Cents app. "I'm the creator, developer, and publisher of the Two Cents app." He turned his phone toward Bear. "Stone Bull is my company. I incorporated last year."

Bear's eyes widened, and his mouth hung open as he stared at the logo Ranger had pulled up on the screen. "You're kidding."

Ranger shook his head, his teeth pressing together. "I want this to be a secret, Bear." He looked at Sammy. "Sammy."

"I'll put it in the Bear box," she said. "But wow, Ranger. I *love* that app. Everyone I know loves it."

"It's one app, for a small town in Texas," Ranger said.

"Bear took me on that moonlit hike last night, and wow. So romantic." She beamed at him. "You should take Oakley for sure. Kissing Bear on top of that hill, with all that silver moonlight shining down?" She sighed and linked her arm through Bear's. "We never would've done that without Two Cents."

Ranger couldn't keep the smile off his face even if he'd wanted to. "I'm glad," he said. "I just thought I'd invest in some app hosting companies to see if they can grow."

He watched Bear, who still hadn't confirmed he'd keep his mouth shut about Two Cents. "Bear," he finally said, and his cousin tore his eyes from the phone. "This is a secret, right?"

"Yes," Bear said, grinding his voice in this throat. "I won't say anything to anyone." He looked at Sammy. "You liked the moonlight hike?"

"Loved it," Sammy said, grinning up at him. "Super romantic."

Bear smiled back at her, and Ranger took that as his cue to get the heck out of there. "This is a secret," he said again. "Repeat it to me."

"It's a secret," Bear said while Sammy said a much longer version of the same pledge.

"All right," Ranger said, though he wasn't convinced Bear could actually keep his mouth shut.

Chapter Eleven

Oakley wiped her wrench on a rag that was dirtier than the tool, the scent of grease and metal, dirt and something burnt hanging in the air. She took a deep breath of it, and something settled in her soul that had started to get knocked loose.

Whenever she felt like an engine with one of the pistons misfiring, she came to garage five behind the dealership. It was contained in its own building, and she possessed the only key. She played soft music in Italian and tinkered with the two racecars she kept here.

She set the wrench on the workbench and got behind the wheel. She'd never drive this car on a regular road. Number one, it wasn't legal, and she didn't need to draw any more attention to herself. Ranger had a lot of money, but probably not enough to bail her out of a ticket if she drove her racecar down the sleepy streets of Three Rivers.

The seat wasn't comfortable, and it was the only one in

the car. The rest of the machine was as stripped as possible. A racecar was all about the engine and the driver. Nothing else.

Oakley flexed her fingers on the wheel, the loud roar of the crowd filling her ears. She closed her eyes and breathed, her heartbeat accelerating the way it always had before a race. Beyond that, the vibrations of the engine told her the car was ready. Her pit team worked to make sure she had everything she needed to drive the fastest and win the money.

If she didn't win, they didn't earn as much either.

The engine chugged, and Oakley missed her days on the track more than she'd thought she would. When she'd walked away, she hadn't looked back. Months had passed before she'd looked back.

"You're not looking back now," she told herself. "You're remembering." She wasn't sure what the difference between the two was. Maybe because she didn't want to go back to racing; she just missed it from time to time.

Her father had often said that motor oil ran in her veins, and on days like today, Oakley believed him. Nothing soothed her as much as being in the garage with one of her babies.

She inserted the key and started the ignition, the familiar sputter-growl-rumble-chug of the engine as it came to life comforting her in a way hardly anything else could.

Mint chocolate chip ice cream usually brought the same sense of rightness to her world. Eating a doughnut right after she'd run five miles made Oakley feel like a million bucks.

"Ranger." His name came out of her mouth before she'd even thought it. He made her feel beautiful and loved. He asked her opinion about things, which made her feel smart and capable. He texted and called, which told her he wanted to spend time with her.

And he still hadn't kissed her again, which indicated that he cared about her as a person and not just a pretty face.

She toed the accelerator and listened to the engine rev up. She wanted to take that energy and that life and infuse it into her own soul. She'd need it for tonight, when she went to dinner with Ranger. They were doubling with Bear and Sammy, and the pressure on Oakley's shoulders intensified.

She wished she still had a racing helmet she could hide behind. Even when she was shown on TV, no one would really know how she was feeling. Behind the helmet, the goggles, and the shouting, she could be relaxed or she could be nervous as someone swimming in an ocean without the shore in sight.

More often than not, she was the latter, and when she'd realized she subsisted on antacids and diet cola, she knew it was time to quit.

The Lord had made that very clear by taking her all the way to the hospital in Germany. She'd earned her twenty-five points for winning that Grand Prix, and she'd collapsed only an hour after the race.

She'd woken in the hospital, and she'd immediately wanted to leave. It had taken three days to get clearance, and she'd nearly missed getting to the Hungarian Grand

Prix. But made it she had, and she'd gotten her twenty-five points there too.

Oakley had won more Prix that year than anyone else at ten, and that record hadn't been broken until last year, when Pierre Laurent had won eleven.

She'd finished as the World Champion that year, as she had for the previous two years. Money came flowing in. Accolades. Interviews. Mercedes had wanted to sign her for another three years with a hundred-million-dollar contract.

She'd walked away from all of it. The most pole positions that year. Poised to win for a fourth year in a row. If she'd have wanted a pet monkey, Gregoris Fontaine would've gotten the animal for her. The manager of the racing team would've done anything for Oakley.

But he couldn't turn back time. He couldn't mend her broken heart. He couldn't make her body do what it couldn't physically do.

He'd at least been understanding. Her father had not.

Oakley jammed her foot on the gas pedal, and the whole car shook. She breathed in the power of the machine and used it to push out the memories she didn't want to dwell on anymore.

She turned off the engine and got out of the car, her back sending a physical reminder of why she didn't race anymore. She sure had enjoyed being on the quads with Ranger, though. That wasn't nearly the same adrenaline rush, but it was something more than feeding her grumpy cat, driving through for coffee, and selling trucks.

She picked up a clean rag and wiped down the car from

front to back, liking the way she could stretch her muscles at the same time she worked.

Ranger called just as she pulled into her garage, and she stayed in the truck so the call would connect via the Bluetooth. "Hey," Oakley said, her voice as bright as she felt, which was much better than she'd been that morning.

"You've been on my mind," Ranger said. "I really have no reason to call, other than to see if you're okay." His voice was lower than she'd heard it before, and she heard other people in the background on his end of the line.

"I'm okay," she said.

"Are we still on for tonight?" he asked. "I'm fine to cancel."

Oakley's eyebrows went up. "Do you want to cancel?"

"Only if you do."

"Ranger."

"No," he said. "I don't want to, but if you're not feeling up to it, I understand. It's Bear and Sammy, and we had a little scare during demolition today." He proceeded to tell her about a flying cabinet that had fallen on Lincoln's calf and pinned his ankle.

Oakley's heart bumped strangely in her chest. She'd only met the little boy once, but she didn't want him to be hurt. "Is he okay?"

"Fit as a fiddle," Ranger said. "I'm using it as an excuse to take it easy this afternoon."

"Oh?" Oakley asked with plenty of flirtatiousness in her voice. "And what does that look like for you, Mister Glover?"

He chuckled. "I'm currently hiding out in my wing,

sitting in my office. I think I might make coffee in my own wing and pop a bag of popcorn and put a lot of salt on it." He laughed quietly, and all the noise from before disappeared. "Bishop doesn't let me put on enough salt."

"The salt and butter are why you eat popcorn at all," Oakley said.

"Agreed," Ranger said. The silence stretched between them, and Oakley found she didn't have anything to say to him either. She didn't need their voices between them, and she laid her head back against the rest and sighed.

"I'm not convinced you're okay," he said.

"I spent the morning with my babies," she said.

"Oh." His tone suggested shock and awe.

Oakley smiled to herself. "My racecars. I have two of them in a super-secret garage behind the dealership."

"Super-secret," Ranger repeated, a laugh following. "Maybe you'd show me your babies sometime."

Oakley automatically bucked against that idea, and she'd have to break down her walls one brick at a time. Ranger was extraordinarily good at removing them by the wheelbarrow-full, and she even felt him taking them out of her heart right now. "Maybe," she said. "I feel like I'm the one sharing all the secrets and revealing all these ugly truths about myself." And she wasn't done yet. "I'm going to need something you've never told anyone before if I'm to consider letting you inside the super-secret shed."

"Is that so?"

"That's so." She covered her mouth as she giggled, hoping it was somewhat muted for his ears.

"I'll think about what I have that fits such criteria."

Something slammed for him, and he said, "Ward just walked in. I have to go, okay? I'll see you at six?"

"Six," Oakley confirmed, and she turned off the truck and opened the door. Inside, she fed and watered The General, who stalked back and forth, his long, black tail held tall and straight, watching her. Judging her.

"It's the same food I gave you yesterday," she said to him, rolling her eyes. "The water is filtered from the fridge." She left him to deal with his substandard diet and got in the shower.

Before she knew it, six o'clock had arrived, and that meant Ranger had too. This time, he held a bouquet of yellow flowers in his hand—daisies, sunflowers, tulips, and roses. "Did you know," he said, his head ducked down as he looked at the flowers in his hand. "That yellow flowers symbolize joy?" He looked up at her, his sky blue eyes wide, somewhat intense, and full of happiness. "They also mean friendship, affection, caring, happiness, and new beginnings." He extended them toward her. "Those are not all exactly how I feel about you, but a lot of them are close."

Oakley melted with his words and the way he leaned into the doorway as she took the bouquet. "They're beautiful," she said. "Just like that little speech." She wanted to tip up onto her toes and kiss him, but someone honked the horn in his truck.

He spun toward the vehicle and waved for whoever it was to stop it. When he faced her again, he said, "Sorry. Someone had to take Link back to his grandparents' house, and he wanted to come with me." He shrugged. "So...."

"Ranger," the little boy called. "There's an armadillo! Look!"

"An armadillo," Oakley repeated. "I want to see that." She'd left her heels beside the door, so she padded onto the porch barefoot. Sure enough, an armadillo skittered down her driveway and along the sidewalk.

"He's a great kid," Ranger said. "Just maybe doesn't understand the finer points of picking a woman up for a date."

Oakley lifted the flowers to her face and smelled them. "Ranger?"

"Hmm?"

"Are you going to kiss me tonight?" She felt the weight of his gaze as it moved from Lincoln in the truck to her.

"I don't know."

She faced him, feeling every bit of that power and energy from her racecars boiling through her bloodstream. "Would you let me kiss you?"

His eyes dropped to her lips, which Oakley had painted to perfection with a pale pink gloss. "Maybe." A smile spread across his face, and that dazzling sparkle ran freely through his eyes.

"You're a tease," she said, hurrying back to the house.

"Come on," he said, laughing.

"You're not invited to see the racecars," she called over her shoulder. She set the bouquet on the side table near the door and stepped into her shoes.

Ranger's hand slid along her waist and leaned toward her. "I've got a secret."

"Is that right?" she quipped. "What? You don't put

your socks in the hamper at the end of the day?" She turned into him, which forced him to back up a step or two. "That's not a secret, Ranger. That's just being a slob."

He laughed, and while a tremor of annoyance for him definitely existed, Oakley did like teasing him.

"I am a bit of a slob," he said. "I can admit to that."

"I pay a cleaning service," Oakley said.

"Will you let me hold your hand, or are you super-mad at me?"

"First, you're impossible to get mad at. Second, I literally just asked you if you'd kiss me, so yes, I think holding hands is within the realm of possibilities."

He grinned and leaned closer. "So is kissing tonight, sweetheart." His lips touched her earlobe. "But not right now, with eight-year-old eyes on us. And that creepy armadillo." He chuckled, and Oakley shivered with the huskiness in his voice.

"Plus, we don't want to be late." Oakley stepped out onto the porch and closed her front door behind her.

They dropped off Lincoln without a hitch, and before Oakley knew it, she was sliding into a booth opposite of Sammy Benton and Bear Glover.

"Sorry we're late," Ranger said. "We saw an armadillo, and I think we all know what Link did with that sighting."

"He loves armadillos," Sammy said with a smile.

"The cartoon ones are okay," Ranger said. "The real-life ones?" He gave a false shiver. "Not okay."

Bear smiled too, but his attention switched to Oakley almost instantly. "How's the dealership?" he asked.

"Amazing," Oakley said. "Great. Ranger said you guys demolished the cabins today. How did it go?"

"Good," Bear said. "A bump here and there." He glanced at Sammy. "But they're cleaned out, and Bishop and Ward have got us on a schedule that leaves very little time for sleeping."

"You don't even like sleeping," Sammy teased, and Oakley smiled at the two of them.

"How long have you two known each other?" she asked, wishing she had a glass of diet cola to hide behind.

They looked at each other, studying one another's faces, both clearly thinking.

"Sammy's been comin' up to the ranch to help with our equipment for what?" Ranger asked. "At least three years."

"Four," Bear said, his throat catching some of the sound and keeping it inside. "Just over four."

Sammy linked her arm through Bear's and leaned into his bicep. "Bear was one of my very first ranch contracts," she said. "I'd always wanted to open my own mechanic shop, and I'd done it only a few months before I got custody of Lincoln, and I thought there was no better time than to try to make it all work."

"Plus," Ranger said. "August Dexter had just announced he was closing his shop, and there wasn't another good option in town."

"I prayed about it, and it was the right time," Sammy said. "Having Shiloh Ridge as a real ranch contract told others they could trust me. It actually helped a lot."

"I didn't know that," Bear said. "You never said that."

"You weren't my boyfriend then," she said, grinning up

at him. He bent down and kissed her, and again, Oakley found them the most adorable couple ever.

She really needed something to drink, and she glanced out into the restaurant to see if a waiter or waitress was coming their way. Didn't seem to be.

"Ranger says you're a racecar driver," Sammy said.

"Yes," Oakley said. "Or rather, I was. I retired a few years ago." She knew she needed to give more than one word or single sentence answers, so she started telling them a little bit about Formula One racing.

The first-place driver in each Grand Prix earned twenty-five points. Whoever had the most points at the end of the season was the World Champion. She talked about what it meant to be in the pole position for a Prix. She answered Bear's question about where the different races were held, and which country she liked best.

Her throat felt like it would crack it was so dry, and she looked for a waiter again. "I'm dying," she said. "How long have we been here? I need a drink."

"I agree," Bear said, his tone darkening. "Two Cents said this place was amazing, but we haven't even been greeted yet." He flashed a look at Sammy, and they both looked at Ranger. Something was definitely going on there, but Oakley wasn't on the inside of the conversation.

She took out her phone and tried to swallow to wet her throat. "Did you know you can tap on the name of a place and leave a rating? We can do that, and it'll move down in the rankings. So it could be number three tonight, but if we give it a lower rating, it'll move down."

"I'm so going to do that," Bear said. "Because I'm dying for a drink too."

"Here he comes," Ranger said. "Be nice."

"I'm nice," Bear said, but when the man arrived, he said, "We're ready for all of it, because you guys seem a bit behind tonight."

The waiter blinked and said, "Sure, let's put everything in."

Oakley quickly scanned the menu and picked the Italian sampler, which came with spaghetti and meatballs and a slice of lasagna. "And double the garlic bread," she said, handing him her menu. "Please."

He nodded and took the cowboys' orders before walking away.

Ranger's hand found hers under the table, and he leaned toward her. "Double the garlic bread?"

"One can never have too much garlic bread," she said, smiling at him.

The food came faster than the drinks had, and the conversation revolved around the ranch, Sammy's shop, and the dealership. Oakley enjoyed getting to know Sammy and Bear, and she got Sammy's number so they could chat about service.

"I'll tell you how I got Link too," Sammy said with a smile as Bear signed his name on the check. "Do you know the story?"

"No," Oakley said. "I'm still pretty new to town." She glanced at Ranger. "Three Rivers has a lot of history and a lot of families who've been here a while."

"That they do," Sammy said.

"Ready?" Bear asked.

She nodded and slid out of the booth. Ranger was still putting something in his wallet, so Oakley waited.

"Well, I haven't been married before," Sammy said. "So Bear and I are planning a huge wedding in March."

"We are?" Bear asked, his perplexed look about the cutest thing Oakley had seen in a while.

"Yes," Sammy said, taking his hand.

Ranger finally stood up, and Oakley slid to the edge of the booth.

"Have you been married before?" Sammy asked.

Oakley looked up and found all three of them looking down at her. She suddenly felt so small and so insignificant. She blinked, and Ranger's dark hair and tan skin morphed into Roberto's. His light blue eyes sat in Roberto's face, and Oakley felt like throwing up.

She managed to shake her head and get to her feet. They moved toward the exit, and Sammy switched places with Ranger. "I'm sorry," she said. "I didn't mean to put you on the spot."

"It's fine," Oakley said, desperate to get outside now. She just needed to clear her head, and fresh oxygen would do it. "I'm fine." She hurried ahead of everyone, practically bursting into the cool night air beyond the restaurant.

She looked around wildly, not finding her truck. It wasn't until Ranger put his hand on the small of her back and said, "You're with me, sweetheart," that she realized she hadn't driven.

She looked at him, so many words teeming on the end of her tongue. She bit them all back, nodded, and went with him toward the truck that smelled like leather and horses and Ranger's fresh, clean aftershave. That would settle her too.

In the back of her mind, though, all Oakley could think about was getting back to garage five, strapping into the racecar, and driving as fast as she could away from Three Rivers.

Chapter Twelve

Ranger kept one eye on Oakley as he pulled out of the parking lot at Sweet and Saucy, his mood already slightly dampened by Sammy and Bear's blatant attempt to get him to admit his ownership of Two Cents.

Oakley was a smart woman, and she'd seen the silent conversation between the three of them. Ranger had some choice words for his cousin once he dropped off Oakley and made it back to the ranch.

He didn't head straight there, though. "I think we need dessert," he said. "I just couldn't stand to wait for it there."

"They really were slow, weren't they?" she asked. "They didn't seem that busy either."

"Maybe they had a new chef or something."

"Maybe." She looked out her window, her countenance completely different than the fun, flirty woman who'd asked him to kiss her a couple of hours ago. "That app is usually right."

For some reason, Ranger wanted to defend Two Cents, but he held back. He had to remind himself that it wasn't a commentary on him or his decisions. He hadn't placed Sweet and Saucy in the number three spot for best baked pasta. The people who'd filled out his survey had.

He'd added the user ratings last night, and Oakley had known about them. "How about you look up the best place to find dessert in this town?"

She pulled out her phone, saying, "It's Heidi's, and you know it. They're also closed by now."

"It's only eight," Ranger said.

"They close at four." Oakley swiped, her face illuminated in the white and blue light. "Things that are open now...you've got Ice Cream Emporium. That's a no for me."

"No?"

"I went there a couple of weeks ago with Vanessa from the dealership. The place was not clean, and just...no."

"Okay," he said. "Is that number one?"

"No," she said. "Number one is closed. So is two, three, and four. Number five is something you won't like, and then we get to Ice Cream Emporium."

"I think they changed ownership a while back," Ranger said, his memory firing now. His survey had likely been before that. The bottom dropped out of his stomach as he realized he'd launched Two Cents with old data. No wonder the lists weren't coming up with the best of the best.

He tried to swallow and found he couldn't.

"We could try Maple's," she said.

"What's the one I won't like?" he asked when he found his voice. "Number five?"

"Empanadas," she said.

"Too doughy," he said. "Though Etta makes a pretty good empanada."

"I like anything fried," Oakley said, but she didn't smile or look away from her phone. She didn't say anything for a few minutes, and Ranger just drove aimlessly.

Tension bled through Ranger, and he thought about what he'd say to get Oakley to talk. He'd told her once that she could tell him what she wanted, when she wanted, and that was still true.

So maybe start there, he thought.

"Okay," he said, pulling into the grocery store across the street from the downtown park. "I know something's wrong. Something happened there at the end, at the restaurant. You don't have to tell me if you don't want to. But if you do...I'd love to talk to you. Know about it." He cleared his throat. "Whatever you want, whenever you want."

Oakley had looked up from her phone after the second sentence. Her eyes searched his, almost like she was looking for proof that she could trust him.

"I'm going to go get ice cream," he said, indicating the store. "They have those little pints, and I'll get some plastic spoons. We'll drive somewhere where it's just us and the stars, and we'll...eat ice cream."

"You'll tell me a secret," she said, still no smile in sight.

"Yes," he said, still unsure of what he should reveal.

He'd considered telling her about Two Cents, but his embarrassment about using old surveys to rank restaurants and other items wouldn't allow him to do it.

He'd fix it by sending out a push notification to the app, asking people to vote for their current favorites. Then he'd tell her.

"Mint chocolate chip?" he asked.

"And the birthday cake one."

"You got it." Ranger got out of the truck and headed inside. The grocery store blasted the space with very bright lights, and they almost hurt Ranger's eyes. He just wanted to be under the wide sky, where he could breathe and where he could hear the Lord better than anywhere else.

Help me know what to do with Oakley, he prayed as he examined the choices in the freezer case. He got one with chocolate ice cream, caramel swirls, and brownie chunks. He picked out her mint chocolate chip. He found the birthday cake container, though he found the flavor too sweet. He also chose a banana flavored ice cream with peanut butter and chocolate, and then he headed for the check-stand.

Back at the truck, Oakley had pulled her knees to her chest and curled into the door. She turned toward him when he got behind the wheel, a small smile on her mouth.

"I got four flavors," he said. She took the bag from him and set it on the floor where her feet should've been. She didn't wear her heels, and Ranger could sense her apprehension like a strong scent.

He cleared his throat and started driving. "Should I just take you home?" he asked quietly.

"No, the stars and the ice cream sound great," she said.

"So you're not going to break up with me."

"No," she said. "Of course not."

"You looked at me like you didn't even know me back there," he said.

"I'm—" Her voice cut off, and a squeak came out. "I did?"

"Yes," he said. "At the restaurant. You sort of blanked for a minute before you got up."

She looked out her window again, and Ranger hated that he had to focus on the road. Maybe he disliked how she wouldn't look at him. "I don't want to tell you."

"Okay."

"I do," she said. "But I don't."

"What do you think is going to happen?"

"I think *you'll* break up with *me*," she said.

Ranger could not think of a single reason why he would, and he suddenly knew what secret to tell her. His throat closed, and his heart raced.

He kept driving, feeling wild and out of control. Time seemed to pass like water over a steep drop, and before he knew it, he'd left the lights and noise of Three Rivers on a Saturday night in his rear-view mirror.

He'd gone north and east—about as far from Shiloh Ridge as he could get—and up into the hills where a new subdivision had gone in a few years ago.

He made a right turn before the gated community began, and bumped over the uneven dirt road to the top of the hill. A sigh passed his lips as he put the truck in park, rolled down all the windows, and killed the headlights.

"Can I have the banana one?" he asked quietly.

The plastic sack rustled as Oakley started to dig through it to get the ice cream and spoons out. She passed him what he'd requested, and Ranger took off the lid.

He peeled back the plastic, the scent of fake banana flavoring hitting him in the nose. His mouth puckered, and he looked out his own window. "I'll go first," he said. "My secret, Oakley, is that I'm already falling in love with you. It's been what? A week?" He released the rest of the air in his lungs and dug the plastic spoon into the ice cream.

"I've never been in love before—maybe that's another secret—but Mother always said I'd know when it happened. And well, I guess I just know."

Oakley said nothing, but she also removed the lid on a container of ice cream and the crackly plastic under that. A moment later, she said, "I can't see the stars from in here. Do you have a blanket or anything in here?'

"Yes, ma'am," he said. "Right behind your seat."

She faced him, putting her legs down. "Want to lay in the back?"

Boy, did he ever. "Sure," he said. "You stay there, since you don't have shoes on. Okay? I'll get it set up and come get you." He reached for her ice cream, and she handed it to him.

He collected the blanket and took everything to the truck bed. It wasn't exactly clean back here, and Oakley's pretty sundress would get dirty. She obviously didn't care, so Ranger went to her side of the truck and opened the door. "All right, baby. Hold onto me." He gathered her into his arms, and she wrapped her hands around the back of his neck.

He carried her the way one would carry their new bride across the threshold of their new home and lifted her right up over the side of the truck after only three steps. "There you go."

She started to get settled as Ranger went to the tailgate to use the step there. He joined her near the back windows of the cab, where she'd bunched up the blanket to make their seat softer.

"This is so much better," she said, gazing up into the sky. "The night sky is incredible, don't you think?"

"Yes," he murmured, taking his ice cream from her again.

They both ate a few bites of ice cream before she said, "I've been all over the world, Ranger. Australia, Germany, Great Britain, Belgium, Russia, Spain, Italy." She sighed and looked up into the sparkling expanse above them. "All over. I've been the Formula One World Champion three times. One year, I won more grand slams than anyone else, and that's hard to do."

"What's a grand slam?"

"It's where you're in the pole position—that goes to the highest ranked driver in the race—you lead every lap of the race, you win the race, and you had the fastest lap time."

"Wow," he said, as if he needed additional reasons to feel inferior to her. "That's pretty amazing, Oakley."

"I was a good racecar driver," she said, her voice breaking.

Ranger wanted to shield her from anything unpleasant in her life. The problem was, all of those things had happened in the past, and he hadn't been there to help her.

You're here now, he said, switching to a prayer. *Help me help her.*

"Do you miss it?" he asked.

"No," she said. "No, I don't miss it. It was time for me to leave, and I left."

"Okay," he said, nodding.

"It was actually the second time I'd left racing."

Ranger simply took another bite of ice cream, thinking the night was a little too cold to be snacking on a frozen treat.

"The first time, I left because I'd met and fallen in love with a man named Roberto Alonso. He was from Spain, and a recruiter for Ferrari, a racing team that was trying to get me to sign with them." Her voice quieted when she'd said the man's name. "We were to be married, and I wasn't going to race anymore. That was the first time my father threatened to cut me off." She gave a mirthless laugh before she filled her mouth with mint ice cream.

Ranger wished he'd bought a couple of bottles of water, and then he remembered he had some in the truck. He didn't want to jump out and get them in the middle of her story, though, so he just sat tight.

"There's nothing embarrassing about falling in love with someone else," he said, not quite understanding her distress.

"Yeah." She sighed, a long, heavy sound. "It took me a

while to realize he loved me, but he didn't want to marry me. We lived together, and I thought he was worth giving up everything for. Everything, Ranger. My family. My friends. My job and career. My morals and beliefs."

She shook her head. "I'm embarrassed by how I acted, and I—Roberto and I lived together. I got pregnant, and I thought that would change everything. He'd certainly want to marry me if I had his baby."

"He didn't," Ranger said softly.

"He did not," Oakley said. "And it wasn't like marriage was a deal-breaker. It wasn't. I would've given up everything for him. I *had* given up everything. When I told him I was pregnant, he asked me to end it."

Ranger sucked in a breath. "You're kidding."

"Turned out, he was married, and that was why he didn't want to marry me. He didn't want another baby. He'd lied about his age, and he was far older than me—twenty years older than me." She sighed, and Ranger stuck his spoon in his ice cream and lifted his arm over her shoulders.

She snuggled into his side, and this way, Ranger could see the stars and smell Oakley's perfume, but she couldn't see his face. "People make mistakes, Oakley."

"Don't stand up for him."

"I didn't mean him," Ranger said, swallowing. "So...you have a child?"

"No," she said. "I lost the baby after only a week. Thank all the stars in heaven I hadn't told my parents yet. I packed everything I'd taken to Roberto's Spanish villa, and

I went back to London, where my father lived. We ended up feeding a story to the media about me needing a year off, and I signed with Mercedes for the next three years."

Ranger's mind had a lot to stew over, and he couldn't do much more than stroke his fingers up and down her arm. He looked at the smear of stars through the sky, wishing he could reach up and touch one if he tried hard enough.

"In the end," she said, her voice loud in the still, silent night. "When I retired the second time, I still gave up everything. But not who I am, and not what I believe." She took a deep breath. "I know who I am. I know where the lines are that I won't cross."

Ranger didn't know what to say to that. He breathed in the soft floral scent of her hair, finding it mixed with something like dryer sheets. He didn't want any more ice cream, and it would all be melted by the time he got back to the ranch.

He couldn't believe he was worrying about melted ice cream when he should be thinking about how to respond to Oakley.

"I understand if you don't want to be with me," Oakley said, sitting up.

His arm fell back to his side, and he looked at the back of her head. "Why would I not want to be with you?"

"Don't you ever feel like you used up your chance at the life you want?" She peered at him over her shoulder, and she was everything Ranger wanted. "That's how I feel." She faced the horizon again. "Or I felt, before I met you. You... you make me feel like I might get a second chance to show myself, the Lord, and my father that I can do it right."

"That's a good thing, right?" he asked.

"For me it is," she said. "But you still haven't said one thing about everything I just admitted to."

Ranger opened his mouth to respond, not knowing what would come out. "I just need some time to think," he said.

She nodded, the tension between them doubling.

Ranger's phone buzzed, and he watched her for another moment before getting it out to look at it. He read the message from Rhett Walker quickly, his smile immediate.

"Hey, Oakley?"

"Hmm?"

He sat up too and gently drew her back into his chest. "Would you go to a graduation party with me?"

"Graduation party?" She tilted her head back and looked up at him. If she hadn't just told him what she had, Ranger would probably kiss her.

"Yeah," he said instead. "For Penny Walker. She just finished all of her coursework for law school, and the Walkers are having a big party for her in a few weeks. I need a date for that." He lifted her phone so she could see it. "They need a count for the food."

"A few weeks, huh?"

"Yep."

"You think we'll be together in a few weeks?"

"Yes," Ranger said.

"So you're really not going to break up with me for acting like a fool and going against what I knew to be right."

"Like I said," he said. "Everyone makes mistakes. Either

I believe people can change and do better, or I don't. I do believe that, because I need the ability to repent and change more than anyone."

"Oh, please," she said. "You're perfect."

"I am not," he said. "And it's dangerous for you to think I am."

"Even your secret wasn't really a secret," she said. "Mine was that I quit racing for a guy, got pregnant, and then lost the baby."

Ranger closed his eyes and breathed in. He did believe people could change and do better. He did. "Will you come to the party with me?"

"Yes," she said, snuggling deeper into his chest. "Yes, I'll go to the party with you."

Great, Ranger said, but only in his mind. If anyone could show Oakley that it wasn't too late to do something, it was Penny Walker. The woman was sixty-eight years old and had always wanted to be a lawyer. She was one of the first women to get into law school in the seventies, and she'd traded it all to raise her family of seven, loud cowboys with her husband.

She'd started working on the degree she'd left behind a year or two ago, and now she'd finished. She was a great example for everyone that just because dreams didn't come true when she'd thought they would, didn't mean the dream was dead.

Ranger knew he couldn't say any of that to Oakley right now. He would later, after he'd figured out how he felt about everything she'd said. He saw her in his future, and while it was fast, Ranger found himself wanting to press on the accelerator of their relationship even more.

He'd always known what he wanted, and he shouldn't expect this to be any different. Now, he just had to figure out if him saying he'd started falling in love with her already had freaked her out at all.

Chapter Thirteen

Cactus Glover smelled the evidence that Thanksgiving dinner was well underway as he rode up to the homestead. The clock had barely struck nine in the morning, but Bishop, Ida, and Etta had been cooking for days.

As his horse started to clop over the driveway and gravel, Cactus looked up at the new mansion that marred the ranch.

Cactus simply didn't know what to do with all that space. He didn't want more than he absolutely needed, because the empty rooms, closets, and air were simply a place for his thoughts to get stuck.

He spent very little time indoors if he could help it, and with rain in the forecast for the next several days, starting tomorrow, he was facing a lot of cold, wet clothes, mud, and grumpy cowboys. He'd probably lead the pack with that one, especially now that Bear had been tamed into a teddy.

Cactus said, "Whoa," and Hammy took one more step and stopped. Sammy stood on the porch already, leaning against the pillar at the top of the steps. She leaned against it, her arms folded and one foot up against the pillar as if waiting for a bus.

He knew she wasn't waiting for no bus. She was waiting for him.

"Go on," he muttered to his horse, and Hammy knew Cactus-speak by now. He plodded forward again while Cactus pushed his cowboy hat further down.

"I still see you," Sammy called, and Cactus grunted. She wouldn't be able to hear that, but she also wouldn't be expecting an answer. "Corral that beast and come talk to me."

Cactus kept the frown on his face while he thought she could see. Once she couldn't, he relaxed, his heart booming in his chest at the mere possibility of retiring his hermit status. If he did, and he got hurt again.... He wasn't even sure who or what he'd morph into then.

He put Hammy in the pasture north of the homestead and walked back to the porch. He climbed the steps to where Sammy stood. She hadn't moved, but her eyes tracked him every step of the way.

"Nice hat," he said in a deadpan.

"Thanks," she said. "Bear and Lincoln got it for me." She reached up and lifted the cowgirl hat, smoothed her auburn hair back, and put the hat on again. "So? What do you think?"

"I think I'm insane," Cactus said, sighing. He moved around her and walked along the railing of the front porch. It wrapped around the house on both sides, with a large deck on the north, and a hidden alcove on the south.

He'd gone south, of course. Cactus didn't air anything, for anyone. And yet, this mechanic had somehow gotten under his skin.

It wasn't Sammy under there. It was the possibility of another woman in his life that had everything he'd become and every decision he made seem wrong.

"I think *you're* insane too," he said as he heard her footsteps behind him. She always gave him a lot of space. She visited with him like he was a normal man, and Cactus appreciated that. She treated him with kindness and respect, something even some of his brothers and cousins didn't do. They simply didn't know how to treat him, and while he'd thought he'd wanted to be ignored and left alone, the truth was, he hadn't. Didn't.

"I think if I do this, everyone is going to know why. I think it's ridiculous to think there will be anyone who could possibly be interested." He looked across the road that ran along the edge of the lawn, and to the southeast, where the small family cemetery beckoned to him.

He visited it often, as his father and grandmother were buried there, and he often needed their advice. Lately, he'd been visiting their graves more than that of his son, which was only a stone's throw from his back porch.

Hardly anyone knew about the four-day-old infant Cactus had loved and lost. He knew how much a person could go through in ninety-six hours, and the ninety-six days after that, then ninety-six months.

It was time to step out of the prickly skin he'd donned a decade ago.

It is, he told himself.

The problem was, he was very brusque, and he had no patience for trivial things. Not only that, but his courage had somehow been buried with his son. That, or Allison had taken it when she'd left Shiloh Ridge, left Three Rivers, and left Texas.

"I think you should keep an open mind," Sammy said, copying his stance down to the T. She leaned against the railing, her forearms resting on the wood, her eyes out over the horizon.

"I think I'm going to be too busy renovating that barn that got condemned on Tuesday."

"I think you'll have plenty of time for a haircut." Sammy turned and grinned at him. "When's the last time you went to town?"

"I can't even recall," he said, refusing to let himself smile back, though he liked Sammy a whole lot and she'd probably like it if he did. He'd gotten to know her over the past month, and he'd asked her to help him get ready to dip back into the dating pool. "You're aware I have no vehicle, correct?"

"I'm aware," she said. "You're aware Ranger just bought two brand new ranch trucks, correct?"

Cactus rolled his eyes. "I'm aware."

"Can you drive?"

"I'm a hermit, not an invalid," Cactus said.

Sammy just laughed at him. When she'd suggested he take the time he needed to feel ready, he'd confessed he'd never feel ready. He'd told Bear that, and he'd been telling the truth.

But Christmastime in Three Rivers was very busy, with a lot of people attending a lot of events, and Sammy had thought perhaps he'd like to start with simply getting off the ranch and interacting with someone whose last name wasn't Glover.

"So you'll come down to my place tomorrow," she said. "My mother will cut your hair and feed you all the home-made bread you want. Then we'll go get a few new things to wear, and you'll be ready for the tree lighting on Saturday."

Cactus swallowed, his memories from before flowing through his mind. "I hate the tree lighting," he said. "Maybe I should—"

"You do *not* hate the tree lighting," Sammy said with plenty of force in her voice. "Bear and I are going, and probably Ranger and Oakley, and you won't be alone."

"You think I want to be a fifth wheel?" He gaped at her. "Dear Lord, woman, I thought you were smart."

Sammy blinked at him, her eyes turning from shocked to displeased in a second flat. "Do not insult me, Charles. I'm trying to help you."

"I'm sorry," he said quickly, bowing his head.

"Sammy?" Lincoln called from around the corner, and Cactus moved away from Sammy as she stepped around the corner and called to her son. Lincoln ran toward her, exclaiming something about a peppermint pie, and Cactus felt a smile twitching against his lips.

"Go say hi now," Sammy said, and Cactus turned toward Lincoln.

He did smile then, because there was something about Lincoln that made everything better. "Heya, boy," Cactus said, accepting the hug Lincoln gave him. "Are you supervising in there?"

Bishop would think he was in charge, but really, it was Etta. Ida had a loud voice too, but she was bringing her boyfriend to dinner, so she'd be on her best behavior.

"I cracked a whole bunch of eggs for a mousse," Lincoln said, stepping back. "Can we go riding today?"

"I'm sure we can," Cactus said, retreating to the fence. Lincoln was only eight, and his son would've been ten, but they were close enough in age and coloring for Cactus's heart to fold itself into a tiny box and try to keep sending enough blood to his whole body. "I'm sure we can."

Lincoln didn't seem to be in a hurry to get back to the kitchen, and the three of them stood there in the Thanksgiving morning. He had no idea what they were thinking, but Cactus felt a spark of gratitude pricking at his hollow, hard heart.

Gratitude that Samantha Benton had been led to Shiloh Ridge Ranch. Not only was she a perfect complement to Bear, but she'd also helped him see there was hope after tragedy. He knew Bishop had been trying harder to meet someone, and Ranger would not be dating Oakley if Sammy hadn't first said yes to Bear's invitation to dinner.

Gratitude that he had his family, as loud and annoying as they could be.

Gratitude for this ranch, and this land, and all those who'd worked it before him.

He cleared his throat and straightened, his eyes meeting Sammy's. "Thank you, Sammy," he said.

"You're welcome, Cactus."

With that, he left her and her son looking at the cemetery and went inside the house.

HOURS LATER, CACTUS EYED THE MASSIVE GROUP OF people, a frown etched on his eyebrows. He wasn't close with a lot of them, and he knew that was his fault. Bear had kept in close touch with Cactus. Surprisingly, so had Bishop, his youngest brother. Ward and Ranger never let him get too far from them, and Judge had been Cactus's saving grace all those years ago.

"Who are we missing?" someone bellowed.

Ward, who stood a few feet away from Cactus yelled, "Ranger's not here. He went to pick up Oakley."

Cactus had not met the woman yet, and something like the beating of bat wings moved through his stomach. Brady Burton had arrived fifteen minutes ago, and he looked like someone had taken a frozen turkey and hit him upside the head with it.

Cactus's head felt like that, and he maneuvered his way through the crowd to the kitchen.

"Nope, get out," Etta said, giving him a look.

"I have a headache," he said. "I'm not going to touch your precious mashed potato sculpture." The moment he spoke, he regretted the words. There was no way Sammy's insane plan was going to work.

He needed a lot more than a haircut and a new pair of jeans. He needed etiquette lessons and empathy classes.

"I'm sorry, Etta," he said. At least he knew how to apologize. Mother had taught all the children to apologize if they said something or did something to hurt someone else.

"It's fine," she said. "I know today is stressful on a lot of levels." She looked from Cactus to where Ida stood with her hand in Brady's. Cactus saw the look of longing on Etta's face before he turned to get the painkillers out of the cabinet.

Cactus saw a lot of what happened on the ranch. He kept his head down and did his work, but that didn't mean he didn't hear the gossip and see the turmoil in other people's lives. He swallowed the pills, thinking of all the joyous occasions he'd missed out on too. For a while there, he simply couldn't bring himself to celebrate anything. Not a stellar market day. Not a ribbon-cutting ceremony on this massive mansion. Not a luncheon to celebrate the removal of all the grasshoppers from the ranch.

Time had started to stitch together his wounds, though, and as Cactus faced the crowd again, a new type of energy poured through him.

"Thank you for cooking for us," he said to Etta.

She turned toward him, plenty of surprise in her

expression. "You're welcome, Cactus." She smiled, and he patted her shoulder as he left the kitchen.

Quite proud of himself, he searched for Sammy to see if she'd been watching him have a normal conversation with someone he usually wouldn't. Before he could find her, someone yelled, "Ranger's here," and cheers and chaos rang out.

He wasn't going to like that, but Cactus supposed he should've timed his arrival better. As it was, the entire family had their eyes trained on the wide arched hall that led into the foyer when Ranger and Oakley walked through it.

They both froze, and Ranger looked around at everyone with a resigned look in his eye. Oakley actually said, "Oh, my," and brought her hand to her mouth. Her eyes widened as if they could take in the crowd that way, and she scanned the huge space too.

"Everyone," Ranger said in a loud voice. "This is Oakley Hatch. Oakley, this is what crazy looks like." He grinned at them, and a few people jeered back at him.

"All right," Bear said, joining Ranger and Oakley and facing the family. "Thanks for coming everyone. We're glad to have you all at Shiloh Ridge this year, whether you live here or it's your first time on the ranch."

He looked around too. "Ward? Cactus? Would one of you say grace, and then we're going to turn the mic over to Bishop, Etta, and Ida, who've been working for days and weeks to provide us with this feast."

Cactus's pulse pounced in his body, and he normally

would've just let Ward take over. Ward knew that too, and he'd done it loads of times.

But today, Cactus wanted to take one step outside his comfort zone. If he couldn't do that with family, he'd never be able to do it with anyone he met in Three Rivers, male or female.

"I'll do it," he said, raising his hand. He was closer to Bear and Ranger anyway.

An actual murmur moved through the crowd, their surprise echoed on Bear's face.

"Okay," Bear said, recovering quickly. "Get on up here, Cactus."

Chapter Fourteen

Oakley kept her hand in Ranger's as his cousin said the prayer over the food. She'd asked him on the way up to the ranch if his family did those rituals where they all had to go around the table and say something they were grateful for. He'd said, no, not really, but Oakley had the very real suspicion that something gratitude-based was going to rear its ugly head.

Not that she wasn't grateful for things. Her life, her health, the fact that the Lord had directed her here. For her business, and her past success that allowed her to have that business. For Ranger, and for his whole family.

She found herself adding to Cactus's prayer, and by the time he said, "Amen," out loud, she added one mentally to her prayer and his.

No one else kept their amen inside, and a flurry of activity followed as the largely male population in the homestead put their cowboy hats back on. "I'm going to lose you in here," she said to Ranger, looking around at all the men wearing a hat like his.

"I'll stay right by you," he said again. "Don't worry. Let's go help Mother." He started to move, but Etta got up on a chair with Bishop's help, and she put two fingers in her mouth and whistled.

"For the love," Ranger said, glaring at his sister.

"Hold your horses," Etta said. "We want to go over the food." She actually used a wooden spoon as a pointer as she went dish by dish down the length of the island. "Two sides," she said. "There's the table in here which will seat eighteen, and the picnic table outside. Ida, has it started to rain yet?'

"Not yet," Ida said. "That table seats eighteen as well. There should be plenty of room for everyone."

Oakley wasn't sure how many people had gathered for turkey and mashed potatoes, but it felt like four times as many as they had seats for.

She kept her hand secured in Ranger's as he led them to his mother. "Hello, Mother," he said, hugging her. "You stay right here. Oakley and I will get you what you want." He brought her to his side, and Oakley beamed at the woman who'd broken her the last time they'd met.

"Oh, hello, dear." His mother reached for her, and Oakley gladly stepped into her arms. Once she'd straightened, his mom said, "I just want turkey, stuffing, and cranberries, son." Her light eyes held the same sparkle Ranger's did. "And get me a little taste of all the desserts."

"Mother," Ranger said with a chuckle. "All of them?"

"You only live once," she said with a smile.

Oakley nodded. "I'll get them, ma'am." She turned to enter the fray, ready to do whatever it took to get Ranger's mother what she wanted. "Divide and conquer, Ranger. I'll hit the desserts. You get the food." She looked at him. "Meet you back here?"

"You got it."

She stepped away from the safety of the table and went to the far end of the counter. No one had quite gotten there yet, and she was able to pick out a sampling of each dessert.

"That's for Aunt Dawna, right?" Bishop asked, looking at the plate in her hand.

"Yes," Oakley said with a smile. "Thanks for having me, Bishop."

"You're always welcome here, Oakley." He put one arm around her shoulder and moved out of the way as the crowd got closer to desserts. "You don't happen to know any single blondes, do you?"

"I thought Brady Burton had a sister," she said.

"What are you talkin' about?" he asked.

"Ranger got her number for you. He didn't tell you?" She watched Bishop search for Ranger.

"He must've forgotten."

"It was last week. When we rode the four wheelers." She'd seen Brady standing next to Ida, so one message had been conveyed. "I'll remind him."

"Thanks." Bishop met her eye again. "I like your dress, by the way."

"Thanks."

Bishop moved away, and Oakley looked down at her

long, mustard yellow dress. It had large, brown, tan, red, and orange leaves sewn all over it, as if a windstorm had kicked them up and they were swirling back to the ground.

She never would've picked out this dress on her own. But the boutique owner had helped her find it, and even she could admit it was perfect for a Thanksgiving feast at a ranch.

She hadn't seen Ranger for a couple of days, and she felt a different vibe between them since her Saturday night confessional. He'd admitted to some things too, and Oakley had felt the weight of what he'd said the following day.

She'd skipped church, because she knew Ranger would be there, and in truth, she'd needed some space too. She knew better than most women that every relationship had an exciting "honeymoon" phase, where the man could do no wrong, and every little touch and each small conversation was the most meaningful thing in the world.

She knew, too, that a relationship needed more than that to survive. She really wanted this one with Ranger to survive, so she'd given him the distance he obviously wanted, and she'd taken the space she needed.

She set aside her thoughts and took the plate of desserts back to his mother. "Here you go, Dawna. One of everything." She sat down at the table with her and smiled.

"Thank you, dear." She picked up the fork and took a nibble of the peach pie. "Did Ranger tell you Ida made you a pecan pie?"

"Yes, ma'am. He brought it with him when he came to pick me up."

"He said you've never had a real Texan pecan pie."

Oakley smiled and shook her head. "I was born here, but I can't say I've really spent much time here until the last few years."

"Ida makes the best pecan pie in the county. She won a blue ribbon and everything."

"That was twenty years ago, Mother," Ranger said, appearing on her other side. He put a plate in front of her with the three things she'd requested.

"So what?" she said. "She still won it."

"Yes," Ranger said, meeting Oakley's eyes over his mother's head. "She did." He was so *good*, and she hoped she could be as good as he was someday. He inspired her to be better than she currently was, and he was the type of man she'd been living to meet for the past five years.

"What about Cactus saying the prayer?" his mom asked, and Ranger leaned closer to her. They had a quick, quiet conversation, and then he stood and extended his hand to Oakley.

"Let's get some food, sweetheart. Momma, save our places, okay?"

She nodded, but Oakley could easily see she wouldn't need to beat anyone off to save the seats. The doors leading outside had been opened, and it was easy to get out there or come back in. Most of the cowboys from the ranch had stuck together and gone out there. Etta had fixed herself a plate already and ate with them, something Oakley noted and would be texting the woman about later.

Ida and Bishop still hovered over the buffet line as people continued to move through it. With both sides available, though, Oakley got her feast in a matter of minutes and returned to the table.

Bear's mother sat across from Ranger's, with Bear and Sammy nearby, and Cactus and another of Ranger's cousins on the end.

Their eyes met, and she smiled. "I've forgotten your name."

"We've never formally met." He reached across the table to shake her hand. "I'm Judge."

"Judge," she said, glancing at Ranger.

"I told you about the names."

"He won't tell me his," Oakley said, leaning toward Judge. "Will you?"

"Not if he won't." Judge glanced at Ranger. "What are you guys doing about that barn?"

Ranger looked up from his food, his eyes skipping down to Bear. Oakley built a perfect bite of turkey, mashed potatoes, and gravy and put it in her mouth. She watched, but holy cow, this food was good.

She moaned, and Bishop sat beside her.

"Good?" he asked.

"Bishop," she said. "This is *so* good."

"We do a little survey afterward," he said. "So make sure you fill it out. It helps us plan the menu next year." He flashed her a smile and scooped up a bite of stuffing.

Next year. Oakley could hardly stand to think she'd be here next year. Gratitude swelled within her, choking her and making her eyes burn.

"I think we should keep the barn," Ranger said.

"And do what with it?" Bear asked, his eyes flashing with bright blue fire.

"Renovate it into something we can use here on the ranch," Ranger said.

"Just spit it out," Bear said. "I know you have an idea you're just not saying."

"A dance hall," Ranger said. "Wedding venue." He shifted in his seat. "Heck, somewhere we can host these big dinners. We fix the foundation where it needs to be fixed. Strengthen the boards. Take out the hay loft. String lights. Paint. Put on new doors. Get tables and chairs." The more he talked, the faster his mouth moved.

Oakley had hardly heard him put that many words together at once, and Ranger stopped when he realized everyone in the near vicinity was looking at him.

He reached for his glass of sweet tea and took several healthy swallows. "Something like that."

"It's a great idea," Judge said.

"Your daddy would love to see that barn stay standing," Bear's mother said. "He and Bull built it with their bare hands, with their daddy."

"The blue barn?" Ranger's mom asked. "I didn't realize that was the one they'd condemned."

"It's the blue one," Bear said. "It's structurally unsound. The inspector said it has to be fixed or razed."

"Oh, dear," Dawna said.

"Since we're not already doing a ton of construction on the ranch," Bishop said sarcastically. "Renovating a barn into an event venue should be easy."

"It's not like you'd have to do it alone," Cactus said.

"Yeah, don't be so dramatic," Bear said with a grin.

"I'm just saying, it's easy for y'all to be like, *renovate the barn. Fix up the barn.* You're not the one who'll do it. I am."

"You'll *oversee* it," Ranger said, smiling at Bishop. "And you'll get all the praise when it's done too."

"I'll need more people," Bishop said.

"Then hire in the seasonal cowboys," Bear said. "We could use 'em with the cabins too."

"Really?"

"Why not?"

Bishop looked at Ranger, who did and said nothing. Oakley watched all of these Glovers, and they seemed to have so many conversations with so few words. A tip of the head, a blink of the eye. They meant something, and they all knew this secret language she didn't.

She didn't care. The food was the best she'd eaten since coming to Three Rivers, and the company was twice that good.

"I think we should go in for a gift for Penny Walker," Bear said next. "What do you guys think?"

"Good idea," Ranger said. "Did you have something in mind?"

"Jeremiah mentioned once that she liked to sew." Bear shrugged. "I don't know."

"Gideon's the one with all the easy stuff," Sammy said. "He loves those miniature horses and he'd have a dozen dogs if Penny would let him." She smiled around at the others nearby.

"Didn't Micah say once that his mom's family owns an egg farm?" Ranger asked.

"That's right," Bear said slowly. "What can we do with that?"

"It's not like Penny needs a gift," Bishop said. "They have plenty of money. It could just be something fun like a whole wall of eggs that spells out *eggcellent job on finishing your degree*."

"It is pretty amazing she did that," Oakley said, watching the Glovers for their reactions.

"It really is," Bishop said. "I never graduated from college."

"There's still time, son," his mother said. "Now, where did Zona get to? She always has good ideas for off-the-wall gifts."

An hour later, Ranger caught Oakley's eye, and they had their own secret conversation with a nod of his cowboy hat toward the front door. She left the bowl of candy corn she'd been snacking out of and went with him.

He took her hand near the Christmas tree in the foyer, and she squeezed to get him to stop. "Talk to me about this tree," she said.

"It's our angel tree," he said. "My grandmother made the ornaments by hand, over the course of her lifetime. Each year, we get together and decorate this tree as a way to remember our ancestors." He stepped over to the tree and trailed one fingertip down the edge of a birdcage that had a red bird inside. "I hung this one for my father."

He turned back to her, a smile on his face. "It's a good tradition."

"You have a tree in the living room too."

"Yes," he said. "And one in the Ranch House. Arizona

and Aunt Lois will have one in their cottage. You saw the mistletoe over the arch when we drove in." He stepped over to the front door and opened it. "Wreath here, and Mister and Preacher put wreaths on every barn on the property."

Outside, Ranger stopped at the top of the steps and took a deep breath. "Bear will hang the lights on the homestead tomorrow, and we'll put white ones on the arch and the main barn. Sometimes, we go even crazier and put pine wreaths around the goats' necks like scarves, and one year, the girls wove red and green ribbons through the horse's manes."

"You guys really are crazy."

"We love Christmas up here," he said. "And the year they did that, they rode the horses in the light parade. So." He grinned at her and started down the steps. "You said you wanted to see the blue barn?"

"Yes, sir," she said, hurrying after him. She caught up to him, glad she'd worn her cowgirl boots with her new dress. He'd stared at her until she'd asked about the pie in his hands, and once he'd put it on her kitchen counter, he'd swept her into his arms and said, "Yeah, it feels just like I'd thought it would. Soft." He'd pressed his lips to her temple, and Oakley thought he'd kiss her in the kitchen.

He hadn't, and they'd settled on her couch for a few minutes.

"How are you feeling?" he asked, interrupting her memory from a couple of hours ago.

"Good," she said. "Believe it or not, I love your family."

He chuckled, his gait even and strong. "I don't believe that."

"When you have no one and nothing," she said. "Anything would be great. But Ranger, your family *is* actually great."

"They're loud and opinionated."

"They belong to you."

Ranger looked at her, his expression probing. "I'm sorry. I didn't mean to sound ungrateful for them."

"Remember when the tornadoes hit earlier this year?"

"Yes."

"Who did you shelter with?"

He didn't say anything, because he didn't need to. Oakley knew they'd all gathered to the homestead, even those living in other houses and dwellings around the ranch.

"I went down into my unfinished basement," she said. "Alone. I have no food and no water down there. No bed or blankets or even so much as a chair."

"Oakley."

"I'm tired of being alone," she said. "There. That's my secret for today."

They walked past chicken coops and an enclosure for goats. A bright red barn, the kind Oakley imagined whenever she thought of the typical cattle ranch, and a huge building with a high center point and two sides that were a story lower.

"Stables," he said. "We have about forty horses here."

"How many cattle?" she asked.

"We're moving into birthing season," he said. "So we'll

keep our mothers close to check on them, and by spring, we'll be back up to about twenty-seven thousand head."

Oakley had no idea what that many cows looked like. "How do you keep track of all of them?"

"We don't," Ranger said. "They don't go far. Our cowboys round 'em up in the winter and bring 'em back. We brand them, of course, and we own all the land up here. The Rhinehart's are to the south, and they send back any errant cows that might wander onto their property. We do the same for them."

"It's a good life." One Oakley found herself wanting.

"About a hundred times slower than what you're used to." He nodded ahead of them. "Right around this corner is the blue barn." They took a few more steps, and then the barn came into view.

"Oh, I love that," Oakley said, stopping to take in the majesty of the barn. It was a muted shade of blue that had probably been bright at some point in the past. It had a cute, curved shape, with a silo next to it that had plenty of rust discoloring it that added to its rustic charm.

A large pine wreath with bright red holly berries hung over the shutters near the top, and everything about it fed Oakley's soul in a positive way.

"You can't knock that down."

"We won't," Ranger said. "You wanted to see the sign? Get a picture?"

"Yes," she said. "I don't have anyone to show it to, but...." She let her sentence trail off, because she couldn't finish it. She'd been thinking about reaching out to her father, but she hadn't quite found a way to do it.

She walked beside Ranger, the wind picking up as the storm blew in. "I love Texas thunderstorms," she said.

"Me too," he said.

They came out from behind the buildings, and Oakley gaped at the wide horizon in front of her. "This is incredible," she said. "Look at that."

"You should see it when the sun comes up," he said. "It's like God dipped Texas in gold."

"I want to see that."

Ranger let a few seconds go by. "You really want to come live up here with me?"

"Yes," Oakley said, still stunned by the view in front of her. She swore she could see all the way to Oklahoma and across the whole state of Texas. Of course she couldn't, but the gently rolling hills stretching for such a long distance made her feel like she could.

She saw another ranch not too far down the road, and Ranger had told her that was Seven Sons. The town of Three Rivers sat to the northeast, and Oakley could see the edges of it, the four-story hospital, and the road leading west up into the hills where she'd told Ranger her biggest life failure.

"You really don't care about my past?" she asked Ranger.

"No, Oakley," he said. "I appreciate you giving me some time and space to think it through, which I did several times. Every time, I came to the same conclusion: I want you in my life." He lifted her hand to his lips.

He'd said the same thing at her house when he'd come

to pick her up, and he was so steady and so calm that Oakley believed him.

"You don't have a secret wife and family somewhere else, right?" She giggled afterward, though the fear had gripped her lungs in an icy fist for a few minutes earlier in the week.

"No, ma'am," he said, starting down the road that led all the way to the highway. It was gently inclined here, and every step Oakley took down she'd have to take back up.

"Good," she said, inching closer to him.

"My father is buried right over there." Ranger indicated a spot to their right, and Oakley looked that way.

"Do you miss him?"

"Every day."

"I bet." Oakley took a deep breath. "Do you go shopping on Black Friday?"

"Sweetheart, do I look like the type of man who goes shopping on Black Friday?"

She laughed, and it felt like it had been a long time since she'd done that. "What do you guys do for gifts up here?"

"We draw names," he said. "Everyone goes in—well, except for my mother's and Bear's. All the siblings and cousins. There's a hundred-dollar limit for the gift, and we get together on a set day and eat and exchange gifts."

"A set day? Not Christmas Eve or Christmas Day?"

"We work all the time, baby. Year-round. Seven days a week."

"I get what year-round means, Ranger."

He grinned and nodded to the sign. "Almost there." He

glanced at her. "We don't do Christmas Eve or Day, because we want to relax on those days. Every year, someone different is in charge of the food, and we order a ton on Christmas Eve. Then we have enough for Christmas Day."

"Then no one has to cook."

"Right."

"Smart."

"We do minimal chores to make sure the animals are fed and watered, and then we just...relax."

"Do you even know how to relax?" she teased.

He laughed, and he released her hand in favor of putting his arm around her waist. "I do, a little."

"What do you do?"

His hesitation spoke volumes, and Oakley wondered what other secrets he still had. "I don't know."

"Hobbies? Interests? Do you, I don't know, work on a Rubix cube? Put together jigsaw puzzles?"

"Nothing as exciting as that," he said. "More like surf the web or look over the ranch investments."

"Yawn," she said. "That *is* boring, Ranger. Guess you're not perfect after all."

"I never claimed to be perfect." He took a few more slow steps and stopped. "In fact, I'm pretty sure I insisted I wasn't." He frowned at her, and Oakley faced him, reached up, and smoothed that crease from his brow line.

"I know you did," she said.

"We're standing under your sign," he said.

"No," she said. "We're standing under the mistletoe."

She pointed up, a smile filling her whole soul, and Ranger tipped his head back and looked up.

"Well, I'll be," he said. "We sure are."

The thunder rolled through the sky, and Oakley was sure they were going to get soaked in a few minutes. She didn't care. In fact, a kiss under the mistletoe, in the rain, with that view stretching before her...it was the stuff dreams were made of.

"What are you going to do about it?" Oakley whispered, her fingers sliding along the short hair on the back of his neck.

He bent his head toward her, taking her face in his hands. "I'm going to kiss you." He did, and everything inside Oakley rejoiced. A sense of adoration came with his touch, and she felt nothing but cherished by this man.

He tasted like sugar and pie crust, and Oakley enjoyed the way he controlled the kiss and yet poured passion into it too. The first drops of rain fell, but neither he nor Oakley broke the kiss.

Pure joy rose through Oakley, and she felt herself falling all the way in love with Ranger Glover, right there on the dirt road that led up to Shiloh Ridge Ranch.

Chapter Fifteen

Ranger moved his hands from Oakley's face and into her hair. He enjoyed the taste of her, the scent of her, the nearness of the warmth of her body. He was aware of the rain wetting his shoulders and back, but he couldn't stop himself from continuing the kiss.

He wanted to kiss her—and only her—for a long time.

She cradled his face in her hands and whispered, "It's raining."

"Mm." He touched his lips to hers again, then moved his mouth along her neck. "We should probably go back."

"Yes," she said with a sigh. "We should." She didn't pull away or make any attempt to walk away from him.

Ranger finally reeled in the reins on his emotions and hormones and stopped kissing her. He stayed right in her personal space though, his heartbeat throbbing through his whole body. "I think you're an incredible woman," he whispered. "I think you're gorgeous on the inside and the outside, and I sure have enjoyed getting to know you the past couple of weeks."

Oakley smiled, and Ranger loved that he'd caused that. She looked at him with soft eyes and said, "Thank you for looking past the exterior."

Several seconds passed, wherein Ranger's clothes got wetter and wetter, and he spiraled further and further in love with Oakley.

"I'm grateful you told me you wouldn't go out with me if I was seeing someone else," Oakley said. She tipped up onto her toes and hugged him, pressing her cheek to his. "I think you're a pretty incredible man too."

He wrapped his arms around her and held her tight. *Don't say it. It's too soon to say it.*

A loud clap of thunder filled the sky, and Oakley jumped in his arms.

"Let's go back," Ranger said, stepping back and reaching for her hand. She laughed, and Ranger did too, feeling like he was fifteen years old as he flirted with his girlfriend.

He was panting by the time he made it up the steps to the porch and under the cover of the roof. Oakley was too, but when she turned to look at him, she still wore the biggest, brightest smile he'd ever seen.

He felt the exact same way, and he laughed again as he wrapped her in his arms and swung her around. She squealed, and Ranger set her on her feet. "You've done it now."

"I have? Why?"

"Ten seconds: someone is gonna open that door." He

kept both arms around her, kept her close to his body—right where he wanted her. "Then I won't be able to kiss you again."

He watched the door. "Five, four, three...two...one."

The door opened and Ward came outside. "There you are. I was about to send Cactus out to find you." He gestured for the two of them to come inside. "Get in here. No one's leaving until the rain lets up."

RANGER WOKE ON MONDAY MORNING, WONDERING whose life he'd started to live over the weekend. Instead of every day holding the same, boring chores, Ranger now felt like each new sunrise brought with it a day of endless possibilities.

He and Oakley had gone to the town tree lighting on Saturday, and Ranger had never paid much attention to the Three River traditions. There was always too much work to do on the ranch.

Somehow, even with him and Bear focusing on their girlfriends, the work still got done. Ranger had slipped away with Oakley right after the lighting, because Sammy and Bear had spent most of the previous hour leading up to it whispering to one another.

Ranger hated whispering in a crowd. If it couldn't be said out loud, it shouldn't be talked about until later. He'd been on-edge right up until he and Oakley had gone to get funnel cakes, thinking Bear or Sammy was about to blurt out something about him and Two Cents.

He'd sent out the push notification to get more data about the restaurants in town, and he'd gotten an amazing response. He and Ward had gone behind closed doors last night to look at the data, and they'd gotten their ten thousand downloads.

"In the first ten days," Ward had said, staring at the screen. "That's incredible."

Ranger showed him a few other stats, including how many people had responded to the push notification, and that had a seventy-four percent click-through-rate. Just over seventy-four hundred people had voted on the Italian restaurant list, and when Bishop had come in from the barn, he'd suggested they do a push every two or three weeks.

"Is that annoying, though?" Ranger asked.

"How else are you going to get the lists to stay up-to-date?" Bishop asked.

"The rating system."

"The what?" Bishop had leaned closer to the computer and then used his own app to rate the places he'd been. "I didn't know about this, Ranger. You should do a push about that, and then see what happens. You could then do periodic pushes for specific things."

"Yeah," Ward said. "Like a survey: What are you most excited about for this year's Harvest Festival?"

"Or what do you look forward to in Three Rivers every spring?" Bishop added.

"Good," Ranger said, typing those ideas into his notes. "What else?" They'd brainstormed for a good thirty minutes, and Ranger had gone to bed on a technological high.

He sat up, ready for a technological war with Bear in that morning's meeting. Ward would be busy this Friday, and Ranger couldn't wait another two weeks for a Friday to come around. He'd set up a meeting with Bear, Cactus, and Ward for that morning.

In only forty-five minutes, in fact. He'd promised it wouldn't take longer than thirty minutes, and Ranger got in the shower so he could get coffee and toast before the meeting and be ready to hit the ground running afterward.

He and Ace needed to make sure all their pregnant cows had made it in from the foothills, take a count, check on their progress, and go over the supplies they had for birthing season. Bishop had texted the family group last night about construction help, and hardly anyone had answered, so Ranger thought he'd check in there.

Then, he was hoping to go riding with Oakley again. "Minus the speeding ticket," he muttered to himself. He couldn't count that encounter as a negative, though, because Ida had a new boyfriend and while Ranger had forgotten about Brady's sister, he'd given her number to Bishop on Thanksgiving.

He'd just taken his last bite of toast when Bear and Cactus walked into his office. Ranger looked up and stirred his coffee, something definitely different about the pair of them. He narrowed his eyes at them as they strode closer. "What's goin' on?"

"Goin' on?" Bear repeated—a dead giveaway that something had happened.

Ranger looked at Cactus, and the realization hit him like a load of bricks. "You shaved." Ranger stood up and took one step toward his prickliest cousin. "Did you...? You cut your hair?"

"I've cut my hair before," Cactus said, rolling his eyes.

Bear grinned at him, and Cactus growled as he dug in his pocket. He slapped a five-dollar bill into Bear's hand, and they faced Ranger again.

"What is happening here?" Ranger asked, looking between them. There was more too. "You've got a new hat, Bear. That's easy enough to spot, but you get new stuff all the time." He focused on Cactus again. "Not only have you shaved and cut your hair—way shorter than normal, Cactus. And it looks like someone did it for you, not that you did it yourself—you've got a new hat, new shirt, new jeans." His eyes slid down Cactus's body. "New boots, and holy steers and silos. What belt buckle is that?"

"Can we not?" Cactus asked and he moved to take the seat he always occupied in these meetings.

Ranger looked at Bear, his eyes wide. "Tell me what's happening."

"Cactus is goin' to town today."

Ranger spun around. "You are? Why?" Cactus didn't even move, and he'd bent his head down enough so his cowboy hat obscured his face.

"He was supposed to come with us to the tree lighting on Saturday," Bear said, a touch of frustration in his voice. It disappeared when he added, "He wasn't ready then, but he is now." He took a seat and grinned at Cactus, who kept his head down. "It's the soldier care package put-together tonight. He's going with Ace and Bishop."

Ranger didn't know what to say. He felt like someone had just told him the name he'd been using his whole life wasn't really his.

"Sit down," Bear said quietly. "He doesn't want this to be a big deal."

Ranger closed his mouth and took his seat. "Ward should be here in a minute."

"Great," Bear said.

"This app says the best place to meet new people is the grocery store." Cactus looked up, a measure of disbelief playing with disgust in his eyes. "Is that true?"

"It's women," Ranger said automatically. "Not people. The best place to meet new *women* is...." He trailed off as he realized how he sounded.

"I just order my groceries online," Cactus said. "They deliver. Do people not know that?" He genuinely looked confused too.

Ranger glanced at Bear. "Most people don't mind going to the grocery store," he said.

"I hate it," Bear said. "But I at least drive to the store and pick up my order."

"Driving takes so much time," Cactus grumbled.

"So does shaving," Bear quipped. "And you did that."

Cactus looked up and met Bear's eye. They had a conversation Ranger understood really well. Cactus was scared out of his mind, and Ranger found his heart softening toward the man.

"It's going to be fine," Bear said. "Ace and Bishop aren't going to leave you alone."

"Are you joking?" Cactus's eyes squinted. "Bishop will run after every blonde who walks by."

"Ace won't do that," Ranger said.

Cactus pinned him with a powerful glare that had Ranger swallowing. "Ace volunteers his brains out during the holidays. He's already texted me and Bishop twice about how he has to stop by the church to talk to Pastor Summers about getting the lists and getting the reminder texts out."

"I forgot about the volunteering," Ranger said. Ace did like to do that. He loved Christmas and the town traditions, and he spent a lot of time working with the pastor and other members of their church to help with the events throughout the month of December. The planning started in October, and some events happened before Thanksgiving even.

"I'll talk to them," Bear said.

"If you do, I will never leave this ranch," Cactus said, his voice as sharp as his name. "I don't need my big brother to run to my rescue."

Ranger thought it was a mistake to unleash Cactus on Three Rivers, but he wasn't going to say so.

"Remember what Sammy said," Bear said, his eyes flashing with blue lightning. "Please."

Cactus seemed to wilt with just four words, and Ranger felt like he was getting whiplashed around. Thankfully, Ward walked in with a box of doughnuts in his hand and the words, "Sorry I'm late. They had a long line at Holy

Fritters. I guess they got moved into first position on Two Cents over the weekend, and they're offering a dozen doughnuts for a dollar and two cents."

He set the box on the table and took the remaining seat. He didn't look away from Ranger, and heat crawled into Ranger's face.

"Let's get started," he said. "First up is the Christmas bonuses. Bear, would you explain, please?"

Bear did, outlining the investment with Netways, and how they'd cashed out for a tidy profit. "We want to offer Christmas bonuses to everyone," he said. "All of us—everyone in the family. That's twelve. And our six full-time men. That's eighteen."

"Mother?" Cactus asked.

"I don't think they need money," Bear said. "They have what they want and need. This is a bonus for working the ranch, and neither of our mothers do that." He looked at Ranger, who nodded in agreement.

"Yay or nay on the bonus?" Ranger asked. Everyone agreed, and he added, "How much?"

"How much did we get?" Ward asked. He had his tablet out, and he'd probably update their investment portfolio, as Ranger hadn't done it yet.

"We invested sixty," Ranger said. "I personally think we should re-invest that seed amount in something new. Which would leave us with two-twenty-seven."

"We don't have to use it all on bonuses," Bear added.

"We don't even need bonuses," Cactus said.

"Our men do," Ranger argued. "If you don't want one, we can offer to invest anyone's bonus in a stock portfolio for them." He loved working with the financials, and he had his personal money in dozens of stocks, bonds, and other investments. Ward did too.

No, not a single Glover needed a Christmas bonus.

"It's a nice gesture," Ward said. "We work hard around here. It's nice to have some money that's just for play."

"Yeah, like Ranger can use his to pay for those ATVs," Bear said, his eyes hooded and his voice dark.

"Let's settle the bonuses before we move to that," Ranger said, glaring at his cousin. "I think five or ten thousand each."

"We could offer one amount to family and another to the boys," Ward said. "We know what it's like to earn a cowboy's wage. They don't have anything."

Ranger nodded, remembering how his father had required everyone to live in a cowboy cabin for a year, working for a regular ranch wage. He'd done it, but he hadn't liked it. The work hardly seemed worth the pay, and if he hadn't loved the ranch and loved working with animals, Ranger would've quit.

He knew the men they employed stayed for the same reason. They loved the ranch, and they loved working the land, and he'd like to believe they liked working for him and Bear.

"I say ten for the cowboys," he said. "Five for us."

"I agree," Bear said. Both Cactus and Ward assented, and Ranger made a note of it.

"Okay," he said with a sigh. "I'll get that out to everyone in an official memo. We'll pay on the twentieth." He looked at the agenda, though he knew exactly what was next. "The ATVs. I personally think it's time for us to expand."

He turned his laptop around and started the presentation he'd put together. Four minutes later, he concluded with, "I think having access to ATVs increases productivity and safety on the ranch. We're not talking about drones or using computers to test soil, though I think those things have their place in the agricultural community too. We're talking about getting hard jobs done faster and easier, and getting around the ranch quicker, which would really be advantageous if a medical emergency came up."

"Or a fire," Cactus said.

"Exactly." Ranger looked at the others. He knew they lived and breathed by the Glover family traditions. He did too. He loved that he thought of how to reuse something instead of just throwing it away. He loved that his father and uncle had taught them all to love and respect the land, themselves, and God. He loved that he knew family came first, and forgiveness was expected, and that he could try, fail, and still be accepted at the dinner table.

"I'm a no," Bear said. "Sorry, Ranger. I think you have solid arguments, but I don't think we need ATVs to do good work and stay safe."

Ranger nodded, his stomach sinking. The others would follow Bear. Heck, he normally followed Bear. "Okay," he said. "The last thing is—"

"I didn't even get to vote," Ward said.

Ranger nearly rolled his eyes, but he managed to wave his hand toward his brother. "Go on, then."

"I'd say no too." Ward grinned, and Ranger did roll his eyes then.

"Cactus?" he asked.

"I'm actually considering it."

"You shaved," Ward said.

Ranger was thrilled his voice had as much awe as Ranger's had.

"You missed that conversation," Cactus said, reaching for a doughnut. "We're fifteen minutes into this, and you get fifteen more." He took a bite of the glazed treat, and the sugary, yeasty smell made Ranger's mouth water.

He plucked a pastry from the box too. "The last thing is what we want to re-invest that sixty-K in."

"And where you're going to store those ATVs." Bear gave him a pointed look.

"They're at Oakley's right now," he said. "Maybe I could at least get a shed or something up here?"

Bear didn't give an inch in his hard expression, and Ranger rolled his eyes again. "I'm surprised you use running water, Smokey," he said.

Cactus burst out laughing, and Ranger hadn't heard his cousin's laugh in so long, it surprised him to the core. All three of them sat there and stared at Cactus as he laughed. Ranger finally joined in, because it was so good to see Cactus again. He'd grown up with the man, and together with Bear, they were the oldest trio of boys on the ranch.

Bear added his voice to the laughter, and so did Ward.

"Smokey," Cactus said. "That was great, Ranger."

"He acts like he needs to warn me of the dangers of

ATVs," Ranger said, refusing to look at Bear. "It's annoying."

"Oh, I get it," Cactus said as the group sobered.

"So the sixty thousand," Ranger said. "Ideas?"

"You have ideas," Bear said, and Ranger's heartbeat jumped. He swung his attention back to his cousin, who wore that dangerous glint in his eyes.

"Bear," he warned.

"I think technology," Bear said over his name. "Ranger has a ton of ideas for app hosting and the like."

"The like?" Ranger asked, scoffing. "Ward, what have you got?"

"App hosting sounds great." He looked from Bear to Ranger, worry plain in his eyes.

"I'm missing something," Cactus said, looking around at everyone.

"Ranger—"

"Bear—" Ranger yelled over him. He rose to his feet. "This is not yours to share. Stop it."

The atmosphere shifted, and Ranger hated that he'd spoken so strongly. He straightened his shirt, smoothing down the blue plaid and touching his belt buckle. "I apologize," he said quietly as he sat down. He studied the printed agenda in front of him, trying to see his way through this.

"No, it's my fault," Bear said.

Ranger looked up, and Bear radiated regret from the set of his shoulders in his black and white striped shirt. "Really," Bear said. "I took things too far."

Ranger gave a single nod as a way to say *I accept your*

apology. Bear did the same, and Ranger drew in a deep breath. "Okay," he said. "We could go with something like an app hosting company. We could go with an established internet giant. We could stick closer to home and invest in something more local."

He looked at Ward. "Have we done any companies out of Three Rivers or Amarillo?"

"Usually Austin," Ward said, tapping on his tablet. "There was one that came across my feed the other day...I thought they were in Amarillo." He swiped and read, and Ranger glanced at Cactus.

He'd folded his arms, and he wore a look as if he was extremely dissatisfied with the meeting. He switched his gaze from Bear to Ranger, and his eyebrows went up.

"Fine," Ranger said. "I own Two Cents." He leaned back in his chair. "Happy now?"

Cactus's eyes widened, and he glanced at his phone. "You...what?"

"He wrote and developed the app," Bear said, practically yelling. A wide smile filled his face. "I keep telling him how great it is, and he keeps telling me he doesn't want anyone to know."

"We're working on bugs," Ranger said. "I'd rather I get it to a place where I'm happy with it, and *then* I'll tell people." He swung his gaze back to Cactus. "So I would appreciate it if you did not say anything to anyone else. Enough people know as it is."

"Who else knows?" Cactus demanded.

"Everyone here," Ranger said. "Bishop. Sammy. Frank Russo."

"Some guy at the newspaper knows, and I didn't?"

"You don't even go to town," Ranger said, smiling. He looked at Ward. "And even he has it."

"You haven't told Oakley?" Cactus asked.

"Not yet," Ranger said. "Like I said, Bishop, Ward, and I are working through a few bugs and brainstorming ways to improve the app."

"Fair enough, I suppose."

"Thanks for your permission," Ranger said dryly. His alarm went off, and he quickly swiped to silence it. He stood. "That's thirty minutes. I have work to do on the ranch, so will you guys submit some companies you think we could invest in? I could just ask Don, but I like to give him something to compare to. It helps him stay focused on what we want."

They all nodded, and Ranger closed his laptop, snagged another doughnut from the box, and followed everyone down the steps. If he wanted to see Oakley that day, he probably wouldn't even have time for lunch, but he was certain he could survive on two doughnuts and half a cup of coffee until evening.

Chapter Sixteen

Oakley fingered the fabric on the shirt, wondering if she'd ever felt something this slick in Ranger's current wardrobe.

"That red one is nice," Dawna said, and Oakley turned her attention to Ranger's mother. She put her hands on the handles of the wheelchair and pushed her toward the rack with the red shirts.

Oakley had personally seen enough red shirts in her life to never want to see another one. But she reached out and took the red, yellow, and white shirt from the rack. The checks were small, with no space between them like some of Ranger's other shirts.

"Is this the right thing to even be getting him?" she asked. Etta had stayed with Oakley and her mother, but Ida had gone off to the beauty section of the department store to see if they had cologne she could get for her boyfriend.

Etta looked at Oakley, clearly distracted by whoever was texting her. “Ranger likes looking good.”

“He said he gets his shirts from The Boot Barn,” Oakley said, examining the red shirt again. “He might hate this.”

“He’s not going to hate it,” Dawna said. “He’ll like whatever you get him.”

“Because he has to,” Oakley said, smiling at her. “I don’t want him to be obligated to like it. I want him to actually like it.” She put the shirt back on the rack. “Men are so hard to shop for.”

“Ranger’s not picky,” Etta said. “He’d probably be super happy if you showed up in a tight skirt and said you were his gift.” She looked back at her phone, so she missed Oakley’s shocked look.

“Etta,” her mother said, her voice full of disapproval.

“What?” Etta said. “It’s true. Men like Ranger just want a cute woman. And food.”

Oakley wasn’t sure if she’d just been insulted or not. She opened her mouth, but she didn’t have the words.

“Etta,” her mother said much sharper this time.

She looked up from her phone and met Oakley’s eyes. She realized something, and Oakley ducked her head. “Oh, I didn’t mean he doesn’t like you as a person, Oakley,” Etta said quickly.

“I know,” Oakley said, but the pinch remained in her chest. “Maybe he’d like—”

“He’s interested in you for more than your cute body.”

“I heard you,” Oakley said, unable to look at Etta.

“Why do you say such things?” her mother asked, and

Oakley patted Dawna's shoulder to let her know it was okay. *No harm done.*

"You insulted her *and* Ranger," she continued anyway, her voice sharp. "He's not some pervert, lusting after every beautiful woman he sees."

Etta looked at her mother in surprise. "I...I know, Momma."

"You owe him an apology."

Etta looked at Oakley, but she focused on the jeans as if she'd buy Ranger a pair for Christmas. She sighed and stepped around her mother. "Oakley," she said, her voice wavering slightly. "I'm so sorry. I didn't mean anything by it."

Oakley looked at her, and Etta drew her into a hug. "I'm sorry. Please forgive me."

"Of course," Oakley whispered, holding onto Etta a little too tightly. She didn't care. She loved Ranger's sisters, and when Ida had suggested they go shopping together so they could help her find something Ranger-appropriate, Oakley had cleared her schedule instantly.

They'd started with lunch, and they'd been at the department store for about twenty minutes now. Dawna wouldn't last very long, and honestly, Oakley really liked browsing and shopping for herself, but for everyone and everything else, she liked to have a plan. Or at least an idea of what she should be looking for.

Etta stepped back, pure frustration in her eyes. "I started talking to this guy," she said quietly. "A week or so ago, and he's just...." She shook her head and kept her eyes down. "He was really only interested in a pretty face."

"Then he's not for you," Oakley said. "There are hundreds of cowboys in Three Rivers, Etta."

"Yeah, for you." She met Oakley's eyes. "You're petite and gorgeous."

"So are you."

"No," Etta said. "I'm short. There's a difference. You wear a size six. I wear a twelve."

"You're gorgeous," Oakley said again, adding more power to her voice. "And anyone who can't see it is blind."

Etta gave Oakley a small smile. "You're one of my favorite people."

"And you're one of mine." Oakley linked her arm through Etta's. "Two things, okay? One, I really need help with a gift for Ranger, so could you put your phone away and help me? And two, who are you texting? Not the loser who's only interested in your pretty face, I hope."

Etta grinned and handed her phone to Oakley. "See for yourself. I'll look around for something for Ranger." She moved away, and Oakley took a peek at her phone.

Etta had exchanged hundreds of texts with a man she'd only labeled as Works for Ranger. Oakley's mind spun. Who worked for Ranger? The Glovers all worked at Shiloh Ridge...and they had cowboys who lived and worked there too.

Ranger was co-owner of the ranch. So this man must be one of those cowboys.

Whoever he was, he was extremely good at flirting, and Etta could hold her own in that arena. Oakley found herself smiling and then laughing right out loud at the conversation. Etta looked over her shoulder at her, some measure of trepidation in her eyes.

"Whoever this is is cute," Oakley said.

Etta gave her a sour look and shook her head.

"Tall, dark, handsome, maybe?"

Etta smiled and turned toward a rack of ties. Oakley was not giving her boyfriend a necktie for Christmas. That was what daughters gave to their fathers, not the man they wanted to cuddle with in front of a roaring fire as they talked about their future together.

"They don't have Denim and Dreams," Ida said, clearly irritated as she rejoined the group. "Where are we?"

"Juniper's," Dawna said, and Oakley's laughter bubbled in her gut again. It came spilling up her throat and out of her mouth, especially when Ida said, "Okay, Mother. Thanks for that," in a very sarcastic tone.

"Etta's texting a tall, dark, handsome man who works at Shiloh Ridge," Oakley said, handing Etta's phone to Ida. "I'm still trying to find something for Ranger that says romantic and thoughtful. Your mother is offering advice."

"We call that lecturing," Ida said, looking at the phone. "Oh, my," she said a moment later. "Who is this?"

"She's not telling." Oakley watched Etta, who could clearly hear them. She turned away, and Oakley started toward her. When she only had a few more paces to reach her, Etta spun and held up a T-shirt.

"This is it."

"A T-shirt?" Oakley looked at the black shirt, which had large, blocky white letters on the front of it that read SPIRITUAL GANGSTER.

"I actually really like it."

"Come look."

Oakley moved to her side and picked up a navy blue shirt that said BEARDED AND BEAUTIFUL. Joy lit her heart, and she held it up for Etta.

"Yes," Etta said with a giggle. "He'll like all of these."

"I've only seen him wear a T-shirt once," Oakley said. "Does he wear T's? Really?"

"All the time," Etta said. "You see him when he wants to look his best for you, or while he's working. Trust me, Casual Ranger wears T-shirts, and he's going to love these." She picked up a bright blue one that said LOVED BY A COWGIRL.

"Hmm," Etta said, and Oakley folded the shirt and put it back. "No?"

"I'm not a cowgirl," Oakley said. "I'm a racecar driver." She smiled at Etta and looked at the two shirts she'd liked. She had felt good about them, but she wasn't sure they were girlfriend-caliber Christmas gifts.

"I'll get them," she said. "But I want to keep looking." She returned to Dawna and showed her the shirts, and Ranger's mother smiled at her and patted her hand. Ida suggested Oakley get Ranger some more outdoor gear, as he sure seemed to like riding the quads with her. He did, and they'd gone out a few times in the past week.

He'd asked her for a recommendation for where he could store them, and she'd offered to have him keep them in her garage. They'd been fine there, and she didn't see why they wouldn't be. Bear was apparently against even having a shed where they sat on the ranch, and Oakley didn't understand it.

But the ATVs brought Ranger down to town, where Oakley got to see him, spend time with him, and kiss him, so she wasn't complaining.

She hugged Etta and Ida in the department store parking lot and helped Dawna get in her sedan. They didn't say much on the way back to the assisted living facility, but as Oakley steadied the older woman as she got out of the car, Dawna looked right into Oakley's eyes and said, "I'm so glad my boy found you, Oakley. You don't listen to a single thing Etta says. You two belong together, and he finds you beautiful inside and out."

"I know that," Oakley said quietly. "But thank you, Dawna." She kept her arm through his mother's as they went inside. She accompanied her all the way back to her apartment, where Dawna wrapped her in a tight hug and just held on.

Love cascaded over and through Oakley, but she didn't cry again. "Please call me if you need anything," Oakley said as she stepped back. "Even just a friend to eat dinner with. I don't see Ranger every night, you know." She smiled at Dawna.

"Oh, I'm not taking you from my son." She hobbled over to her recliner and sat down. "Bring him by to see me one night if you have time. Mothers miss their sons."

"Yes, ma'am," Oakley said, and she went back downstairs to her car, basking in the warm glow of the family that she'd somehow been accepted into.

She did a little more shopping on her own, finding a

shirt and a sweater that were absolutely perfect for Penny Walker's graduation party before she went home.

There, she was greeted by a very perturbed cat. The General yowled at her as she closed the garage door behind her, and he paced back and forth, his long, black tail straight up in the air.

"You hungry?" she asked the cat. "All right." She put her purchases on the kitchen counter and stooped to get his empty bowl. She scooped food into it from the bag in the mudroom and put it back in place.

The General eyed it like she'd tried to feed him poison instead of cat food. "It's the same stuff you scarfed this morning," she said dryly. "You're so fussy."

Aloof was a better word for the cat. Snobby would work too. Oakley did love him, though, and she rinsed out his water bowl and refilled it too, before she took her shopping bags down the hall to her bedroom.

She added the two T-shirts she'd found for Ranger to the growing pile of gifts she'd picked up over the past week. She had gone out on Black Friday, and she'd found a couple of blankets that she thought he might like.

Reaching out, she ran her fingers along the hem of one. It was downy soft, and done in black, burnt orange, and blue, which she'd seen Ranger wear several times. He lived in a brand new house, though, and she didn't peg him for the type of man who needed a lap blanket to keep him warm while he watched TV at night.

She wasn't even sure if he watched TV.

She pulled out her phone and texted him. *Favorite TV show? Or movie?*

The Office, he sent back. *It's really funny. Favorite movie – The Man From Snowy River.*

Oakley smiled at the device and asked another question. Then another. The minutes turned into an hour, and she could not get enough of the kind cowboy who'd somehow stumbled into her life.

She'd never felt like this about a man before, not even Roberto. She knew now she was infatuated with Roberto. She'd truly believed her life would end if she didn't have him in it. But he'd chosen his wife and family over her, and she'd survived.

She'd learned who she was, and who she really wanted to be. She'd learned how to turn to the Lord, and she'd learned how to repent. While she didn't want to repeat the experiences she'd had with Roberto, she now knew so much more about herself, life, and what she really wanted.

She opened Two Cents while Ranger sent something about one of the horses on the ranch. She'd seen a new category come up in her notifications last night, and she hadn't tapped on it yet.

Best things to do on short dates.

She wanted to see him again. Tonight. Tomorrow. Definitely before the party, which was this weekend. She didn't want to wait five more days, and she tapped to open the list.

The ten items sat there, and Oakley started reading.

Grab coffee at Brewed.

Pick up cookies from Ackerman's and drop them by her house/office.

Everything in the app was geared toward a man reading

it, as if only men needed ideas for or how to plan amazing dates.

Go fly a kite.

She smiled at that one, because it actually sounded fun. Just her, Ranger, and the wind. It reminded her of their night in the back of his pickup truck, looking at the stars. She'd like to repeat that night too, minus the part where she told him all of the mistakes she'd made in the past.

Make ice cream sundaes at home and eat them while the sun goes down.

Walk a dog together.

Go horseback riding.

Sign up for a class together. Pottery. Dancing. Yoga.

Her phone rang, and Ranger's name covered the app. She grinned as she thumbed it on. "Hey, cowboy."

"Hello, sweetheart." He didn't say anything else, and Oakley basked in the warmth between them.

"When will we get together again?" she asked. "Are you super busy with the cattle?"

"Yes, ma'am," he said, sighing. "I'm waiting for Ace to check a cow that's down. A cow lying down is not good."

"I see."

"There's the Walker's party."

"That's on Saturday," she said. "It's Monday."

"Oh, I see how it is. Someone's missin' me." He wore a smile in his voice, and Oakley liked the strength and confidence in his tone.

"Are they?" she teased. "What about if I came up there for an hour? Brought coffee and those lemon bars you like so much? Or you could finally show me how to ride a horse." She didn't even care that she sounded too hopeful. "There's also that Letters to Santa thing tomorrow night, and the free miniature golf afternoon is on Wednesday...."

"There's Wassail Weekend too," Ranger said. "But that's not until the weekend, obviously."

"They're doing those sleigh rides in the downtown park," Oakley said. "I drive by there every day. Seems like stuff for children though."

"Yeah," he said. "We could drive around and watch the light shows. The last day to vote is Friday."

Oakley wasn't sure what that was, but she didn't care. If she got to be with Ranger for a little bit, she'd be happy.

"It's hard for me to plan right now, baby," he said. "If a cow goes into labor, I have to be here."

"I'll come to you, then."

"I could be busy."

"I am *so* good at waiting," Oakley said. "You have tons of family. Someone will feed me or entertain me."

He chuckled, and she could just see him leaning against a fence post somewhere on the ranch, his head bent down as that smile filled his face. She sighed with the fantasy alone.

"You do what you want, Oakley," he said. "I'm sorry I can't come take you to dinner."

"Oh, dinner is overrated," she said. "We've been to all the best places, at least according to Two Cents."

"Mm."

"I'm just glad I don't have to go out to eat by myself anymore," she said. A sting of shock moved through her. "I mean—"

"Did you eat alone before?" he asked. "I kinda thought you had a lunch date and a dinner date every day."

Oakley's mind raced for a way to get out of this embarrassing situation. In the end, she opted to tell him the truth. "That's why I dated multiple men at once. So I wouldn't have to be alone. If one guy didn't work out, I always had another to take his place."

"Mm," Ranger said again, and Oakley didn't like it. "I don't mind being alone. Now, if it's a choice between being alone and being with you, I'd choose you every time."

"Me too," she said.

"Yeah? You don't have someone waiting in the wings, ready to step on stage, if we break up?"

"Why would we break up?" Oakley didn't even like thinking about that.

"I'm just asking," Ranger said.

"No," she said. "Of course there's no one waiting in the wings."

"You've been alone for a long time," he said. "I'm never alone. I think how we feel is normal for us."

"I agree," she said.

"Are you comin' tonight?" he asked.

"Should I?" Oakley was actually thinking of calling the animal shelter and finding out about their dog rental program. She'd seen a flier cross her desk about the new program, and she thought it would be amazing to take a dog up to Shiloh Ridge and hold Ranger's hand while they all walked around.

"You do what you want," he said. "But I'll take a lemon bar morning, noon, or night."

She laughed, and Ranger did too. Soon enough, though, Ace called his name, and he said, "I have to go, sweetheart. Talk to you soon." With that, he was gone, and Oakley sighed as she let the phone drop to the bed in front of her.

She laid back, her mind swirling through her possibilities. She could stay right where she was, and stroke The General until he forgave her, something meaningless playing on the TV. Or she could go get a treat and see her boyfriend.

"No contest," she said, getting to her feet. "Now, Lord, if You could please make sure they don't sell out of lemon bars until I get there, that would be fantastic." She hurried into the bathroom and looked into her eyes. She looked more tired than she'd like, but Ranger would take her face in his hands, tell her what a sight for sore eyes she was, and kiss her like a man in love.

"And if You could bless this relationship I have with him, I'd appreciate that too," she whispered. "I like him so much."

So much, she might be in love with him, but she wasn't ready to say that out loud quite yet.

Not quite yet.

Chapter Seventeen

Ranger washed his hands in the calving barn, the air actually cold against the back of his neck. Ace had the fans running high, as the humidity had soared with a small heat spell that was moving through the Panhandle.

By the end of the week, there was supposed to be snow on the ground. Ranger had just bought himself a new coat, and he was ready to face the winter. Three Rivers was one of the coldest places in Texas, and from what he'd seen on the weather radar, they'd have snow on the ground for a couple of days at least.

It usually didn't stick around much longer than that, but he was counting it as a win that it hadn't snowed yet this December. January was fairly cold too, with more snow days. It snowed in February and March too, and sometimes as early as November, but those storms usually only accumulated a skiff of the white stuff that melted by afternoon.

Ranger shivered and wished the sink out here spit out

hotter water. He washed twice, and then started for a third time, feeling grimy and slimy at the same time. He and Ace had been up for most of the night, shining spotlights through their fields and helping heifers deliver their calves.

This morning, they'd brought in three that had calves the wrong way in the birth canal, and he'd been assisting them all day. The last one had just been born twenty minutes ago, and Ranger needed a hot meal, a hot shower, and a soft bed.

Ward and Judge were taking the shift tonight, and Ranger didn't have to report to work until seven the next morning. He yawned and looked left when he heard a heifer lowing. Ace had separated her from her calf as he rubbed the infant down and tried to get him up and moving. They'd reunite them in a few minutes, and she was just indicating her impatience.

They'd had a good birthing season already, and Ranger hadn't recorded a single death yet. He knew there'd be some. That was just the way of the world. He prayed every morning and every night for a healthy herd, and he knew Bear did too. They probably all did.

Ace opened the gate to let the mother and baby into the same pen together, and her calf went right to her side. Ranger's soul smiled, because he loved the bond between mother and baby, even in animals.

His brother approached the industrial sinks and stepped on the pedal to release the water. "Hey, did you know Etta is dating Russ?"

"She is?"

"That's what he said. I just talked to him." Ace

scrubbed with water first and squirted soap into his hands. "He was all dressed up, and I asked him where he was goin'. He said he and Etta were going to dinner and then to the Snow Ball fundraiser."

"Huh," Ranger said. "Aren't you goin' to that too?"

"Yeah, but not with a date." Ace focused on getting himself clean. "We're okay here? I have to get showered and get down to town. I'm in charge of the raffle tickets, which means I have to be there early."

"We're okay here," Ranger said. "Ward and Judge should be out in the fields already. I'll update them as to the situation here."

"Thanks, bro." Ace grinned at Ranger, who just shook his head. He reached for a paper towel and leaned against the sink. "What do you think of Etta dating Russ?"

"Think of it?" Ranger asked. "I don't think anything of it. Good for her. Good for him. Everyone deserves to be happy, you know?" He shut off the water too and gathered his own paper towel. "Why do you look so sour about it?"

"Do you think there's just one right person for everyone?" Ace asked.

Ranger took a moment to wipe his hands. He and Ace started for the doors together. "No," he said as they exited the barn. The sun was almost all the way down already, and Ranger glanced at his watch. Only four-thirty. It felt like midnight.

He peered west, the golden globe of the sun casting everything in a hue that reminded Ranger of heaven. "I don't think there's one right person for everyone. I think there are a lot of people for each person. Just like you get along with a lot of people. I think there are probably several women you could meet and fall in love with, and when you do...." He shrugged as he thought of Oakley. "But is she the only one? No, I don't think she's the only one."

"Maybe the only one you'll ever meet in your life," Ace said quietly.

"Yeah," Ranger agreed. "Maybe that, especially for men like us, who don't leave town very often."

"I think you mean ever," Ace said with a grin.

"New women come to Three Rivers," Ranger said. "Look at Oakley."

"Oh, I can't look at Oakley," Ace teased. "I've seen the way *you* look at her, and I'm not getting in between that."

"Come on," Ranger said, scoffing.

Ace jogged ahead of him. "See you tomorrow." He left in much better spirits than before, and Ranger thought that at least was a win. He continued toward the homestead, his legs and back throbbing and protesting with every step.

He focused on his phone and sent Ward and Judge a text to let them know how things had gone with calving that day. He and Ace had cleaned up the barn so it was ready if it was needed. Once he tapped on the arrow to send the message, another yawn consumed him. His stomach growled, and all he wanted was someone to bring him something to eat. Anything to eat.

He approached the homestead, easily picking out the pickup truck he'd driven before. Oakley was here.

A smile filled his face, chasing away his aches and pains

and discomforts. She'd come last night too, with hot coffee and a box of lemon bars he still hadn't finished.

He checked his phone, but he didn't have a text from her. Perhaps someone had grabbed her when she'd arrived, and he'd find her inside.

A dog barked, and Ranger frowned. It sounded like the sound had come from the homestead. That couldn't be right, as Bear didn't allow their ranch dogs inside the house. They had a pretty cushy situation in the supply shed, where Bishop bought furry and fluffy beds for them and put them down on the paved part of the barn near the doors.

He climbed the steps, and sure enough, the dog barked again. It was definitely inside the house. He opened the door cautiously, anticipating a big beast to bowl him over as he tried to escape.

There was no beast, and Ranger entered the house to a blast of warmth and the sight of the angel tree. He paused and admired it, thoughts of his father flowing through his mind. The tree was placed there for that very reason, and he tapped the birdcage as he went past.

"He is the cutest thing ever," Arizona said as he entered the large space that housed the kitchen and living room. She giggled as a dog licked her face. He wore a harness and a leash, but he wasn't trying to get away from Zona at all.

"Can you adopt him?" she said.

"Yes," Oakley said, and Ranger scanned the area to find her, his pulse doing funny things in his chest. "I just rented him for the night."

"You can rent a dog?" Zona asked, grinning as the pup continued to lick her neck.

"Sure." Oakley came out of the kitchen, a tall glass of water in her hand. Ranger could only stare at her. She wore a pair of black jeans, her feet encased in sexy, black boots that went all the way to her knee. She wore a sweater that looked like cotton and chicken fluff that was pure white, with a slash of orange in it that was clearly meant to indicate a snowman's nose.

He wanted to see her waiting for him in this house every evening. Or morning. Whenever he came in off the ranch.

"Hey," she said when her gaze moved to him. "I didn't hear you come in." She grinned at him as she walked toward him, and Ranger scanned her from head to toe again. Her hair was down, which meant she hadn't worked that day. Or, if she had, she'd been home to shower and change already—something he needed to do very badly.

"Aren't you a sight for sore eyes?" He slid his hands through her hair and down her shoulders. He didn't care if Zona saw him kiss her. Anyone could watch for all he cared. He lowered his head and kissed Oakley, feeling himself fall down the last step. He was completely in love with her, and he could feel it all the way to the ends of his hair and the tips of his boots.

Oakley kissed him back, and because they weren't alone and she had more sense than him, she pulled away before he'd even really gotten started. "I brought a dog. I thought I could steal you away for an hour and we could take her for a walk."

Ranger's plans for a hot supper, a shower, and sleep vanished, and he didn't care. "Yes," he whispered, sliding his nose down the side of her face. "As long as there's more kissing."

She giggled and pushed one palm against his chest. "I might have to wrestle her away from Zona."

Ranger straightened and took Oakley's hand in his. He'd seen her last night, but they'd only sat on the front steps for twenty minutes before Ace had texted to say he'd found another heifer down in the fields.

He'd drank half his coffee and had eaten one lemon bar while she'd talked about Two Cents. She'd suggested the app should add the ability to reply to the reviews, and Ranger had coded it that morning. He'd kissed Oakley once, and not for long enough.

"Yeah, she loves dogs," Ranger said, watching his cousin with the pup. "What is she?"

"They're not sure," Oakley said. "Maybe a mastiff mix. Her name is Wallflower."

The dog looked over at her name, and she spun and bounded for Oakley and Ranger. Oakley laughed, and Ranger seriously thought it was the best sound in the world. She wrapped her arms around the dog and hugged her. "Come on, Wallflower," she said. "We're gonna walk now that the cowboy is here." She picked up the leash and straightened, looking at Ranger.

"I just need to grab a snack," he said. "Wait for me on the front porch."

Oakley nodded and started in that direction while he darted into the kitchen to grab a lemon bar and a granola bar. He glanced at Zona, who'd taken a spot at the bar. "You're staying?"

"I have grits on the stove," she said, swiping on her phone. "I'm hosting a card game here tonight." She looked up. "Bear didn't tell you?"

"Yeah, he did," Ranger said. "I just forgot." He tapped the brim of his hat. "Bye, Zona."

"Be careful with that woman," she called as he strode into the foyer. He wanted to go back and ask her what she meant by that, but he didn't want to waste time talking to his cousin when he could be with Oakley. He had her number. He could text Zona later.

He took a bite of the lemon bar as he went outside, and he joined Oakley at the top of the steps. "Ready?"

She went down the steps, Wallflower on her left side. The dog's claws clicked against the wood, and then all of their feet crunched over dirt and gravel.

"We have maybe an hour of light left," Ranger said. "What do you want to see?"

"Just you," Oakley said quietly, and Ranger shoved the rest of his lemon bar in his mouth so he could hold her hand.

She looked at him as he put his fingers between hers. A smile touched her mouth, and Ranger thought she was saying more with her eyes than she'd ever said with her voice.

"So," he said with a sigh. "Small wedding or big affair?"

"Small," she said. "You forget I have no one to invite."

Ranger's heart squeezed at the same time his fingers did. "Sure you do. You can invite your parents. Maybe they'd come. Maybe it would be exactly what you guys need to mend the fences between you."

"Maybe," she said.

"Are you thinking about talking to them again?"

"Yes," she said. "I don't think I ever stop thinking about it."

"Maybe that means you need to do it," he said. "Whenever I feel like that, the Lord won't stop pestering me until I do it."

"I can't figure out what to say," she said.

Ranger watched the path in front of them and led her past the barns, the chickens, and the stables. "You just say, 'Dad, I'm living in Three Rivers, Texas now. Did you know it gets cold here? I didn't know it actually snowed in Texas, and of course, I picked the one place in the whole state where it does.'"

She smiled and leaned into him on the next step.

"Then, you can say, 'I met this amazing man. He's good to me, and he loves me, and I think I'm going to marry him.'" Ranger's voice quit then, and he paused as the blue barn she loved came into view. He could see the lights in the rafters and hear the music they'd dance to on their wedding day.

He saw the brand new cowboy boots all of his brothers and cousins would wear, and the tasteful flowers she'd pick out for their tables and wedding cake. He could smell the barbecue they'd serve their family and friends, and he could feel the sun rise on the day after their wedding, with her beside him in bed.

Oakley stepped in front of him, interrupting the perfect fantasy. "Ranger Glover," she said. "Is that true?"

"Which part?" he whispered.

"Any of it." She looked up at him with wide eyes filled with hope and fear. Oh, boy, did he understand those two emotions and how often they came as a pair.

"All of it," he whispered before he took her fully into his arms and kissed her again. She ran her fingernails along his neck and into his hair, dislodging his hat. It fell to the ground, but Ranger barely noticed.

He could not get enough of this woman, and he absolutely thought she was the one for him. He might have another soulmate out there somewhere, but he didn't need her. He'd found Oakley Hatch, and he loved her.

She traced her fingers down the sides of his face and across his beard before sliding her hands inside his jacket and around to his back.

He kissed her for as long as he wanted, finally stopping when Wallflower barked. Oakley turned toward the dog too, quickly taking a few steps to scoop up her leash. "It's okay," she said, her voice a bit rusty. "It's just the wind."

She returned to Ranger, stepping into his arms and letting him hold her again. "I have met this amazing man," she said. "He is kind, and he is good to me, and I do think I might just marry him to make sure everyone in Three Rivers knows he's mine, and I'm his."

Ranger's smile bloomed with her very first word and only grew with every single thing she said. His arms tightened around her, and he felt like he needed to make sure she understood what she was getting into.

"Ranching is hard work," he said. "All the time. Twenty-four-seven. I got up at one-thirty this morning, and I've been working since."

"You've told me that."

"Sometimes there isn't time to walk a dog or sit on the front steps or talk on the phone."

"Okay."

"The animals don't care if it's Christmas or Easter. They don't care if it's snowed or if it's a hundred degrees. They have to be fed and looked after."

"I understand."

"I love the ranch," he said. "I don't want to leave it or sell it. I love living with Bear and collaborating with him and everyone else here. My goal is to have a family so I can pass it to them when it's time."

She looked up at him, her expression open and vulnerable. "I want a family."

Ranger nodded and kissed her again. "You don't have to stop working at the dealership," he said. "You can still be yourself."

"Thank you," she said. "I don't know what I'll do. I guess we'll have to see what actually happens."

"Impossible to predict what'll happen," he murmured, bringing her back to his chest again. He could honestly stand with her like that forever, but the sun dipped lower and lower. The initial rush of adrenaline at seeing her was wearing off, and Ranger needed to eat and sleep.

"I wanted to tell you something," he said, swallowing.

Oakley stepped out of his arms then, surprise on her face. "You have something to tell me now?"

"Yeah," he said, clearing his throat. "Let's head back to the homestead." He took the leash from her, hoping Wallflower would suddenly sprint away so he'd have to chase her.

"If you say you have a wife and family at another ranch, I'm going to explode," she said, her voice very, very tight.

"It's not that," Ranger assured her. He couldn't find the words he needed. Why was telling her about Two Cents so dang hard? He hadn't been able to untangle his feelings surrounding the app, and none of that made sense.

"I have this thing I do on the side," he said, realizing how scandalous that sounded. He shook his head. "I mean—"

"Ranger."

He turned toward the panicked sound of Ward's voice. He ran toward Ranger and Oakley, waving both hands above his head.

Ranger shoved the leash at Oakley and jogged toward Ward. "What? What is it?"

"There's the glow of fire on the west side." Ward turned as Ranger met him. "Near Cactus's place."

"I'm calling it in," Ranger said. "Let's go." He wasn't sure what they were going to do, though. The commercial hoses were all located here at the epicenter of the ranch. They couldn't take a truck out there, as there was no road.

"Judge is saddling right now," Ward said, and Ranger really wished he had those two ATVs sitting in Oakley's garage.

Oakley.

He glanced back at her, still standing there with Wallflower. "Go," she called. "Call me later."

"Nine-one-one, state your emergency."

Ranger spun away from the woman who was far too good for him and barked, "It's Ranger Glover up at Shiloh Ridge Ranch. We've got fire on the west side of the ranch and need a truck."

He swung into the saddle behind Ward, as Judge had only saddled two horses, and hoped he could hold onto his phone, his brother, and his exhaustion for just a little longer.

Please, he prayed. "Hey," he yelled to Judge. "Have you called Cactus?"

"He's not picking up," Judge yelled back, and he spurred his horse into a gallop. Ward got their horse going as fast as he dared with both of them on the back of him, and Ranger kept his silent prayer running as he answered the periodic question from the emergency operator.

Chapter Eighteen

Bishop laughed at Cactus, because the man could do some spot-on impressions. Cactus laughed too, and Bishop had never seen him like this. His haircut would've qualified him for military service, and Bishop hadn't seen him wearing ripped or dirty clothes in almost two weeks.

They'd gone to town last night, and while Bishop had seen three or four women at the soldier care package event that he would've liked to talk to, he hadn't left Cactus alone. Ace had run off to talk to a couple of people about the fundraiser happening tonight, but he'd only been gone for ten minutes.

They'd stuck to Cactus like glue, and his brother had done great. Really great. The whole thing had taken two hours, and Cactus hadn't said a word about it since.

He swung out of the saddle once they reached his barn, and Bishop did too. They worked in silence, both of them so familiar with the equipment and tasks that Bishop's mind was allowed to wander.

He cleared his throat, and Cactus said, "Don't."

"Don't what?"

"Ask me anything," his brother said. "I went, and I didn't die. Obviously. That's enough."

"No, it's not," Bishop said, hanging up his blanket. He didn't look at Cactus. "Can we do a yes-no thing?"

"Fine," Cactus clipped out.

"Did you have fun?"

"Yes."

"Were you nervous?"

"Yes," he growled.

"Did you want to talk to anyone but me or Ace?"

"No."

"No one?" Bishop dared to cast a glance over his shoulder.

Cactus looked confused, his eyebrows all scrunched up. "Maybe." He shook his head. "No."

"Do you want to go to the pony ride tomorrow?"

"Absolutely not," Cactus growled. "I'm going in." He left the barn, and Bishop let a hissing sigh out as he finished up with his horse. He stroked his hand down the side of the animal's neck and followed Cactus at a much slower pace.

He paused and bent over to scratch the dogs that had followed him out to the edge of the ranch. "Did he say anything to you? Huh?" He glanced toward the house, which had a golden glow on it from the setting sun.

Bishop straightened and stretched his back, a groan

pulling through his body. He had to be up at three o'clock in the morning to go out into the fields to relieve Judge and Ward, and Bishop should head back to the homestead.

Cactus had said he'd feed Bishop dinner, though, as Zona was using the house for a card game tonight. His stomach grumbled, and Bishop once again looked at the cabin.

Sighing, he walked toward the house and went up the steps to the back door. He knocked and entered at the same time, but Cactus wasn't standing in the kitchen. He wasn't in the living room either.

"Cactus," Bishop said, turning toward the bedroom. That was the only other place he could be, unless he'd gone out the front door. Hesitating, he took a few steps toward the bedroom, his boots making no noise on the rug there.

Cactus stood with his back to the doorway, his head down, clearly looking at something on the dresser.

A strange, almost reverent feeling hung in the air. "Cactus?" Bishop said, keeping his voice low as the situation seemed to call for it.

His brother didn't move, and Bishop approached the way he would a wild animal. He went all the way to Cactus's side and looked at the dresser too.

A book sat there, and Bishop pulled in an audible breath as he saw pictures of a happy, smiling Cactus from a decade ago. He stood next to a sandy blonde, who had her lips pressed to Cactus's cheek. They were both laughing, and the happiness on both of their faces hit Bishop straight in the heart.

"Allison," he whispered.

Cactus nodded, which meant his ears still worked. He swallowed and turned the page. The few pictures here showed Cactus and Allison, and Bishop hadn't been around a lot of pregnant women, but he knew one when he saw one.

"Cactus," he said, his eyes rounding. His pulse sprinted through his whole body, and his fingertips tingled. "She was pregnant."

Cactus didn't nod this time. He just flipped the page. Bishop gasped as he looked at the only picture there. Cactus and Allison, both of them red-eyed and obviously crying. She held a bundle of blue blankets, and Cactus was pressed right against her back. They were both smiling at the camera, but it was not a happy picture.

Bishop's heart tore right in half. He opened his mouth to say something, but he honestly didn't have the mental capacity at that moment.

"He died," Cactus said.

"What?" The word came out as mostly air, and Bishop finally tore his eyes from the picture to Cactus's face.

"He would've been eleven in March. He was born with congenital heart failure. They'd just told us he would not live longer than a week, and we'd wanted a family picture."

Bishop couldn't make sense of anything, but tears burned behind his eyes, and he simply grabbed onto Cactus and held him tightly. Surprisingly, Cactus gripped him back, and Bishop took a long breath in and then pushed it out. He did so again, and Cactus stepped back.

"Would you like to visit his grave with me?" He raised his eyes to Bishop's, and while they barely looked like they belonged to the same family, Bishop had never felt closer to one of his brothers.

"Of course," Bishop said.

Cactus closed the book and put it in the bottom drawer of his dresser. Without another word, he left the bedroom, and Bishop scrambled to catch up to him. He let Cactus walk a step or two ahead of him, and he didn't go far past the paddock to a tall sycamore tree. Beneath the branches of the tree, a tiny headstone stood, and Cactus crouched down in front of it and brushed his fingers over the letters.

"We named him Bryce," Cactus said. "Allison spent hours teasing me with what we'd call him instead." A smile flashed across his face, but it was mostly made of pain. "I keep thinking I won't feel so devastated one day. That the wound inside me will heal."

Bishop couldn't guarantee it would, and he had no idea the turmoil Cactus had been dealing with all these years. He knelt in the dirt and put his hand on Cactus's shoulder. "Why didn't you tell me?"

"It was too much," Cactus said. "But I'm talking about it now, and you know what? It helps." He glanced at Bishop. "I'm going to move past this. I think I've been using them to keep myself in the past, and while I don't want to leave them behind, I want to move forward."

Bishop nodded and tried to smile. It felt all wrong on his face. "I will do whatever I can to help you. I'm sure we all would."

"I know that," Cactus said. He put his hand against the trunk of the tree and used it to help himself get to his feet.

He groaned and gave a light chuckle. "I'm too old to crouch down like that."

Bishop looked at the name on the headstone. *Bryce Charles Glover.* He straightened. "It's a good name."

"It is, isn't it?" Cactus started back toward the house, his steps slow and heavy. "Allison wanted to call him Deacon." He chuckled again, the sound much lighter this time. "I tried to tell her it didn't work that way. That the nickname had to start with the same letter as the real name."

"What did you suggest?" Bishop asked.

"Boone," he said, still smiling. "Barker. Bowie. Bolt. Bronc." He shook his head. "She said things like Bash and Barney."

Bishop laughed, and he wished he'd have known Cactus's wife. They went into the house, and Cactus opened the fridge. Bishop sat down at the table and watched him, which he knew Cactus hated.

He looked down at his phone. "So, you and Allison...."

"We broke up after Bryce died," Cactus said. "I still love her. She said she loved me the day she left."

Bishop looked up in time to catch him shrugging. "She moved to Georgia. I haven't heard from her in years. I don't do social media, so I don't know." He left it there, and Bishop let him have his silence for a few minutes.

"I am going to get past it," Cactus said. "I'm going to keep going to town, and I'm going to stop being a hermit. I'm going to see if I can have a better semblance of a real life."

"You can," Bishop said. "You can do all of that."

Cactus nodded and stuck something in the microwave. He'd just put a couple of bowls on the table, along with a loaf of sourdough bread and a plastic container of ham and corn chowder, when they heard someone whistling.

"What's that?" Bishop asked.

Cactus groaned as he sat down. "You look. I'm too tired to get up again."

Bishop rolled his eyes and went out the back door. Judge came flying toward them on horseback, with another horse a bit back, carrying two people. "What?" Bishop asked, hurrying down the steps. Maybe something had happened at the homestead. Maybe something with Mother, though as the second horse came closer, he saw Ward and Ranger. Maybe something with Aunt Dawna.

"There's a fire out here," Judge said, swinging out of the saddle.

Bishop looked around, breathing in deeply. "No, there's not."

"We saw fire," Judge said, panting as he ran to the corner of the house. "There's nothing on fire?"

"No," Bishop said, turning back to Ward and Ranger. "There's nothing on fire."

Judge yelled, and Bishop swung back around, jogging after him. He stood past the barn and pointed. "There it is."

Bishop ran to his side, Ward and Ranger not far behind. The sun was almost down, with only a sliver left on the horizon. It glinted off an old piece of machinery with violent rays.

"If the sun was up higher, it would be brighter," Judge

said. He turned to Bishop. "I can't believe I rode all the way out here for this."

"Cactus has soup," Bishop said.

"And a goldarn phone he didn't answer," Ranger snarled, stomping back toward the house. "I'm going to find out why he couldn't pick up a call."

"Ranger," Bishop called after him, but he didn't break his stride.

They all ended up in the cabin, and Cactus apologized, saying, "I left it in my bedroom when I went out to look at Bryce's grave." He opened the cabinet and got out three more bowls. "Who wants to eat?"

Ranger looked around at Judge and then Bishop. "He told you?"

"Yes," Cactus said. "I told him. Judge already knows. You know." He looked at Ward. "If I'm talking, I have to have something to eat. I'm starving."

BISHOP DRILLED ANOTHER HOLE, THE GIANT BIT punching through the wood in only seconds. He'd spent an hour sketching out where the holes needed to be to spell out the message he and the other Glovers wanted to give to Penny Walker.

Eggcellent job!

They'd gone back and forth on the C. Ranger wanted it to be an S. Bear too. To Bishop's surprise, not everyone just caved after that, and when they'd finally put it to a family vote, the C had won.

Excellent is spelled with a C, Etta and Ida had both said, and after that, everyone had voted for the C.

Bishop had been working on the sign, which barely fit in the back of his truck, for a few days now. Ranger, Bear, and Cactus were going to Wilde & Organic a few minutes before the party to get the eggs. They sold them in a variety of colors, and they wanted the sign to be pretty for Penny Walker.

Behind him, the barn door opened, and he turned as Bear and Sammy entered. "Hey," he smiled at them, his heart shriveling a tiny bit. He told himself he didn't need to feel like that. He was doing good things around the ranch right now, and he could sacrifice his love life for a couple of months if it helped his brother move past the tragedies he'd endured.

"This looks amazing."

Bishop backed up to stand beside them. "You can tell what it says."

"It's amazing," Sammy said.

"I just have the exclamation point left," Bishop said. "I told you I'd have it done in time for the party. I've got a whole twenty-four hours still." He swatted at Bear's chest. "It's going to be a great party." He started to walk back to the sign.

"It's snowing," Bear said.

Bishop spun back to his eldest brother. "What?"

He hooked his thumb over his shoulder, a giant grin on his face. "They're moving the party to the rec center."

"We can get this in the rec center," Bishop said. "It'll make it more farm-like."

"Ranger sent me out here to find out how many eggs we need to buy to fill it."

"Two hundred and seventy-seven." Bishop had no idea how many dozen that was. He didn't have to know. He just knew he'd get this sign to the rec center, make sure it stood upright, and help fill it with all the eggs.

"It's going to be so great," he said after he finished drilling another hole. "Do you know if the Walkers know any blonde women?"

Chapter Nineteen

"Hey, it's okay, bud," Rhett Walker said to his son in the back seat. He'd brought Austin with him and left the other three kids with Evelyn, who'd been plaiting their daughter's hair so it would look just like hers for Momma's party.

Austin continued to fuss, because the boy always seemed one breath away from a complete melt-down. He tried Evelyn's patience most days, and Rhett had taken him with him everywhere more than any of the other kids.

"Gramma's gonna be there," Rhett said. "It's going to be a big party." He ducked his head and looked out the windshield and up to the sky. At least he hoped it was going to be a big party. The snow's arrival in Three Rivers couldn't have come at a worse time.

All of Momma's roommates had confirmed their attendance. They had spouses and families they were bringing, and none of them lived in the Panhandle. All of Momma and Daddy's neighbors were coming. All of her sons, of course. The grandkids.

Several of the Glovers had confirmed, and a dozen cowboys from Three Rivers and Courage Reins. Daddy had been riding out there for over a year, as had Jeremiah and Wyatt, and they knew a lot of the men and women who worked with the therapy horses.

Wyatt had invited everyone from Bowman's Breeds, where he still worked a day or two each week, and many were coming. Jeremiah knew all the ranch owners in the area, and several of them were coming.

"*Supposed* to be coming," Rhett muttered as the snow thickened enough to warrant windshield wipers.

Not only that, but Momma's brothers and all of her nieces and nephews were coming. Rhett, as the oldest, knew all of them, though he didn't get down to Sweet Creek in the Hill Country to see them very often.

They all still lived there; only Momma had left the egg farm and the small Texas town in her rear-view mirror. Her oldest brother, Darren, had just signed over the farm to his oldest son, Peter, who already had a son in his twenties.

Daddy's brothers were coming, and now that Rhett's grandparents lived in Three Rivers, they'd be there too.

"Everyone loves Gramma," he said. "So we have to be on our best behavior." He turned into the parking lot and pulled as close as he could. Wyatt's truck was already in the lot, praise the stars above.

Rhett got out and stepped to the back door. "Austin," he said, glad the little boy had calmed. "Did you know Gramma and Grampa lived in Austin for a couple of years?"

He'd heard the story of his parents' courtship and first few years of marriage dozens of times.

"Daddy was born only a month after Gramma finished her bachelor's degree." She'd gone to one year of law school before Jeremiah had been born, and then she'd quit. None of the boys had even known she'd started taking classes again until six months ago.

As it was, Daddy had told them. Rhett could still hear his words as plainly as if he'd just said them.

Your mother has had three dreams her whole life. To be a mother. To have an amazing wedding. And to be a lawyer. She got the first two, and she's finishing up the third.

Rhett loved his mother with everything he had, because she was sixty-eight years old now, and about to graduate from law school at the top of her class.

Rhett unbuckled his son and scooped him into his arms. "I'm gonna run for the door. Hold on to Daddy."

Austin wrapped his arms around Rhett's neck, and Rhett slammed the door and ran for the entrance to the rec center. Once inside, he took a deep breath and set Austin on his feet. "Hold my hand, bud."

The little boy did, and they pushed into the heated part of the building. He took out his phone and called Evelyn.

"I swear I'm leaving right now," she said.

"You've got time," he said. "No rush. Listen, it's snowing pretty hard. Drive real careful, okay?" He looked around for the sign to the Starlight Room, which he'd rented for this celebration. He'd done it over the phone, and when he'd come a couple of days ago to see the room, he'd been disappointed in how small it was.

This party was meant to happen at Seven Sons, with a big deck, the massive kitchen, the front porch, and tons of sunshine. Too bad Momma was finishing up her coursework in December, in a town in Texas where it actually snowed.

"Okay," she said.

"Text me when you get here, and I'll come help with the kids. They don't even have the sidewalks cleared yet." He found the sign and went that way, walking slowly so Austin could toddle along with him.

"Okay."

"Evelyn?" Rhett asked.

"No, Elaine," she said to their daughter. "Don't put that in your mouth."

He waited for her to get whatever the girl had picked up, and when she said, "Hmm?" he took a deep breath.

"Have you achieved all of your dreams?"

"What?"

"Nothing." Rhett shook his head. "I'll see you when you get here."

"Okay."

The call ended, and Rhett picked up his son so he could walk faster. In the Starlight Room, Wyatt was already there, setting up tables with Micah, Tripp, and Skyler.

"Afternoon," he said to his brothers. They all turned toward him, and Oliver came into the room behind them.

"There's no more. That's all there is."

Rhett looked at the six tables. "It's not enough."

"I can call Jeremiah," Skyler said. "He'll bring some

from the ranch." He already had his phone at his ear, and Rhett nodded as he passed Austin to Ollie.

He sighed as he stepped next to his brothers. "This isn't going to work. Do you know how many people we have coming?"

"I'm going to go ask about opening that divider," Wyatt said, nodding to the wall that could be pushed back to make the space bigger."

"I already asked," Rhett said, but Wyatt just waved his hand over his head and kept going. Rhett frowned, because he knew Wyatt would come back with good news. His brother possessed a charm people couldn't say no to. "He'll offer them five thousand dollars for the room next door," he grumbled.

"Let him," Micah said. "We need it."

Tripp nodded and swatted Micah's chest. "Come help me get the drape."

Rhett had stuff to bring in from his truck too, and he looked at Oliver. The fourteen-year-old wore a smile as he pretended to run away from Austin. "You okay with him?" he asked the teen.

"Sure thing," Oliver drawled, and Rhett smiled at him. Tripp sure had gotten lucky when he'd found Ivory and Oliver. She nearly ran into him as Rhett started to exit.

"Oops," she said, smiling at him. She reached out to detour Isaac, a rambunctious four-year-old who ran everywhere he went.

Rhett bent to pick up the boy. "Conrad's coming," he said. The two cousins were close in age. "Want to come help me bring in the cupcakes?"

"Yep," Isaac said, smiling at Rhett. He grabbed onto his whole head and hugged him, and Rhett laughed as he took the older boy with him.

Liam arrived with his family, and steadily, as the minutes passed, they brought in everything they needed for the party. With all the brothers there except for Jeremiah, the food, and the tables, the room was practically full.

"This isn't going to work," Rhett said, thinking of the dozens of other people expected to attend.

"Maybe the snow will keep them away," Micah said.

"That's not what we want either," Rhett said. His phone chimed, and it was Evelyn saying she'd arrived and needed help with the toddlers. "I have to go help my wife."

Before he could get out of the room, Bear Glover started to enter it, a massive piece of wood gripped in his gloved hands.

"Holy cow," someone said.

"What is that?" another asked.

"Leave it to the Glovers to make a big scene."

Rhett smiled at Bear, though his anxiety about this party only tripled with the sign. Bear's youngest brother held the other end of the sign, and Bear's family walked through the door behind the two of them.

"We need to open this up," Bear said. With that he set down his end of the wooden sign and reached for the latch holding the two halves of the temporary wall together. Rhett stared as he pushed one to the left while Bishop pushed the other to the right.

"Yeah, let's take it over here, Bish." Bear picked up the

sign and moved it so it stood beside the newly opened curtain, in the other room. That done, he turned and looked at the Walkers.

"They said we couldn't use that room," Rhett said when no one else said anything.

"Hogwash," Bear said. "What are they using it for?" He turned and looked at it. "Nothing. They canceled their classes this morning."

"I even asked," Wyatt said. "I said I'd pay a lot to have it."

"I'll talk to Miriam," Bear said. "You have to know what button to push." He nodded and left the room.

"I wonder what button that is," Rhett said, watching him go.

"Miriam Bunce plays by the book," Bishop said, gesturing for his family to bring forward the cases in their hands. "Bear will get her to see that letting us use the room is by the book. You'll have to pay for the room." He looked over his shoulder, and Wyatt nodded.

"I want to pay for it."

"You can open that one too," Bishop said. "He wasn't kidding when he said they canceled all their classes and sports this morning."

"Because of the snow?" Rhett asked.

"Yep."

"Maybe no one will come," Rhett mused. At that moment, he remembered Evelyn and the kids, and he rushed out of the room and down the hall. She was struggling with both of the smaller kids in her arms, Conrad with one hand in her coat pocket, when Rhett burst out of the rec center.

"I'm coming," he said, and he jogged down the sidewalk to help her. He took Easton, the biggest of the triplets, and swung Conrad into his arms too. "Come on, boys. Let's go get this ready for Gramma."

Jeremiah was stopping by the farmhouse to get Momma and Daddy, and as Rhett held the door for Evelyn, Tripp and Ivory left to go get Gramma and Grampa Walker.

He started to follow his wife when someone called his name, and he turned to find Momma's family coming toward him. His heart grew and expanded, and he waited for her oldest brother to creep slowly down the sidewalk to the entrance.

"You made it," Rhett said.

His uncle Darren grinned at him. "This is my baby sister graduating from law school. I wouldn't miss it." He took Rhett in a hug despite the two children, and ended up taking Easton with him as he entered the rec center.

"Look at that boy," his wife said. "It's been a while since we've had little children. Can I?"

"Go on," Rhett said to Conrad, and he passed him to Beth. "She's my aunt, buddy. You'll be fine."

He hugged Uncle Brandon and Uncle Andy too, gratitude for them filling him from top to bottom. They'd brought their wives, and Uncle Andy had brought one of his grandsons—a boy about ten named Jason.

"We have a Jason too," Rhett said. "Jeremiah's son is named after Momma's father. He gave his daughter the name Jean after Momma's mother." Out of all the brothers, Rhett alone had known his maternal grandparents, but he'd been a very small boy, and he didn't have many memories of them.

Uncle Andy smiled at him, his eyes as bright as Momma's.

Back in the expanded Starlight Room, Rhett was pleased to see more tables and more chairs. The drape Tripp had designed and printed showed the Aarons egg farm in Sweet Creek, which was where Momma hailed from. The Glovers had put their spectacular egg sign next to it, and it read *Eggcellent job!*

Colored eggs from white to brown to light blue filled the holes, and Rhett knew his mother would love it.

He'd heard her stories of crating eggs seven days a week and feeding layer hens. She'd talked of a trucking arm of their business, and Rhett thought he should take his family down there to see some of their roots.

Daddy came from Sweet Creek too, and while his parents hadn't known each other growing up, they'd met in Sweet Creek, and all of the boys had lived at the Walker family ranch after Daddy had once lost everything.

His parents were prime examples for Rhett. They never quit. They didn't quit on each other, and they didn't quit on their family. They didn't quit when they failed, and they didn't quit just because a dream had been put on hold.

He stepped over to Evelyn, who was child-free due to all the extra adults there without kids. She put her hand in his and looked up at him. "I have accomplished all of my dreams, Rhett," she said.

He looked at her. "Have you? There's no unfinished law school in your past?" He loved her with a love that ran deep and wide, and he thanked the Lord for her each and every day.

"You made me a mother," she said. "That was what I wanted."

He brushed his lips along her forehead and looked at the pictures Liam and Callie were hanging on the far wall. "Are those of Momma and Daddy?"

"Callie asked your mother for them." Evelyn went with him over to the wall, where the enlarged black and white photos showed his mother as a young woman, her eyes lit with laughter as she looked at a much younger version of Daddy.

He looked a lot like Rhett had in his twenties, and a sense of belonging moved through Rhett.

"These are their wedding pictures," Callie said. "And your mother's graduation from UT-Austin the first time." She grinned as she tacked the photo of Momma in her graduation cap.

She'd never once told him or any of the boys all she'd given up to be their mother, and Rhett loved and appreciated her more than ever at that moment.

The noise level behind him increased, and Rhett turned to find the cowboys from Three Rivers had arrived. Every one of them seemed to have a gift in their hands, and Mal started taking them and piling them on another table in the second room that had been opened up.

There was definitely enough space now, and Rhett tugged on Evelyn's hand. "Let's make sure the food is ready." They worked to get main dishes by main dishes, and salads by salads. Everything needed a utensil, and plates, silverware, and cups were set near the beginning of the line.

Bear Glover returned, and he had Miriam Bunce with him. She carried a microphone and got it set up. She tested it by saying, "Testing, testing. Can I have your attention, please?"

With all the people, it took several long moments for the noise to quiet. Miriam didn't look happy, but she said, "We have canceled all of our other events for today. Yours is the only party here, so you can use the gym across the hall also, if you wish." She shot a glare at Bear, who simply looked back at her. "Enjoy your party." She nodded and walked toward him, and Rhett jumped in front of her.

"How much for the extra rooms?" he asked.

"It's taken care of," she said, patting his shoulder.

Rhett turned and watched her leave. "Taken care of?" He looked at Bear, who now had his hand in that of a beautiful brunette, his head bent toward hers as he said something to her. His face lit up when she laughed, and Rhett could feel their love and affection from several paces away.

He knew what had just happened. Bear Glover had paid for the extra rooms.

"They're here," someone said, and Rhett hurried toward the microphone.

"All right," he said, his voice really loud. "We're going to have them come in this middle door. Gather around. She knows she's here for a party, but she thinks it's just a family Christmas party. Hurry, now."

Rhett joined Evelyn, who'd found Elaine somehow, and they stood together, right in front of the doorway his mother would come through. All his brothers and their families crowded in around him.

Rhett saw people he hadn't spoken to, and he wondered when Momma's roommates had arrived. He wondered if the decorations were good enough. He hoped the food would be.

He told himself to stop worrying about it. If Momma had wanted someone to plan elaborate parties for her, she would've kept having kids until she'd gotten a girl. She had seven sons; she had to know what to expect by now.

"A little further," he heard Jeremiah say from outside in the hall. "Right there, Daddy, where the light is coming from."

Daddy entered the room first, his eyes sweeping the crowd easily. He stopped, his limp hardly noticeable anymore but his wide eyes broadcasting his shock.

"Don't stop in the doorway, Gideon," Momma said. "Land sakes." She squeezed around him, and she froze too. Pure surprise covered her face, and Liam counted in a loud voice, "One...two...three!"

He and Tripp did something, because a huge load of balloons spilled from the ceiling then. Everyone shouted, "Congratulations!" and then various forms of "Penny" or "Momma" or even "Gramma."

Momma covered her mouth with both hands, and tears spilled down her cheeks. She turned into Daddy, who gathered her into his arms as she moved her hands to hide her whole face.

Rhett glanced at Wyatt, who stood a few feet from him. Jeremiah was behind Momma, and Rhett and Wyatt stepped out of the crowd first. He heard footsteps behind him, and soon enough, all seven of Momma's sons had converged on her.

"It's a party, Momma," he said.

"For you," someone else said.

"You finished law school."

"Daddy told us."

"What?" Wyatt asked. "Did you think we wouldn't find out? Or wouldn't celebrate?"

"Come on, Momma. Don't cry. No one got married without you."

They all smiled at Jeremiah's last comment.

"Look at your boys, Penny," Daddy said, and Momma finally emerged from his chest. She looked at all of her sons, one at a time, her eyes bright and full of fire, just like they'd always been.

"We love you, Momma," Tripp said, and they engulfed her in a hug. Rhett alone could bury her in his arms, and all seven of them were simply too much for her.

She laughed and started swatting at them. "Okay, okay," she said. "Get off me, you brutes."

Most of them did, but Wyatt lifted her right up off her feet and hugged her. "You're the best momma in the whole world," he said, setting her down. "We have Gramma Lucy's macaroni, and so many cupcakes, I hope I get sick." He beamed at her, set her down, and the brothers backed up so she could see the decorations and guests.

Momma was a born leader, and she'd make the rounds

and talk to every person there, thanking them for coming. She kept her hand in Daddy's as she went past the food and commented on it.

They made it to the egg display, and she burst into tears again, this time gesturing for all the Glovers to come to her. "Get over here and hug me," she even said. They obeyed, and Bishop told her about the display and the eggs.

"I loved that egg farm," she said.

"We made a banner of it, Momma," Tripp said, and she and Daddy stood in front of it for several long minutes.

"Pictures," Momma proclaimed, and she stood with her siblings in front of the printed version of their family farm. She stood with her roommates. She made all of her sons stand with her and Daddy. She made every Walker do it too, even all the little kids.

"No way they were all looking," Jeremiah said, and Rhett just smiled. Absolutely no way.

Finally, he sensed everyone looking at him, and once again, Rhett was expected to know what to say and how to say it. He got behind the microphone and said, "We're all incredibly proud of our mother, as you can see."

People turned toward him, and Momma and Daddy came out of the crowd to face him.

Rhett's emotions choked him, and he took a few seconds to swallow them back. "I was told that Momma had dreamt about three things for her life. She wanted to be a mother." He looked out at the many Walkers there, across four generations. "She got seven sons, who likely drove her to the brink of madness at times."

She smiled and touched two fingers to her lips. Rhett cleared his throat and ducked his head. "She wanted as many children as the Good Lord would give her, and I think she got them. On top of that, she wanted the best wedding she could have. Daddy didn't have a lot to offer back in those days, though he was working for one of the top companies in Austin. Momma's family wasn't rich by any means, but she sewed her own wedding dress, and she and Gramma Jean put on an amazing wedding at the egg farm."

His voice broke on the last word, because he'd made the mistake of looking at his mother. Tears streamed down her face, and he could not imagine what she'd felt when she'd learned about the deaths of her parents. They'd died in a car accident, at the same time, leaving their grown children in the world alone.

Momma had only been twenty-six. She'd had two little boys, and two more on the way, and Rhett could not imagine not having his mother there with him as he had his own children.

Thankfully, his weren't the only wet eyes in the room. All of her brothers crowded around her, and they stood with their arms around each other's shoulders in a display of strong sibling bonds.

Rhett cleared his throat. "Momma wanted to be the first female to graduate from law school at UT-Austin. She wanted to be an amazing lawyer. She wanted to show that women are as smart as men, and that they had every ability to be in courtrooms and technology firms." He smiled out at everyone. "She wasn't the first woman to graduate from law school at UT-Austin, but she just finished all of her coursework there, done through their online program, and she's going to take the next few months to study for the bar exam. I have no doubt my mother will become the lawyer she's always wanted to be, whether she chooses to practice or not."

"Yeehaw!" Wyatt said, taking off his cowboy hat and throwing it into the air. That set off every other cowboy in the room, and cheers, whoops, and applause filled the room as hats went flying.

Rhett smiled through his tears as he clapped for his mother, and he waved at Daddy to come to the mic. "All right. Daddy's gonna say grace, and we're going to eat. Then you can mingle and talk for as long as you want."

The crowd settled down, and Daddy took his hat off his head and pressed it to his chest. He opened his mouth to speak, but nothing came out. He tried again, and then again, finally saying, "Lord, we thank Thee for a bountiful life and all of its beautiful blessings. I personally thank Thee for Penelope Aarons and the influence she's had on me to be a better man, a better husband, and a better father. Her sons thank Thee for the gift of being her children, and we give glory to Thee for all we're each able to accomplish. We miss those who can't be here with us, whether because of the snow or because Thou has already called them home to Thee. We love Thee, and we are grateful for the opportunities life gives us to try, fail, and try again. Amen."

"Amen," a chorus of voices repeated, and the noise started up again.

Rhett stood beside Daddy and just took it all in. He finally looked at his dad, and Daddy's eyes were glassy too. "You're an amazing man, Rhett," he said.

"I guess I inherited it." Rhett smiled at his father and hugged him. When they separated, Momma stood there, and she took Rhett into her arms and held him with the fierceness of love he'd always felt from her.

"I love you, my oldest boy."

"I love you too, Momma."

Chapter Twenty

Oakley sketched out the racetrack on her front driveway, glad the sun had returned, however weak it was. It had been enough to melt the snow from last weekend, and she finally felt like it would stay dry enough to redo the chalk racetrack she'd been drawing on her driveway for a few months now.

Every time she made one, she took a picture of it so she didn't repeat herself. She had a huge driveway that was mostly flat, with enough room to park five cars across it. The three-car garage had a massive bay to the north of it, with enough room to park an RV and a boat.

She'd noticed that every evening, starting about June, a little boy would ride his bike up onto her driveway, triggering her video cameras. She got notified when one of her cameras registered motion, and she'd watched the little boy motor around on her huge driveway while his parents walked by the house with their two dogs.

Sometimes, it was just the dad, the dogs, and the child. Sometimes just the mother. Sometimes all of them.

No matter what, the little boy came onto her driveway and rode around in circles or swirls until he had to go get caught up to his family. Once, she'd heard him making racecar noises with his mouth, and an idea had bloomed in Oakley's mind.

She'd bought sidewalk chalk on the way home from the dealership that evening, and she'd turned on her bright spotlights that night to draw her first racetrack.

It had been basic—just a few curves with an entrance and an exit.

It had taken the little boy only five seconds to spot the blue and pink chalk on the cement, and he'd looked to his mother for permission before zooming up onto the track. Oakley had cheered right there in her office as he maneuvered through it.

It had rained the next week, and the track had been mostly washed away. Oakley got rid of the remnants with her hose and drew another one.

This time, the little boy wasn't alone, and he and his friend had circled through the new track, which had twice as many curves, one of which was a hairpin they struggled to stay upright on. Oakley got such joy from watching them, and every time it rained—or now, snowed—she drew a new track.

The little boys weren't the only ones using it either. Teens rode their bikes back into the cul-de-sac and went through her track. A tween had navigated it on his scooter.

Even an elderly couple walking by had come up and walked through it, laughing together as they did.

Oakley liked bringing that small ray of joy to whomever she could, and today, she used exclusively red and green chalk to make a holiday-themed track. This one had a bridge she indicated with lots of horizontal slashes of red chalk and the words WATCH OUT – BRIDGE written on the side of the track.

She would've liked some warning signs when she was behind the wheel of her racecar. She needed to get over to garage five soon, because the light parade was coming up in just eleven days, and she'd been asked to drive in it. She'd agreed readily, because she wanted the publicity for Mack's Motor Sports.

She honestly didn't need it, and she let her mind wander as she sketched out the track. By the time she finished, sweat ran down her back despite the cool temperatures. She'd invested in a pair of knee pads from the gardening department at the hardware store a long time ago, and they helped as much as the leather gloves she wore. Together, those two items made the hour it took to draw a new track easy to bear.

Inside, she washed up and stored her chalk in the cabinet next to the sink where she had a salt and pepper shaker set. She checked Two Cents, which had become an obsession of hers over the past few weeks.

It seemed like new sections were added every day as the Christmas holiday approached. First, she checked on the car dealership list, where Mack's was still number one.

She smiled, and then asked herself, "What would you do if you were number two?"

She didn't know, because Oakley's dealership hadn't ever been anything but number one. She tapped on the ratings, and saw they'd gotten twelve more since she'd checked last night. People seemed to be enjoying the buying experience there, and Oakley made a note to herself to praise her senior salesmen and let them know to pass the good vibes along to their individual teams.

She looked up, thinking about a bonus for them. Perhaps she could have Vanessa pull anyone who'd sold at least two vehicles a month that year and give them a holiday bonus. She tapped that idea into her notes app as well, and went back to Two Cents.

After tapping on the Seasonal tab, she saw several new things sitting there. *Best locations for hot chocolate* and *Best holiday locations for a Christmas proposal* caught her eye. She adored hot chocolate, and while Three Rivers had a lot of coffee, they didn't seem to have many bistros or cafés serving hot chocolate.

Her favorite came from Belgium, where she'd done several chocolate tours over the years she'd gone there to race. They knew exactly how much peppermint to put in so the chocolate flavor didn't get obscured. The caramel was never too sweet, and the dark chocolate hazelnut hot chocolate she'd sampled there at the chocolate bar was the best she'd ever had.

"Holiday locations for a Christmas proposal," she mused. She tapped there first, and it was just a list of places around Three Rivers. "The downtown park?"

Oakley did not want to get engaged in the downtown park. When she thought of a cowboy down on both knees, she saw the whole wide world of Texas in front of her, because she stood under the entrance arch to Shiloh Ridge Ranch.

Ranger's ranch hadn't made the top ten, not that Oakley was surprised. It wasn't like they were a dude ranch or a commercial operation. Etta and Ida brought up school and community groups, like the Girl Scouts and the local 4-H chapter.

No, what this app needed was the top ten holiday proposal *ideas*. Something she could look at and go, "Yes, that's how I want to be proposed to."

Oakley looked up from the app as The General yowled at her. "I fed you already," she said, looking at the disdainful cat. His bowl was still half-full too. "You have plenty."

She went back to her app and navigated back to the Seasonal menu. *Best places for a Christmas meal* sat there, but Oakley was going to be eating at Shiloh Ridge again. Ranger had offered for her to let her employees come up to the ranch too, and Oakley had sent an email to everyone yesterday morning.

She tapped around, reading a few reviews for places she hadn't visited yet, and she found she could waste as much time on Two Cents as she did social media. There was something charming and unique about the app, and she'd learned about mom-and-pop restaurants with only three tables in them. She'd never known Three Rivers had thirty-one parks she could visit, one as small as a football field.

She hadn't known a coalition of food trucks descended upon Three Rivers every Wednesday night, and she still hadn't gotten Ranger to take her to eat at the rodeo grounds, where the food trucks congregated, set up tables, chairs, and umbrellas, and played loud country music.

She answered every push notification that was sent, and she was excited and happy to do it. In fact, she tapped on the red circle with the four in it at the top of her screen and found that two people had responded to her review, and two more had left reviews after hers.

She tapped on the top one, and the app spun for a microsecond before it went to The Ugly Duckling, which was a brand new car wash in town. They'd opened up only half a block from Mack's, and Oakley's crew had been taking their cars and trucks there to get them washed before their new owners drove them off the lot.

Someone with a handle about cats and tea had said, *If a car dealership uses them, they must be great!*

The comment below that just had a smiley face, and it came from The Ugly Duckling themselves. Oakley stood up straight, not realizing she could now respond to comments on her own business items.

Her handle was Racecardriver, and she should probably change that to be more official before she did anything like that. Once she finished doing that, she went to Mack's Motor Sports to leave a few comments on the reviews that people had left.

About halfway down the first screen, she saw one that had been left by someone called Admin. No profile picture.

She tapped on that, her curiosity piqued. The profile didn't reveal much, but she'd never seen an Admin profile before.

She scrolled down and saw the words *This user has lost their ability to review.*

"Huh." Out of habit, she tapped on the words, though they weren't hyperlinked. To her surprise, the app flashed white and took her to another profile. This one was for Two Cents itself, and she'd never seen that user either. At least not with this more hand-drawn logo and not the more digitized one that sat on the front of the app or that waited for her on the home screen of her phone.

The words beside the slightly different logo read, *Ranger recommends the best of Three Rivers to other cowboys looking to plan the best dates possible for the special women in their lives.*

She stared at the words, not quite comprehending them. She pulled in a breath only because breathing was something her body would do without direct instruction from her mind.

She finally said, "Ranger? How many men are named Ranger in this town?" That got her moving, and Oakley swiped her keys from the drawer in the kitchen and headed for her truck. In her haste to back out, she nearly collided with a teenager on his bicycle, and she braked hard.

"Sorry," he called, and she waved as she backed out. He was with three friends, and they pointed to the track and clapped for her.

A smile touched her face, but it didn't stay long. She couldn't believe Ranger.... Was Ranger...? She couldn't even get her mind to form the questions that had sprung up in her mind.

"He owns Two Cents," she said as she turned onto the highway and left Three Rivers behind. "He has to."

She didn't even know how that was possible. He'd never said one word about it, and she felt like a real schmuck for thinking that there was no way Ranger could be the brain-power behind Two Cents.

"Why couldn't he?" she asked next. She'd certainly been underestimated plenty of times in her life, and it was not a pleasant feeling. Her feelings changed instantly, and she grew excited the closer she got to Shiloh Ridge.

Her boyfriend was the genius behind Two Cents.

She pulled up to the homestead, realizing that it was the middle of the day, and Ranger could be anywhere on the ranch. Still, her nervous stomach urged her out of the truck and up the steps to the front door. She rang the doorbell and knocked, and no one came.

She noticed a new wreath on the door, though, and it was made from a rodeo rope, bluebonnets, and mistletoe.

"Oakley," a man said, and she spun around. Bishop climbed the last of the steps, his smile instant. "What are you doin' here?" He was definitely lighter than the other Glovers, Ranger included. His hair was almost golden, and his eyes resembled the bright spring sky early in the morning.

"Does Ranger own Two Cents?" She held up her phone, though it was off and had a black screen.

Bishop froze, his smile sliding right off his face. He looked over his shoulder and ran his hands over his beard. "Uh, yeah, he didn't want you to know about that."

Oakley went from excited to have such a man on her arm to the scared woman she'd been in Spain when she'd left the villa with two suitcases and as much dignity as she could. "What?" she asked.

"He's real secretive about it," Bishop said. "He's out in the west stable if you want to talk to him."

Oakley took a deep breath, because she needed the air for what she needed to do next. She needed to say all the things to him that she'd never said to Roberto. She said nothing as she brushed by Bishop and ran down the steps.

"Oakley?" Bishop called after her, but Oakley did not slow or turn back.

"He didn't want you to know," she said to herself, her breath coming fast despite the time she put in on the treadmill. "He didn't share anything with you, Oakley. You let yourself get duped by another man."

Her footsteps sounded like stomps, and she couldn't lighten them. She'd bared her whole soul to him. She'd told him everything about her past, including all of the embarrassing mistakes she'd made.

He'd told her nothing.

"Nothing," she bit out. Not even something simple and easy like he owned Two Cents.

How many times had she talked about the app with him? Practically every time they were together, because she liked the app so much. That should've made it easy for him to tell her.

"Ranger?" she called as she pushed into the west stable.

The blue barn she liked so much sat just beyond this, but she didn't want to see it. She wasn't sure she ever wanted to come up to this ranch again.

Her heart warred with itself then, and she called, "Ranger," again.

"Yeah?" He came down the aisle, a pair of reins in his hands. "Hey, sweetheart."

She shoved her hands in her pockets, suddenly not as confident in what she should say to him. So many things flew through her mind, from what she wished she could've done when her relationship with Roberto had ended to how stupid she'd been.

"Oakley?" Ranger had come closer, and he wasn't smiling anymore.

"Do you think I'm stupid?" she asked, keeping her eyes on the front of his coat.

"Of course not." He reached for her, but Oakley stepped out of his reach. "Hey, what is going on?"

"You've been lying to me," she said, her fingers clenching around her phone. "You own Two Cents, and you never told me." She looked up at his face then, because she wanted to see his reaction and know if she was right or not.

He cleared his throat and dropped his chin to his chest. "I was going to tell you."

"You were going to tell me?" Oakley scoffed and wanted to push him further from her. "I cried my eyes out in front of you. I told you things—" Her breath hitched in her chest and stole the air from her next words.

She would not cry again. She would not. When she left here, *he* was the one who would be crying.

"I told you things I've never told anyone, Ranger. Anyone. I told you about my mother, and my father, and everything about what a horrible person I was in the past." She fell back a step from him, needing space and distance and a whole lot of mint chocolate chip ice cream.

"You just sat there and said nothing." She panted, her chest so tight. "Why?" She threw her hands up into the air. "Why?"

He raised his eyes to hers, and while he looked to be in a certain measure of agony, he also wore an edge of defiance. "Two Cents was new," he said. "I was—*am*—working out the kinks. I haven't told anyone but three or four people here on the ranch, and trust me, that wasn't voluntary either."

He'd made an excuse, just like Roberto had.

She was so tired of excuses. "I thought we were serious."

"We are." He reached for her again, but Oakley stumbled away from him.

"No," she said. "You're more serious with whoever you told here." She spun and walked away.

"Wait," he called after her, but Oakley did not wait. He burst out of the stable behind her. "I was going to tell you."

"I wouldn't have told anyone," she said. "I'm smart too, Ranger. I could've helped you with this." She shook her phone at him as she turned back toward him. She walked backward, wishing with all of her might that she hadn't run into Bishop, that he hadn't said anything. "In fact, I'm pretty sure you added review replies because of me."

He said nothing, which was all the confirmation she

needed. She'd suggested that replies would be a good move last week when they'd sat on the front steps with the lemon bars she'd brought him.

She rolled her eyes, shook her head, and spun around to keep walking forward.

"Are you breaking up with me?" he called after her.

"I just need some time to think through everything," she said. "You got that after I exposed my whole heart and soul to you. I'm sure you can find a way to give me the same courtesy."

By the time the vehicles in front of the homestead came into view, Oakley was running. She had to get off this ranch before she started crying. She would not give any of these men at this ranch the satisfaction of seeing her cry. Not again.

She got behind the wheel and got the heck out of there. "You're so stupid," she said as the first tears rolled down her face. She'd made a drive exactly like this before, when she'd left the villa in the hills above the water in Spain. "This is why you date two or three men at once, Oakley. Then, when one acts like a complete jerk, you have someone else to take you to dinner."

She made it to the highway with no one to take her to dinner and no one she'd go with even if someone asked.

Chapter Twenty-One

Cactus watched Tracy Jacobs walk by again, the little paddle in her hand enticing him but not nearly as much as the woman herself. He shifted on the chair he'd brought, Ace on one side and Bishop on the other. If he wanted Milk Duds to go with this holiday feature film, he'd have to crawl over one of them.

He didn't really want Milk Duds, but Tracy was selling licorice too, and popcorn, and Cactus wouldn't have to really eat anything he bought from her. He just wanted to get close enough to see if she smelled as amazing as she looked.

"Stop staring," Bishop said out of the corner of his mouth.

Cactus jumped and looked back at the permanent screen that stood at the end of the field. At least two hundred people had bundled up and brought blankets and hot chocolate for the movie. Cactus sat among families and teenagers, couples and children. People brought their dogs and their coolers and Cactus had enjoyed the energy here.

"If you go talk to her," Bishop whispered. "I'll go talk to that blonde you wanted me to."

"I didn't want you to," Cactus hissed back. "I saw you *drooling* over her and said you could go if you wanted to. I'm fine."

"Yeah, well." Bishop looked at Cactus, his eyes alight in a way that told Cactus he was about to say something that would make Cactus roll his eyes. He'd put his defenses up, and then he'd stew over whatever Bishop said and start to adjust his thinking.

"Well what?"

"Let's go at the same time," Bishop said. "I'm out of practice, and then Ace won't know what's going on."

"He knows," Cactus said.

"He does," Ace said. "And he'd go too, because one, Ace is thirsty, and two, Holly Ann is sittin' over by the drinks with her dog."

"Let's go," Bishop said.

"Go where?" Cactus asked, his panic rising.

Bishop looked at him and then past him to Ace. "I'm going to go talk to Pauline. Ace is going to get a drink and 'suddenly' notice Holly Ann. You're going to go buy a snack from that pretty redhead you keep starin' at. You're going to introduce yourself and get her number."

Cactus's throat turned dry. "How do I do that?"

"You say, 'hey, I'm Cactus Glover. Do you have a boyfriend?'" Ace said. "Then, when she says no, you say, maybe we could go out.' See what she says from there."

Cactus couldn't even swallow. "What if she says she has a boyfriend?"

"Then you buy your snack and get out of there," Ace said.

"What if she doesn't, but she says she doesn't want to go out with me?"

"Same thing," Ace said. "Let's meet back here in ten minutes. Goal: All of us have a woman's number when we get back." He and Bishop stood up, but Cactus had suddenly lost feeling in his legs.

"Let's go, cowboy," Bishop said, putting his hand under Cactus's arm and hefting him to his feet.

"I don't want to do this," Cactus said.

"Yes, you do," Bishop said. "At the very least, get me some licorice." He walked out into the aisle, and Cactus had no choice but to follow him. He turned right when Bishop went left, and thankfully, Ace came with him.

"She's by the drinks, Cactus," he whispered. "I'm right by you."

Cactus felt like a fool, but he kept walking. As he approached Tracy, he pulled his wallet out of his back pocket. Ace veered toward the drink stand, thankfully, because Cactus was forty-three years old, and he did not need an audience to ask a woman out.

Tracy bent down to hear the little boy in front of Cactus, and her smile lit up his soul. "What can I get you, sugar?"

Cactus took a deep breath, and he smelled flowers and candy and salt. Beneath all of that was a hint of perfume, and it made him a little lightheaded. The little boy told her what he wanted, handed her the money, and she gave him a box of candy.

He skipped away, and Tracy watched him, her smile still stuck in place. She switched her gaze to Cactus, and the smile actually bloomed. "What can I get you, cowboy?"

"Um," Cactus said, looking at the placard in the box she carried. "Red licorice." His mind buzzed. What was he supposed to do? What questions had Ace fed him? "Popcorn, please. And I'll take a couple cans of that ginger beer."

She looked down into her box and up at him. "Have you had this before?"

Their eyes met, and Cactus's pulse pounded. "No, ma'am."

"It's pretty spicy." She handed him the licorice and the bag of popcorn, and he passed her a twenty-dollar bill.

"Maybe just one can, then," he said. "And give me a root beer so if that's too spicy for me, I have something I like." He added a smile to the statement, glad when Tracy returned it.

She handed him the cans of soda, and they were like ice in his hands. He had no way to take his change, and he juggled everything he'd bought until she could slide the bills between two of his fingers.

He stood there, and Tracy's smile faltered. "Did you want somethin' else?"

"Uh, yeah, I wanted to maybe ask you out."

Tracy's smile returned, and she ducked her head and tucked her hair behind her ear. "I don't even know your name."

"Oh, right." He was supposed to lead with that. "I'm Cactus Glover." He tried to reach out to shake her hand, but he'd ordered way too much, and the licorice fell to the ground. The popcorn followed, and Cactus was left with two cans of soda and plenty of embarrassment heating his face. "Um." He stooped to pick up the things he'd dropped, wishing the popcorn hadn't spilled quite so much.

"Do you know my name?" she asked.

"Yeah," he said. "Tracy Jacobs."

Her eyebrows went up, and she settled her weight on one hip. "You come stand over here," she said, indicating her right side.

He wasn't sure why, but he did as she said. "All right, sugar. What can I get you?" She started to help another child, and as she plucked out a box of Lemonheads, she looked at Cactus. "How did you learn my name? I've never seen you before."

"You were at the soldiers care package thing," he said, looking out over the crowd. At least they weren't having this conversation in the middle aisle, with dozens of people around. As it was, probably five or six people could overhear them if they cared to. "I, um, asked around."

"Aren't all you Glovers up in the hills?"

"Yes, ma'am," he said, suddenly remembering the first question he was supposed to ask. "Do you have a boyfriend? Because if you don't, I know a great place for lamb chops."

She handed the candy to the little girl, took her money, and looked at Cactus. "You think I look like a woman who likes lamb chops?"

Cactus wasn't sure if she was flirting with him or not, but it sure seemed like it. She had laughing, light-green eyes he wanted to look into some more, and he put a smile on his face. It pulled a little strangely, and he couldn't recall if Bishop or Ace had told him to smile or not.

His eyes cut away from Tracy, and they happened to land right on Ace, who'd somehow managed to get himself invited to sit on the same blanket with Holly Ann and her dog. He tipped his head back and laughed as the pup tried to lick his face.

Holly Ann gazed at him with stars in her eyes, and Ace would definitely be returning to the chairs with her number—if he returned at all.

"Cactus?"

He flinched, his candy falling to the ground again, and looked at Tracy. "Yes, ma'am."

"I don't have a boyfriend."

Cactus blinked at her, and he lost all control of himself, because suddenly everything he was holding slipped from his hands and landed on the ground. He grabbed onto Tracy and hugged her, which was awkward and ridiculous, as she wore a strap around her shoulders to support the concessions box she sold from.

"That's great," he said, stepping back. Heat ran from the tips of his fingers to the soles of his feet.

"I didn't say yes to dinner with you," she said.

Horror moved through Cactus. "Uh, right. Okay." He stooped again, humiliation stomping through him. His heartbeat felt like a whimper in his chest as he straightened. He touched a can of soda to the brim of his hat and nearly knocked himself in the forehead with the aluminum.

Go, he told himself. *Go, go, go*.

He'd taken a few steps away from her, his throat on fire. He didn't look at the soda can as he fumbled with the tab. It made the classic *spit-hiss* sound, and the next thing he knew, soda shot into his face.

Cactus froze, his nose burning with carbonation and his embarrassment intensifying. He licked his lips, getting the spicy flavor of ginger in his mouth. "That is not good," he muttered to himself.

"Cactus," Tracy said, and he should've pretended he hadn't heard her and taken himself back to his family.

Instead, he turned around and faced her, dripping with soda and burning with embarrassment.

Tracy's eyes widened, and she scanned him down at his boots and back to his eyes. "I owe you something still." She stepped toward him and tucked another dollar between his fingers. She nodded and turned back to a teenager standing there, waiting to order.

Cactus had no idea how much the stuff cost that he'd bought, and he dropped the ginger beer into the trashcan as he went by. He took everything back to the chairs, but Bishop hadn't returned yet.

He shoved the money in his pocket and headed for the restrooms to wash up. With everything he could wash clean, he went back to the chairs. Much longer than ten minutes had passed, but Cactus sat in his seat alone.

He ate his way through the whole bag of popcorn

before Bishop returned. Cactus handed him the licorice without a word.

"How'd it go?"

"Terrible," Cactus said. "Can we leave?"

"Ace isn't back." Bishop opened his licorice and cut a look at Cactus out of the corner of his eye. He hated it when his younger brother did that. It made Cactus feel like such a beast and such a loser at the same time. He was far too old to feel like either, and he wasn't sure how he could feel more embarrassment, but he did.

"It really went terrible?"

"Feel my shirt," Cactus said.

Bishop frowned, clearly confused, but he reached out and felt Cactus's shirt. "Why is it wet?"

"Well, after I completely forgot to tell her my name before I asked her out, and then I told her that I'd asked around to learn *her* name, I asked if she had a boyfriend." Cactus had nothing left to stuff into his mouth to get himself to stop talking.

"She doesn't, by the way, and I literally grabbed onto her like she was my personal savior." He shook his head. "She didn't say yes to going out with me, as she so kindly pointed out, and I walked away, opened a can of soda I'd already dropped, and it sprayed all over me."

Cactus looked at Bishop, who stared back at him with wide eyes now. He blinked a couple of times.

"Then, she said my name, and because I apparently like to be humiliated until I'm buried, I faced her, dripping wet, holding all this idiotic stuff, and she gave me another dollar in change." He shook his head. "Then, I came back here and sat by myself while you and Ace are off getting women's numbers like it's as easy as breathing."

Familiar darkness gathered in Cactus, but he pushed against it. He wanted to be off the ranch. So he was rusty. Big deal. Tracy was beautiful, but there would be other women that caught his eye.

Bishop tilted his head to the side. "She gave you another dollar in change after you'd already finished buying stuff?"

"Yes," Cactus said. "She made me stand by her while she helped other customers so we could keep talking." He sighed, his misery starting to bloom. "She thinks I'm a stalker, and I am. She thinks I'm desperate, and I am." He shook his head, wondering how fast his blunders would get around town. Perhaps the women here had a network, and he'd land at number one on the list of *men who are creepy and who you should never go out with.*

"Where's the dollar?"

"What?"

"The dollar," Bishop said, holding his hand out.

"I already bought your licorice," Cactus growled.

"Give me the dollar," Bishop said.

Cactus rolled his eyes and dug in his pocket for the sticky money. He slapped it in Bishop's hand and watched as he unfolded it. A piece of paper fell out, and Cactus pulled in a breath as Bishop went after it.

He unfolded that too and started to laugh.

"What?" Cactus asked.

Bishop handed him the paper, his eyes glowing and his smile a mile wide.

Cactus looked at it, and it said *Tracy Jacobs*, with her phone number below that. The air left his lungs. "What in the world?"

"You got yourself a date, cowboy," Bishop said. He leaned closer. "And don't tell Ace, but I got two."

Cactus stared at the digits on the paper, still in awe that Tracy hadn't filed a protective order against him. He looked at Bishop. "Of course you did."

"He's comin'," Bishop said. "Not a word."

"As long as you take everything I just told you to the grave."

"Deal."

Ace stepped over both of them, saying, "I got it." He sat down. "You guys?"

"Yep," Bishop said, looking at the screen again.

"Cactus?"

All he had to do was lift up the lined piece of paper. Ace whooped, and several people turned around to shush him. He didn't care at all. He plucked the paper from Cactus's hand and said, "I knew it. I *knew* it. Good job, Cactus."

"Yeah," Cactus said, glancing at Bishop, who smiled like a hyena. Cactus looked away from his brother, determined not to ever tell anyone else what had happened in the five minutes before Tracy had given him her number.

Ever.

Chapter Twenty-Two

Ranger avoided everyone he could for three days. Friday came, and Ranger wasn't sure how long Oakley needed. He'd managed to keep himself from calling or texting her, but it had taken all of his willpower, all of the time.

"You have to do something," he said to himself as he paced past his office. Ward and Bear would be there in a few minutes, and maybe he could call Oakley real quick.

The problem was, he didn't know what to say. He couldn't believe she'd gotten so upset about the app, and he felt like he was missing a crucial piece.

He went downstairs to get coffee, because he'd been too distracted to make any in his own kitchenette. Bishop sat at the table, texting.

"Morning," Ranger said.

"Morning," Bishop said, obviously not even knowing

who he'd spoken to. He'd been going to town a lot, and he'd probably met a dozen new women to flirt with and take to dinner. Just as Ranger put a spoonful of sugar in his coffee, Bishop got up. "Hey, whatever happened with Oakley the other night?"

Ranger lifted his head and looked at Bishop. "What do you mean?"

"I ran into her on the porch, and she knew you owned Two Cents." Bishop actually looked concerned, and Ranger reached for that missing piece.

"Did you tell her?" Ranger asked.

"No, she knew." Bishop flipped on the faucet. "I told her you didn't want her to know."

"What? Why would you tell her that?"

"Because you...didn't want her to know?" Bishop scrubbed and reached for a towel.

"I started to tell her earlier this week, when we thought Cactus's cabin was on fire."

"I didn't know that."

"Did she say how she found out?"

"She did not."

"You didn't tell her."

"I did not." Bishop's eyes flashed with annoyance. "What happened?"

"She broke up with me."

"She what? Why?"

"Because." Ranger rolled his head, because he held so much tension in his shoulders and neck, and he couldn't have this conversation right now. "I have a meeting." He took his coffee back upstairs, and he'd just reached the landing when the front door opened.

A few seconds later, Bear and Ward entered Ranger's office.

"New agendas," Ranger said. "Coming to your phones right now." He sent the text, and he sat down in front of his computer.

"Whoa," Ward said, practically falling into his chair.

"What does it mean *get Oakley back*?" Bear asked. "What happened?"

"I'm talking for five minutes about this," Ranger said. "And I need your best ideas afterward." He laid out what had happened, and how he was supposed to go down to town that evening to help her decorate her racecar for the light parade and, "She's coming to the family gift exchange tomorrow. Or she was supposed to."

Ward looked at Bear, and Bear looked at Ward. They both looked at Ranger.

"She loves that app, right?" Bear asked.

"Yeah." Ranger focused on his computer. He wanted to take down the app all of a sudden. It had been a wild ride for the last month, but it had come between him and Oakley.

"You control the app, right?" Ward asked.

Ranger looked up at something in his brother's voice. "Yes."

"You can send a push notification to all users of the app," Ward said. "Anytime you want. You can build a new list—any time you want." He exchanged another glance with Bear. "So push something out to her."

"It'll go to everyone in town," Ranger said, mildly horrified. He'd lived his whole life out of the spotlight, and he didn't want to step into it now.

"It'll show her that you want her and trust her above everyone else," Bear said. "That you don't care if everyone in town knows you own this app, as long as she's yours." He leaned back in his chair. "It's genius, actually."

"Glad I thought of it," Ward said, and the two of them laughed.

Ranger thought they'd lost their minds. "You guys are terrible at giving advice, for the official Shiloh Ridge Ranch meeting record." He glared at them. "Next item on the agenda. We need to get the temporary cowboys scheduled for branding."

THAT AFTERNOON, RANGER PACED THE LENGTH OF THE porch, his phone in his hand. He could send out a push notification with about five taps and a message. The whole town would know who he was, and how he felt about Oakley Hatch, before dinnertime.

"She needs to know how serious you are about her," he said. "That would do it." The more he'd thought about what Bear and Ward had said, the more it had made sense. He still felt slightly crazy, and he turned and walked back the way he'd already come.

"Dear Lord," he said. His breathing slowed, and his pulse stopped hopping around erratically. "Help me to know what to do." He sat down in one of the chairs on the porch and looked out over the front yard.

The whole family was gathering tomorrow evening for dinner, a reading of the Savior's birth, and their gift exchange. Ranger normally looked forward to the event, because while his family could be loud when they all got together, he knew he belonged to them, and he loved them all in their own individual way.

He'd drawn Preacher's name, and he'd bought the man the complete set of Batman movies, as he loved superheroes. He'd stopped by the bakery on one of his trips to town to spend time with Oakley and ordered a gift basket specifically for movie-watching. It had bags of popcorn, flavored salts to sprinkle on the kernels, chocolate-covered pretzels, and gift cards for the bakery.

He hoped Preacher would like it, and he had no reason to think he wouldn't. Most of the Glovers were fairly easy to please, and Ranger was sure he would like whatever he got from Cactus. The man usually had very good ideas for his gifts, because he spent so much time observing everyone.

He'd invited Oakley to the family dinner and gift exchange, because Bear had invited Sammy. Ida was bringing Brady. They wouldn't have gifts for anyone, but Oakley had said she didn't mind watching.

"I want her there," he whispered, and he closed his eyes, trying to hear someone telling him what to do.

His mind cleared, and he knew exactly what he needed to do.

He opened his eyes and breathed in through his nose.

One swipe, and he got his phone open. One tap got Two Cents to pull up. Another took him to the settings, where he could construct and send a push notification to all ten thousand, five hundred, and forty-two people who'd downloaded the app in the last thirty days.

His pulse stayed steady as he tapped out the message. *Oakley Hatch, I'm in love with you. Please know that I wanted to tell you I was the creator of Two Cents, but my own insecurities got in the way. Please forgive me. PS. Check out the new list for How to tell if you're in love with a racecar driver.*

He smiled, saved the message but didn't schedule it, and tapped back out to create a new list. He could set them to go live at the same time, and he worked on the list for several minutes. He checked, double-checked, and triple-checked his spelling to make sure the list was perfect.

It was four-ten, and it would take about a half an hour to push out the new list to the app. So the push notification couldn't go out until then.

His thumb hovered over the publish button for the list, and he drew in another long breath. "Now or never, Lord. Should I do this?"

The wind seemed to be whispering, *yes, yes, yes*, and Ranger tapped the publish button. He went back to the push notification and scheduled it for four-fifty and sat back.

"It's done."

He wondered if he should drive down to the dealership like they'd made plans for him to do. She was going to show him her racecars and he'd promised to bring dinner and help her with whatever she needed.

He wanted to go, but not if she didn't want him there. Not if he proclaimed his love for her and it wasn't enough.

Wait, he thought. *You'll have to wait and see what happens after the push goes out.*

Chapter Twenty-Three

Oakley pulled into her garage and got out of the truck. She retrieved the few bags of groceries she'd picked up at the grocery store and took them inside. After putting everything away, she went back outside to put away the rake she'd been using before she'd gone to pick up her groceries.

She was so tired, as she hadn't slept much in the past few nights. Oakley laid there, thinking about Ranger and what she'd said to him. She tried to figure out if she was hurt by him, or just embarrassed that she'd fallen so fast for him.

She'd done the same thing with Roberto, and she'd been blind to his flaws.

Ranger had told her multiple times that he wasn't perfect, but Oakley hadn't been able to find any imperfections.

She had some now. Even though she'd asked him to tell

her his secrets, he hadn't. He'd kept them to himself. Or rather, he'd shared them with people that were more important than she was.

She'd roll over, trying to erase the thoughts from her mind. They never went far, even after she took sleeping pills, rubbed lavender on her temples, or meditated for a full thirty minutes.

Just when she'd get to sleep, her alarm would go off. She still had a massive dealership to run, and while she had plenty of people in management positions, a lot of the big decisions still had to be made by her, on a daily basis.

"Go say thank you."

Oakley looked up at the sound of the voice, and she saw the little boy she'd originally drawn the track for. A smile popped onto her face, and she abandoned the rake against the garage again.

"Hello," she said.

The little boy looked back at his mother, and she nodded for him to go on. He got off his bike and started walking toward her. By the time he reached her, he was running. She crouched down and hugged him, her eyes closing with happiness.

"Thank you for dwawing the twack," he said.

"Of course," Oakley said. "Which one have you liked the best?" She pulled away from him and looked into his eyes. He was so cute, with those baby blue eyes and his golden, sandy hair.

"I like this Chwistmas one."

"It's red and green," she said, looking at the lines on her concrete.

"Has a sleigh," the boy said.

"Yeah." Oakley's heart squeezed, because tears were starting to pile up behind her eyes. She stood up, and the little boy skipped back to his mother.

Oakley raised her hand for the woman, and she called back to her, "Thank you."

Oakley nodded and hugged herself as they continued their walk. She sighed and left the rake where it was. Inside, she closed the garage and went to feed her cat. As she did, she wondered if hugging that little boy would be as close to motherhood as she would ever get.

"You don't know how to be a mother anyway," she muttered to herself as she opened the can of wet cat food. The General rubbed between her legs, and she scoffed at him. "You're so manipulative, you silly beast."

He definitely liked wet cat food better than the dry, and Oakley just wanted one of them to be happy.

Ranger had not called or texted, and she wondered if three days was long enough to take a break from him.

She set the cat food bowl on the floor and The General streaked toward it. No matter what, she knew she wasn't happy. Would she somehow find happiness tomorrow? If so, how?

She didn't believe in magic. The only way to fix what had broken between her and Ranger was to go talk to him.

Oakley wasn't sure how to do that. She had not reached out to her mother or her father yet, because she didn't have the right thing to say to them.

She moved to the couch and looked at her phone. Normally, she'd have Two Cents open by now, checking her status on the car dealership list and then seeing what was new. She hadn't been able to open the app since she'd left Shiloh Ridge Ranch three days ago.

She tossed the phone onto the couch beside her and leaned back, closing her eyes as she exhaled. She'd set up a small Christmas tree in her living room, but the only presents beneath the branches were those she'd purchased for Ranger. She'd wrapped everything she'd bought for him, knowing she still hadn't found the one exact right gift.

They hadn't planned anything specific to exchange gifts yet, as Ranger struggled to make plans during birthing season.

She thought of her racecar in garage five. She'd scheduled herself off today, because she needed to have the car ready for the light parade, which was taking place in just seven days. She'd done nothing to prepare for it, because Ranger had planned to bring dinner to the garage and help her get everything lit up.

She didn't want to go anywhere right now.

Sighing, she left her phone on the couch and went through the house to her bedroom. She changed into a loose pair of black pants and a ratty T-shirt, called to The General that she was going to take a nap, and climbed into bed.

The cat jumped up onto the bed several minutes later, and Oakley smiled to herself. At least she had him, even if he was crotchety and vocal. The cat didn't keep secrets from her, that was for sure. The cat lay against her legs, the rumbling of his purring lulling Oakley into a blissful state of slumber.

OAKLEY WOKE SOMETIME LATER, HER HEAD POUNDING and her feet cold. She groaned as she sat up and switched on the lamp. Darkness had fallen, and Oakley knew she'd be miserable when it was time for bed.

The General was gone, and Oakley had no idea where her phone was. She got up and padded into the kitchen to get some painkillers and a drink for her cottony throat. Her stomach grumbled, and she got the carton of mint chocolate chip out of the freezer. She sat at the bar and dug right in with a spoon. No bowl needed.

The clock on the stove said it was just after five o'clock, and she should've been at the garage a half an hour ago. She'd have to get her own dinner now, and she started looking for her phone.

"Couch, couch," she said, remembering how she'd tossed it down when she'd considered opening Two Cents. She retrieved her phone from the couch and saw a blue light flashing.

She swiped on the phone to find she had notification icons all across the top of her device. Surprise lifted her eyebrows, and she instantly felt overwhelmed. Over a dozen texts sat in her messages app, and Oakley hardly knew where to start.

A little TC sat at the top, and that was a push notification from Two Cents. For some reason, she really wanted to see what it was. Her finger moved as if it had a brain of its own, and she pulled down the notification. She tapped on it, and Two Cents opened, the push notification popping up over the lists she loved so much.

Oakley Hatch, I'm in love with you. Please know that I wanted to tell you I was the creator of Two Cents, but my own insecurities got in the way. Please forgive me. PS. Check out the new list for How to tell if you're in love with a racecar driver.

Her heartbeat thrashed in her chest, and she closed her eyes as tears overflowed. A sob came up her throat, and she let herself cry.

He loved her. He'd just told the whole town he loved her and that he was the creator of Two Cents. At least for those who knew Oakley had been dating Ranger.

Her eyes snapped open, and she tapped *okay* on the push notification to get it to close. Right there at the top of the home screen sat the new list he'd mentioned.

How to tell if you're in love with a racecar driver.

She tapped on it and blinked so her blurry, watery vision wouldn't obscure the words.

1. *You miss her the moment she leaves the ranch.*
2. *The first time you kissed her, you never wanted to kiss anyone but her.*
3. *You've wanted to press on the accelerator with every step in the relationship.*
4. *She makes you want to be a better man.*
5. *You sacrifice eating and sleeping just to be with her.*
6. *You appreciate the life experiences that have made her into the faithful, loyal woman she is today.*
7. *You want to stand beside her for all the storms life will*

bring. You need her beside you, or you'll stumble and fall.

8. *You've started fantasizing about your life together: where you'll live, how many kids you'll have, and even what they'll look like.*
9. *You said you loved her, and it felt like the truest thing you've ever uttered.*
10. *You've bought the woman an engagement ring, and you're currently gathering data from everyone in Three Rivers for the best way to propose, the best place to do it, and the best time of year to do it.*

Richard "Ranger" Glover

OAKLEY BLINKED AND READ THE LIST AGAIN. "THE truest thing he's ever uttered." She got to her feet, her heartbeat crashing against her ribcage.

Her phone rang, and she saw Etta's name on the screen. Oakley quickly swiped on the call, and said, "Hey."

"Praise the Lord, she answered," Etta said. "Ida, I've got her. I'm putting you on speaker."

"What is going on?" Ida asked. "Did you see everything on Two Cents?"

"I can't believe he did that," Etta said. "I didn't even know Ranger was the creator of Two Cents."

"I suspected," Ida said.

"You did not," Etta said, scoffing. "Oakley? Are you there?"

"I'm here," she said. She didn't know what else to say.

She sank back to the couch and ran her hands through her hair.

"We're coming over," Etta said.

"You really don't need to do that."

"We've already talked to Ranger. He said he was supposed to bring you dinner and help you decorate your racecar, so we know you don't have anything to eat."

"I picked up some groceries on the way home," she said. And there was all that ice cream she'd just eaten.

Etta laughed. "We know you don't cook. Ida's already ordered. We'll be there in twenty-five minutes."

Oakley knew better than to argue, so she just said, "Okay," and let Etta disconnect the call. She looked at her text messages, and they were mostly from Etta and Ida. Sammy had also sent four, and Vanessa three. All of them were talking about Ranger.

Her phone rang again, and Oakley didn't have the number in her phone. Sometimes she got calls from out-of-town buyers, and she swiped right to connect the call. "Hello?"

"Oakley, my dear."

"Dawna," Oakley said, her voice breaking.

"I wanted to see if you'd come over in the morning and take me to the hairdresser."

"Of course," Oakley said.

"Etta and Ida are baking for the family party."

"I can do it."

Dawna clearly didn't use the Two Cents app, and she hadn't spoken to Ranger in a few days. "They'll bring me up the ranch for the party. You're coming to the party, right?"

Oakley's voice stuck in her chest, and she shook her head. She should be talking to Ranger, and she sighed. "What time in the morning, Dawna?"

"Ten-thirty, dear."

"I'll see you then," Oakley said. "I have to run. I have another call coming in."

"Okay."

Oakley ended the call, feeling a tiny bit guilty for her little fib. She thought of Ranger, and what he'd be doing right now. If she'd sent that push message out, and then she didn't hear from him, she'd be a ball of nerves.

She tapped and tapped again, and the line to Ranger started to ring.

"Oakley," he said, plenty of relief in his voice.

"Richard?" she asked. "Your real name is Richard?"

A beat of silence came through the line. Then he asked, "That's what you got out of that list?"

She giggled, and he joined in with a chuckle. She sobered quickly, and so did he. "I miss you," she said. "I miss you the moment I leave the ranch."

"Can I please come help you with the racecar tonight?"

"I'm not doing the racecar tonight."

"Where are you? I'll just come there."

"I'm at home," she said. "Your sisters are on their way with dinner."

"You're kidding."

"You sent a push notification to the *whole town*." She grinned at The General, who stalked past her like she was interrupting his nap time with her phone conversations.

"I know what I did," he said. "Oakley, I am very serious

about you. There is no one more important in my life than you."

She nodded. "I appreciate that. I also know that you sending that push notification was very difficult for you."

"It was," he said. "Now everyone knows about me and Two Cents. I fully expect them to start uninstalling by the hundreds."

"Why would they do that?"

"Because, Oakley, who am I? Who am *I* to tell them what's the best in Three Rivers?"

She frowned, confused. "What do you mean? Why not you?"

"I barely leave the ranch," he said. "I haven't eaten at half of the places on that stupid app."

"It's not a stupid app," Oakley said. "It's amazing, and people love it. You don't have to know everything. You have people contributing their opinions to the app, and that's what's genius about it."

He exhaled, and Oakley wished she was there, so she could take his face in her hands and remind him what an incredible, smart, generous man he was.

"How fast can you get down here?" she asked.

"I can leave now," he said. "Thirty minutes."

"Your sisters will be here in twenty," she said. "How about you plan to arrive in an hour? They'll leave when you show up."

"You don't know them very well," he grumbled. "But okay."

"An hour?"

"I'll see you in an hour."

Oakley hung up and jumped to her feet. If Ranger was going to be here in sixty minutes, she needed to shower. She sent a quick text to Etta and Ida on the same thread. *Going to shower. Come in when you get here. You guys have one hour from right now before Ranger will be at my house. I love you both, but I want to talk to him a little bit more than you.*

Yay! Etta said. *We'll be there in fifteen and gone in fifty-nine minutes.*

Chapter Twenty-Four

When Ranger pulled up to Oakley's house, he saw the new racetrack on the driveway and smiled. He almost felt like he shouldn't pull onto the cement, but Ida's car was parked there, so Ranger eased to a stop next to her.

He'd felt every second since the push notification had gone out, but he wasn't entirely sure if he was early to Oakley's or not. "Does it really matter?" he asked, peering up at the house. His sisters would leave when he walked in, and then he'd be able to explain everything to Oakley.

She had such a good heart, and he had to believe she'd called as soon as she'd seen the message. He wished the backend of his app would tell him which individual users saw the notifications and when, but it didn't. All he could see was how many had seen it.

His throat tightened at that number. Over eight thousand people had seen the notification. Eight thousand people in Three Rivers knew he'd made a mess of things with Oakley, that he loved her, and his real name.

He hadn't deliberately kept that from Oakley. She wanted to know so badly that it had become a game. She'd throw out random names that started with R while they were in the middle of texting or send him memes she'd made at work with a guess for his name.

Richard was so common, he was surprised she hadn't guessed it yet.

He drew in a deep breath and got out of his truck. He went up the sidewalk, his palms starting to sweat. He rang the doorbell and stood back, remembering the first time he'd done that. He'd kissed Oakley right there on her front porch before their date, and he wondered if he could simply do that again.

The door opened, and Etta stood there. She looked down to his boots and back to his face. "Hey, Ranger," she said as if she owned this house.

Annoyance nipped at him. "Hey, Etta." He stepped up to her and gave her a quick hug. "How are you?"

"Still waitin' for you to set me up with a handsome police officer," she said with a smile. He saw the flash of pain in her eyes before that smile reached all the way up there.

"I thought you were dating Russ," he said.

Etta's face hardened for a moment. "That didn't work out."

Ranger disliked the unrest in his sister's eyes. "I'm sorry, Etta."

"Maybe I'm not meant to have a cowboy." She sighed.

"Which would be fine if I didn't like them so much." She shrugged and shook her head. The movement ran through her body, all the way down to her legs.

She looked at Ranger again. "It would be nice to have my older brother set me up the way he did Ida."

"Why didn't you say something?"

"I thought it was implied that all of my brothers should be trying to find me a date." Etta laughed, and Ranger managed to smile.

"You might want to put that on the group text," he said. "I don't think any of us knew that." He stepped into the foyer when she stepped back. "How is she?"

"She's good," Etta said. "We heard you pull up, and she and Ida raced into the bedroom to touch up her makeup."

"She doesn't need to do that." Ranger glanced toward the mouth of the hall that led down to Oakley's bedroom. He'd been that way once, but he didn't step that way now. "What did you bring for dinner?"

"Those spicy meatballs and the noodle salad from Dragon Garden," she said, preceding him into the kitchen. "I'm assuming you didn't eat?"

"No," Ranger said, and he let his sister get down a plate for him. He took it from her with a, "Thanks," his mind still whirring. He did love this Chinese noodle salad, and he took plenty of that and topped it with a few of the mini meatballs that would likely burn his tongue.

He looked at the food, suddenly not wanting to eat it. Then he'd be kissing Oakley with Chinese dressing on his breath. Or worse, sriracha and barbecue sauce.

"Yeah, I'd wait," Etta said. "They're coming." She

smiled at Ranger and added, "I'm very happy for you, Ranger. I feel like you've waited a long time for someone to sweep you off your feet."

"Thank you, Etta," Ranger said quietly. He hated that his sisters knew how lonely he'd been. That the whole town knew of his desperation to get Oakley back into his life. At the same time, he'd once told Oakley that he didn't want her if he couldn't have her all to himself. That had been humiliating and hard too. He'd survived.

Maybe some of the other cowboys—his brothers and cousins for sure—would tease him for a week or two, and then something else would happen in Three Rivers, and everyone would forget about Ranger.

He could hope and pray for that, at least.

"I just want to say hi," Ida said, and she came into the kitchen. "Hey, Ranger." She hugged him tightly and held on. Ranger returned her embrace, as Ida had always been the more touchy-feely of the twins. That made her more approachable, and it was no wonder she'd dated more often than Etta.

Etta was more like Ranger in that regard. She was almost aloof, especially in new situations, and some people took that as stuck-up or disinterested. Etta was neither, and she was great with kids. She just needed a single guy with his head on straight, and she'd fall head over heels in love with him.

Ranger knew of a lot of people in town, but he wouldn't say he knew them well enough to set them up with Etta. Ward definitely dealt with more men in Three Rivers, as did Bear. Ranger would put a bug in both of their ears and find someone for Etta to at least try a first date with.

"Okay," Ida said as she straightened. "We'll get out of your hair." She smiled, turned, and linked her arm with Etta's as they walked toward the front door.

Ranger slipped from the barstool and started to follow them. He paused when he saw Oakley standing in the foyer. She waved to the twins and closed the door. When she turned and saw him, all of the nerves in Ranger's body fired.

A smile spread across his face, and Oakley grinned at him as she walked toward him slowly. She wore a light blue dress that wafted around her body, with a pair of red cowgirl boots. Her dark hair had been curled, and she had put on makeup but not too much.

Those pink lips sure did call to him, as did the vastness of her spirit.

She opened her mouth, but Ranger held up one hand. "I want to talk first," he said. "Please?"

She nodded for him to go ahead, and she stopped a few paces from him.

Ranger's heart started to pound, and he wasn't sure why. He'd already laid everything out for her, and she'd called.

She called, he told himself.

The desperation that had been thick on the back of his tongue disappeared, and he saw everything clearly in that one moment. "I love you," he said. "I think I may have fallen in love with you the very first time we went out. I'm not sure. I know it's fast, and I know I made mistakes, but at the very foundation of us, there's my love for you."

Oakley nodded, her eyes filling with tears.

"I don't care about the past," he said. "I think our pasts make us who we are today, and the woman in front of me is strong, and faithful, and kind. She draws racetracks on her driveway for children instead of getting mad they're coming onto her property uninvited, interrupting her day with security camera notifications. She knows how to have fun. She taught me how to get outside the drudgery of my life and do something new. She's beautiful, and she makes my heart pound every time I look at her, and I'd be lying if I said I haven't thought about you living in my wing with me."

Oakley stepped toward him, and Ranger opened his arms to receive her. She flew into them, and the solid warmth of her settled Ranger even further. He closed his eyes and breathed in the floral, fruity, clean scent of her hair and skin and perfume.

"I'm sorry I didn't tell you about Two Cents," he said. "It's something I've been working on for three years, and I guess I was very protective of it."

She sniffled and held him tight.

"I should've just told you my real name too," he said. "That was more of a joke than anything, but if it made you hurt, I'm sorry."

She nodded against his chest.

"I'm not perfect, Oakley. I'm not great at talking, and I never want the spotlight on me. I'm sure I'll hurt you again in the future, and all I can do is apologize and ask for your forgiveness." He ran his hands through her hair, and she stepped back slightly.

She tilted her head to look up at him, and Ranger smiled at her. "I'm gonna kiss you now unless you have any objections."

She shook her head, a glint in her eye now instead of tears, and Ranger closed the distance between them and matched his mouth to hers. He was infinitely grateful he hadn't eaten so he didn't have to kiss her with noodle salad breath. She tasted like mint, and she kissed him back with a passion Ranger had only experienced with her.

Oakley pulled away far too soon in Ranger's opinion, but when she said, "I love you too, Ranger," he decided he could take a break from kissing her to hear that.

"Do you really?" he asked.

"Yes," she said, opening her eyes and looking right into his again. "I know how hard you work around the ranch, and I can only imagine how much of yourself you've poured into Two Cents. I know telling people was—*is*—extremely difficult for you, and I didn't mean to force you to tell the whole town."

"You didn't force me to do anything," he said. "Except admit how very important you are to me."

She fiddled with the collar on his jacket, and her touch sent sparks down both of his arms. He hoped he'd always feel this electric charge when they were together, and he kept one hand on her hip to keep her close.

"You want me to come live in the east wing with you?"

"Desperately," he said.

"We'll have to get married first."

"Mm hm." He pulled her close and swayed with her, glad when her hands moved up his shoulders. She traced the fingers of one hand up into his hair, and Ranger shivered. "Do you want to keep this house?" he asked.

"It's too big for me already," she said. "Why would I need to keep it?"

"I don't know. Maybe if you're working late at the dealership one night, and you don't want to drive back up to the ranch. Maybe I'll buy it from you so I have somewhere to store the ATVs."

She burst out laughing, and Ranger joined in. Holding her and talking to her and laughing with her was a version of heaven Ranger wanted in his life forever.

"I could move the racecars here," she mused. "Instead of keeping them in garage five."

"Yeah, stuff like that."

She stepped out of his arms again. "We can still go tonight, if you want to."

"I do want to," he said. "Can I eat first?" He gestured to the plate he'd fixed for himself. "And maybe you can talk to me some more about what else you want your life to be." They'd talked a little bit about children and a lot about her family, but he still wasn't sure what dreams she held in her heart for those things.

He went back to the barstool and Oakley joined him. "I want kids," she said. "Lots of kids. A big family like what you've got."

"All right," he said. "We should definitely keep this house, then. The east wing is only three bedrooms." He scooped up a bite of salad and put it in his mouth.

Oakley smiled. "I want to call my mom and my dad and tell them when I get engaged." A new set of nerves entered her expression. "I want to invite them to come, knowing it'll be here and they probably won't make it. I want them to know I *want* them here, even if it'll be hard."

He nodded. "I can sit with you while you call if that'll make it easier."

"It might." She reached up and tucked her hair behind her ear. "I want to get married at Shiloh Ridge, and I want your mother there in the front row."

Ranger gazed at her, this perfect creature he felt God had made just for him. "I think that's doable."

"I'll keep the dealership for now," she said. "But honestly, it's a lot of work, and if we have a lot of kids, I don't know." She shrugged. "I could let it go."

"It's a ways off," Ranger said. "That's not something you need to decide right now."

"Right." She nodded as he continued to eat. "And one more thing...." She cut a look at him out of the corner of her eye. "I want you to ask people where's the best place to buy a wedding dress in this town." She grinned at him, her whole countenance lighting up. "The best appetizers to serve. All of it."

Ranger chuckled. "Oh, boy. I see what's happening here."

She linked her arm through his and laid her head against his arm. "I loved that app, Ranger, but I love it even more now that I know *you* created it. You're so smart, and so capable, and so amazing."

Ranger didn't feel like any of those words described him very well, but he did like hearing her say them. "Thank you, sweetheart," he whispered, pressing his lips to the top of her head. That moment between them became beautiful and peaceful, without anything said and nothing but him and her and the love between them.

An animal yowled, and Ranger dang near fell off his barstool. "What in the world was that?"

"My cat," Oakley said, slipping away from him. "He likes to let me know exactly how displeased he is with me when I don't feed him on time." She smiled at Ranger and got to work refilling the feline's bowl.

"I didn't even know you had a cat," Ranger said, eyeing the black beast like it would claw his face off. "Is he coming to live with us in the east wing too?"

Oakley looked at him with wide eyes. "Of course."

Ranger frowned and popped his last meatball into his mouth. After he finished eating, he said, "Of course," in a dark tone. "You know, cats on a ranch are only good for one thing—catching mice in the barns and stables."

"Oh, The General loves catching mice. Don't you, buddy?" She grinned down at him, then looked at Ranger again. "He'll be fine. You won't even know he's there."

The General gave another yowl, and Ranger's eyebrows lifted. "I think I'll know he's there." The whole ranch would know he'd moved in, and Ranger could only imagine what Bear would say.

That actually tickled his funny bone, and he started to laugh.

"What?" Oakley asked, setting the refreshed water bowl on the ground.

"Nothing," he said. "Let's go see the racecars."

Ranger went around the back of the dealership as Oakley directed him.

"My shop's back here," she said. "Five is way down on the end there."

He went past the other four bays, all of which were still open, with cars and ATVs being worked on. "Busy tonight," he said.

"We stay open late on Fridays," she said. "Close early on Saturdays and Mondays."

He nodded and eased to a stop in front of the last garage, which didn't have a number anywhere to be seen. By all intents, it looked abandoned, and he imagined cobwebs everywhere, dust on everything, and old grease stains on the floor inside.

"Okay," Oakley said, but she didn't get out of the truck.

"Okay," Ranger repeated.

She looked out her window, and her shoulders lifted as she took a deep breath. "I think I know how you felt about telling me about Two Cents," she said. She suddenly faced him, a bit of panic in her gaze. "These cars mean a lot to me. They're going to look like trash to you, but they're not. They're actually in really good condition, and I come out here when I need to find my center again."

Ranger absorbed what she'd said. "I understand," he said quietly. "I'm not going to laugh at them."

She nodded. "I have all the lights. I just need some help getting them in the right place to make the picture I want to make." She reached for the door handle, and Ranger got out too. He met her at the regular door, where she fitted a key into the lock and twisted the knob.

She stretched her arm out and flipped a switch, flooding the garage beyond with light. Looking up at him, she smiled. "Here we go."

Ranger took her hand and let her lead him into garage five. It smelled like asphalt and motor oil, just as he thought it should. There was no dust on anything, and no cobwebs. Oakley kept a tidy shop, and while there was probably some grease stains on the floor somewhere, Ranger couldn't see them right now.

He gaped at the two racecars sitting side-by-side in the space. "They're great," he said. "These are the same ones you actually raced in."

"Yes," she said. "How did you know that?"

"I watched some videos online," he admitted.

She smiled and shook her head. "I had to pay a lot for the cars when I retired," she said. "See, you race for a team. It's not just you out there. You're sponsored by a company—usually a car company, but not always—and they can actually win in Formula One too."

She continued to tell him about her time with the Ferrari team, and then the Mercedes team, and how she'd come to get the cars and ship them here. "They came in on semis," she said. "Middle of the night type of deal." She ran her hand along the top of the orange car. "This one runs the best, so I thought I'd drive it in the light parade."

She glanced to the other one, which was black. "But that one's the right color to attach all the lights to and practically disappear during the parade."

"Start it up," Ranger said, admiring the cars. They didn't look like anything he'd ever seen in real life before. The people in Three Rivers would love seeing her in the parade, and Ranger grinned as he thought about it.

The wheels on either side of the car were almost as tall as the car, and Oakley would sit way down inside the vehicle, right in the very center of it, the fins above her head behind her.

"I honestly don't think the color matters," he said. "There's very little paint as it is."

Oakley stepped over to a cabinet and opened it, took out a set of keys, and climbed into the cockpit of the black racecar. A single-seat vehicle, they'd never be able to drive together. Not that this type of car could go on the roads around here anyway.

"It's going to be loud," Oakley shouted, and Ranger nodded. He backed up as far as he could, and Oakley started the car.

The engine roared, and Ranger thought he'd been ready for loud. He hadn't been. He clapped his hands over his ears and grinned as the engine settled into a chugging rumble that reverberated through his whole body.

Oakley hadn't put on a helmet, and she was easily the sexiest woman in the world sitting behind the controls of the racecar. She turned it off and climbed out. "Now listen to this one." She got in and started the orange car, and while it roared in the beginning too, its engine almost purred once it settled down.

She revved it, a grin on her face, and Ranger laughed.

She turned the car off and got out, joining him as they faced the two of them together. "See?"

"I see." He turned toward her and took her into his arms, kissing her with a newfound passion he honestly had no idea he possessed. "That was amazing." He kissed her again. "*You're* amazing." And again. "I think you should drive the orange one." His breathing ragged, he leaned his forehead against hers. "I'm only disappointed I can't ride with you."

He couldn't believe she could drive that thing at two hundred miles an hour. He looked back at the car and then at Oakley, who barely stood five and a half feet tall. "You're absolutely incredible. It's so different seeing it in person than on a video." He stepped over to the car, where the front bumper barely sat a couple of inches off the ground.

"It pulls more Gs than the space shuttle when it launched," Oakley said. "I can get to sixty miles per hour in under two seconds."

Ranger gaped at her again. "Even now?"

"Even now, cowboy." She grinned at him. "There's a lot of horsepower in this thing." She put one hand on the wheel closest to her. "Can you imagine if I showed up at the ranch in it?" She grinned at him wickedly.

"Bear would lose his goldarn mind." Ranger burst out laughing. "Will you *please* drive it up for the gift exchange tomorrow? *Please?*"

"No way," Oakley said. "Brady's going to be there, silly." She pushed her palm against his chest. "We barely escaped a ticket for going five over the speed limit on a legal vehicle." She gazed at the racecars with love in her expression though.

Ranger put his arm around her again. "I want to go from zero to sixty with you," he said. "In less than two seconds."

"Is that a proposal, Richard?" she asked, plenty of teasing in her voice.

Ranger laughed and shook his head. "Not a proposal," he said, though now ideas for how he could ask Oakley to be his wife shot through his mind. "Let's get this thing decorated. I've got an early morning."

Chapter Twenty-Five

Ward Glover arrived at the blue barn last, having had a heck of a time getting out of the house that morning. Ace had already been gone by the time Ward had entered the kitchen for coffee, and it had been stale in the pot.

"Morning," he said to the other three cowboys who'd gathered there. "Sorry I'm late." If he'd had an ATV in his garage, he'd have been on time, but he pushed the thought away.

"It's fine," Bishop said. He already wore a tool belt, though, and Cactus had gloves on. "We were just hearing about Ace's date with Holly Ann."

"Oh, right." Ward looked at his brother, wishing the jealousy now spiraling through him didn't hit so hard. "How'd it go?"

"Amazing," Ace said with a smile. "I'll catch you up later."

Ward nodded, not looking forward to that. But he'd listen to his brother, because that was what brothers did. Ace dated a lot more than Ranger or Ward ever had, though Ward had definitely had the most serious relationships over the years. He didn't usually date casually. Since Paige, though, he'd been trying to be a little less intense.

He'd been out with a few women, especially lately, but things just hadn't worked out. He'd only been out with Sabrina Hendrick the one time, and when he'd called again, she'd said she was real sorry, but she hadn't felt anything for him.

Ward thought she'd used the words "like a brother," but he'd ended the call quickly after that and deleted her number from his phone.

Before that, he'd dated Victoria Smith for a couple of months. In the end, though, he'd found her expectations for him a bit too high. He couldn't answer her calls ten times a day, and he couldn't text back within ten seconds. He worked on a ranch, for crying out loud.

"All right," Bishop said. "I've been going over some plans, and I just wanted twenty minutes with you guys to see if you're willing to help me with this project." He looked around at the group, his light blue eyes wide and concerned. "It's fine if you're not. I know we have a lot of construction still going on with the cowboy cabins, and we're not even close to being done with birthing season." He sighed and swept his cowboy hat off his head.

After running his hand through his hair, he reseated his hat and stepped over to an old barrel. "Something Ranger said struck me," Bishop said, spreading out a roll of papers.

"This barn has been on the ranch for decades, and we shouldn't just knock it down. He said event venue or dance hall or even just a place to host big family dinners."

"Which we all know are going to get bigger," Ace said. "I mean, Bear and Ranger both have fiancées now, and—"

"Whoa, hold up," Cactus said. "Did Ranger ask Oakley to marry him?"

"No, not yet," Ward said. "But he will." He exchanged a glance with Ace. "Soon, too, is my prediction."

"Wow, he doesn't waste any time, does he?" Cactus grumbled.

"He sure doesn't," Ward agreed, wishing his tone wasn't as dark as Cactus's. The two exchanged a glance, and Ward looked away first. They'd been good friends growing up, and they still were. Being second oldest was a tough job, and no one understood it like Cactus did.

"Anyway," Bishop said. "I want to preserve the barn exactly like Ranger suggested. I think we need to gut the inside and keep everything on the exterior. The foundation will need to be repaired, and I was thinking we'd put in a kitchen out here, install heating and air conditioning, and then have one big room for dancing, eating, weddings...." His voice trailed off, and he looked at the others.

"I want it to be a surprise," he said. "A wedding gift for Bear and Sammy."

Ward was already nodding when Bishop looked at him. "I'm in."

Bishop grinned. "That's what I needed to know. I can hire seasonal cowboys to come help me. Heck, I could hire someone to do the whole project. But I want to do it, and I wanted to know if you guys did too. It could be a gift from all of us."

"We'll have to work on it in our spare time, is what you're saying," Cactus said, peering at the plans Bishop had sketched out.

"Yep," Bishop said.

"I'm still in," Ward said.

"I want to," Ace said. "But I just started dating Holly Ann...I might not be able to help as much as the rest of you."

Ward dang near rolled his eyes, but he caught himself in time. He focused on the dirt at his feet so he wouldn't clobber his brother upside the head.

"It's fine," Bishop said, and Ward looked up again. "We can go over plans and make assignments. Set deadlines, and then you can plan your work according to your own schedule." He looked at Cactus. "Cactus?"

"What the heck?" Cactus asked. "I don't do anything. I'm in."

"What do you mean you don't do anything?" Bishop asked, glancing at Ace. Ward had the distinct feeling he'd missed something the three of them shared, and he cursed himself for not going down to town with them earlier this week. They'd gone for the Christmas movie, and Ward hadn't felt like tagging along. Bishop and Ace seemed to get any girl they wanted, and Ward always ended up feeling bad about himself when he was with them.

But even Cactus had returned to Shiloh Ridge with a woman's number, and Ward wished he'd gone.

"Yeah," Ace said. "You're going out with Tracy. That

could be something, Cactus. You could find yourself with limited time too."

"Nope," Cactus said, reaching for a hammer as if he'd start knocking down pillars and walls right now. "I'm not going out with Tracy."

"What?" Bishop demanded. "Why not?" He turned completely from the plans to face his brother.

Cactus looked like he might start swinging the hammer, and Ward tensed.

"Cactus," Ace said. "Give me the hammer and tell me why you can't go out with Tracy."

"You worked hard for that number," Bishop said. "You should use it."

"I have," Cactus said. "She had to work last night, but we texted a little bit. When she got off, she called me." He handed the hammer to Ace, and Ward relaxed a little bit.

Cactus looked at him next, and Ward just looked back. "Go on," Ward said. "You talked to her last night. Things were going well, and now, you won't go out with her."

Cactus turned around and paced away. "She's twenty-three years old."

Ward sucked in a breath, and Bishop and Ace looked at each other with identical stunned expressions.

"So it doesn't matter if I think she's beautiful and she gave me her number," Cactus said. "It doesn't matter that she's the easiest woman to talk to, or that she suggested we go to dinner on Sunday evening. None of it matters."

Ward's heart wailed for his cousin. Bishop stepped over to him and put one hand on Cactus's shoulder blade. Ward thought he was begging to get slugged, but Cactus didn't start punching.

"I'm sorry," Bishop said.

"Yeah," Ace said, going to Cactus too. "What a bummer."

Cactus glared at Ace, and Ward joined them again too.

"Let's go to that gift donation on Sunday," he said to Cactus. "Just me and you." He glanced at Ace and Bishop. "No offense, guys, but you're hard to be around when we want women to look at us."

"What?" Bishop asked, obviously oblivious to his own charm and good looks.

"Deal," Cactus said. "We'll pick ornaments off the tree and see if there are any single women there." He looked at Ward, new hope in his eyes. "How can we tell if they're at least in their thirties, though?"

Ward found that funny, and he smiled and chuckled as he shook his head. "I don't know, Cactus. I guess we'll have to work it into the conversation."

"Oh, come on," Ace said with a laugh. "You two not being able to get dates has nothing to do with me and Bishop, but your own inability with women." He scoffed and swatted at Bishop's chest. "Can you imagine asking a woman how old she is the first time you meet?"

"It would've saved me the last three days of my life," Cactus growled. "And plenty of humiliation." He looked at Bishop, and there was a story there Ward hoped he'd get to hear later.

"We can get dates just fine," Ward said, glaring at Ace.

"Believe it or not, little brother, not everything has to be done your way to work out."

"Are you kidding me right now?" Ace asked as Ward started back toward the barrel and the plans for the barn. "I know what you've been doing this year." He followed Ward, who ignored him.

"You haven't really tried. You've been stuck on Paige Anders since she—"

"Enough," Ward growled, and thankfully, Ace stopped. He glared at him, his pulse skipping several times. He'd dated Paige for almost a year, and yes, she'd left Three Rivers after breaking up with him. He'd been healing for as long as they'd been together, and that was Ward's typical MO.

Date someone for a long time. Get broken up with. Vow never to date again. Start to heal. A year or two later, he tried again. The cycle was vicious, and Ward was trying to break it.

Seeing Bear and Ranger find amazing women and keep them had certainly helped, and Ward wanted a family and a life all his own too.

"We can go to the gift donation too," Bishop said. "We'll just go separately."

"Aren't the two numbers you got on Wednesday enough?" Cactus asked, plenty of snap in his voice.

"You got *two* numbers?" Ace asked, spinning around.

Ward started to laugh at the incredulity in his brother's voice. He was always competing with Bishop over women, and he obviously hadn't grown out of it yet.

Cactus stepped to Ward's side as the two younger men

started to argue, and he looked at the plans too. "I'm in for this," he said. "And I'm in to go to town with you whenever you want. I think we're both ready to find someone to spend our lives with."

"Yeah," Ward said, because he suspected Cactus might be right. He glanced at Cactus. "Do you think we can really do that?" he asked quietly. "It doesn't always work out, you know."

"Then we keep looking until it does," Cactus said. "Plain and simple." He stuck out his hand, and Ward grinned at him.

"You've got yourself a deal," Ward said, shaking Cactus's hand. "I know Ranger has unpublished data on the best places to meet women," he added in a near-whisper. "I'll get the list and we'll get to work."

"Can't wait," Cactus said dryly, and then they both burst out laughing.

"What's going on over here?" Bishop asked, and Ward just shook his head. Nothing was going on with him or Cactus...yet.

Chapter Twenty-Six

Oakley pulled up to the homestead at Shiloh Ridge Ranch and put her truck in park. She had not driven the racecar, despite Ranger's continued pleas for her to do so. The police car two vehicles down was a good reminder as to why.

She reached over and picked up the grocery bags on the passenger seat. She wasn't a Glover, so she hadn't drawn a name for the family gift exchange. But she hadn't wanted to come empty-handed, and she'd bought enough candy to feed a small army—which was about how many people waited for her inside the house looming in front of her.

The front door opened the moment her foot touched the porch, as if there was some mechanism there that had triggered it. Ranger came outside and then came to a screeching halt. "There you are. I was just comin' to see if you were close, and I couldn't even hear myself think in there."

He lowered his phone just as Oakley's started to ring. "That's me." He smiled and touched his screen to end the call.

"You're sure it's okay I'm here?" Oakley asked. "We're not engaged. Heck, we haven't even been together very long." She took the few remaining steps to him and kissed him.

"Yeah, it's fine," he said. "We're casual." He put his arm around her and went with her inside. They both took a moment to admire the angel tree, and Oakley looked up at the pine boughs laced through the banister on the staircase that went up to the wings.

He led her under the mistletoe that hung above the arch and into the main part of the house, where all of the Glovers had gathered. She saw an empty spot next to his mother on the couch, and she knew that had been saved for her.

Dawna looked amazing too, her hair all set just-so for the holidays. She wore a bright red sweater with loads of candy canes knitted into it, and she laughed at something someone had said.

Oakley took a moment to breathe in their energy. It was almost like being on the racetrack, strapped into that machine that could literally hurl her to her death.

"Oakley's here," someone said, and Ida came toward her. "She brought candy."

"That's for—" Oakley cut off as Ida took the bag from her and ripped it open. "I guess it's for you." She smiled at her friend, and everyone thanked her for the candy as the bag went around. She looked at Ranger, who watched his family with a mildly horrified expression on his face.

"Aren't we eating dinner soon?" she asked.

"Yeah," he said. "You must not have looked at Two Cents today."

"I was on the floor all afternoon." She pulled her phone out of her pocket and tapped to get the app open. Several new lists popped up, signified by the *new!* next to them at the top of the home screen.

"How to live like a kid," she read, tapping. Her eyes scanned quickly. "Oh, well, eating dessert first will do it." She watched as Ace threw a piece of candy into the air for Bishop to catch. He did so, quite spectacularly too, and several people erupted into cheering.

"Get over here," Ida yelled, and Bishop, still laughing, got up to join her in the kitchen.

"This is wild," Oakley said. She'd eaten with his family before, but this felt like a new level of insanity. They'd all been eating candy for eight straight hours, and they were hopped up on the sugar.

"I warned you. They'll calm down once we eat." Ranger looked at the huge dining room table that extended partway into the kitchen and partway into the living area. "We won't eat outside today though, so the noise is going to be contained in here."

"It's time to eat," Etta said, her voice actually louder than Ida's. "Everyone come over here and calm down."

They all obeyed her, and Oakley wondered which twin was older. She was guessing Etta, though Ida could certainly hold her own when it came to conversations and standing in the spotlight. Oakley had done that for enough of her life, and Ranger hated having eyes on him, so she was fine with the way they blended into the background as the others did what Etta had asked.

She, Ida, and Bishop looked out over the crowd. "Where's Zona?" she asked. "I thought she was here."

"She was," Bear said, also glancing around. "I know she was. Sammy asked her about that Zumba class she takes." He looked at Sammy, who nodded.

"Is her car here?" someone asked.

"It has to be. She brought Mother," another Glover said.

Sure enough, Bear's mother was in the crowd, and she said, "I don't know where she went."

"Ranger, go see if her car is here," Bear said, and Ranger stepped away from Oakley to get the job done. Before he'd even reached the front door, it opened, and Arizona walked in. Oakley didn't know her real well yet, but she knew enough to be able to recognize the woman.

She did not recognize the man that came in behind Zona, though he was tall, well-dressed, and wearing a cowboy hat. Zona reached for his hand at the same time Ranger froze.

Oakley had a front-row seat to see into the foyer, but many didn't. Little conversations broke out, most of them grumbling about why Zona would leave now, when she knew they were about to eat.

Bishop came to stand next to her, saying, "What's going—?"

She put her hand on this chest and said, "Shh."

He quieted, and they watched as Arizona introduced Ranger to the man. They shook hands, and Zona looked toward the kitchen. Pure anxiety lived on her face, and Oakley knew exactly how she felt—and this was *her* family.

Bishop started laughing. "Well, I'll be." He strode away from Oakley then, saying, "Duke, when did you get back into town?" He obviously knew the man, and Duke smiled and shook Bishop's hand too. Arizona glared at her brother, quickly switching her gaze back to the doorway.

Oakley gestured in a way that she hoped would make sense. *Do you want everyone out there? Or are you going to introduce him here?*

Zona shook her head and tugged on Duke's hand. Everyone moved back toward the kitchen, and Oakley turned around.

"She's coming," Etta said. "Right, Oakley?"

"Yeah, she's coming," Oakley said.

"Right, quiet down, everyone. This doesn't have to be this hard."

Ranger stepped back to Oakley's side. Bishop went back into the kitchen. Arizona arrived in the arched doorway and stopped, though she now stood right underneath the mistletoe with Duke's hand in hers.

"Everyone," she said, and since they were all staring at her already, it wasn't hard to get their attention. "Most of you know Duke Rhinehart." She looked around the room, and Oakley did too. Yes, these Glovers knew Duke Rhinehart.

"The Rhinehart's own the ranch that borders ours to the south," Ranger whispered in her ear.

"They look like they might eat him alive," Oakley whispered back. "Bad blood?"

"Not that I know of." And Ranger co-owned Shiloh Ridge, so he would probably know.

"Duke," Arizona said. "Here they all are. I'm sure you'll get to know them by name soon enough."

Bear stepped through the crowd and also shook Duke's hand with a smile, so there definitely wasn't too much drama. "Come in," he said. "Come in. We're just starting."

Duke didn't come in very far. He glanced at Oakley and nodded, and she could only offer him a sympathetic smile.

Thankfully, Etta took over again, saying, "Now that we're all here, we want Zona to come up and tell us about the desserts she made." She smiled at Zona, who released Duke's hand and left him standing by himself. He looked like he'd just lost a limb, but he said nothing.

Oakley had to look away so she wouldn't giggle, though she'd feel exactly the same if Ranger had done that to her the first time she'd been to his house.

Arizona went over the pound cake she'd made with peppermint icing, the mint hot chocolate, the banana cake with maple frosting, the brownie cream cheese bars, and the pumpkin cookies.

"I see why we're eating dessert first," Oakley said.

"You didn't see what else was on the app, did you?" Ranger asked.

She shook her head as Zona went by her and Ida started talking food. Oakley had learned that they'd go over all the food and say grace before anyone was allowed to touch a plate. Bishop said it reduced the number of yelled questions and sped up the serving line, but Oakley wasn't so sure about that. She could look at a casserole dish and know she was getting stuffing.

On Two Cents, she navigated back to the home screen and saw the next new item. *Best places to buy a wedding dress.*

A smile filled her face.

Best appetizers to serve at your wedding.

The grin grew to fill her whole soul.

Best ways to propose to a racecar driver.

She burst out laughing, which wouldn't have been a problem if the rest of the family had been operating at their normal level. As it was, Ida had just stopped talking, and Oakley's laugh was the only sound in the room.

Everyone looked at her. She decided she didn't care, and she held up her phone. "Have you guys seen this?" She turned to Ranger. "I love you so much." She kissed him right there, his surprise evident in the way he stood like a brick wall.

Then the Glovers really made some noise, whooping and hollering like they'd just won a family vacation to the Bahamas.

Ranger laughed against her mouth, and Oakley pulled away, giggling too.

"I guess we're ready," Ida said, and Oakley didn't dare tap on the list to see what people had suggested for Ranger as proposal ideas. She could wait until after the prayer.

"Mother," Etta said. "It's your turn. Ace, help her, you lug nut."

Oakley barely stifled a laugh as Ace jumped to help

their mother. He steadied her while Dawna surveyed the group gathered in the homestead.

"Lord," she said. "We thank Thee for Thy bounteous blessings. We're grateful for each other, for this food, and for all those who have chosen to join our family this holiday. Please bless Duke, Oakley, Sammy, and Brady that they won't be too scared off by us, and bless this ranch."

Warmth flowed over Oakley to be prayed for, especially by someone as sweet and good as Dawna.

The older woman paused for a moment, and her voice was thick when she continued with, "We miss those who have already passed, but we know they are here with us at this time of year. Bless us all to keep livin' good lives and remember whose names we bear. Amen."

"Amen," Ranger said beside Oakley, and all of their voices together sealed Dawna's prayer in such a way that God would definitely hear it.

As the crowd surged forward, Oakley thought about what it meant to be a Glover. To have that name on her shoulders.

"You don't want to eat, sweets?" he asked when Oakley stayed where she was.

She looked at him, looking at her, and she hoped she could be good enough one day to carry Glover as her surname. "Of course I want to eat," she said. "Your family makes really good food." She slipped her hand into his and together, they joined the line.

"SHOOT," OAKLEY MUTTERED TO HERSELF. SHE WAS LATE getting the car out of the garage, but she just needed to submit one more thing. Then they'd get the license plates they needed before the New Year.

"Oakley," someone said from the doorway, and she looked up.

"Sorry, Brady. I need two more minutes." She looked back at the paperwork in front of her. She still caught the way he looked at his watch and frowned.

"We can't be late."

"We won't be," she said. "Formula One cars can go up to two hundred miles per hour."

"Very funny," Brady said, though he did suddenly wear a smile.

Oakley typed faster than she ever had before. One more line.... She hit return and straightened again. "I'm ready." She'd already changed, and the car had been decorated.

After the light parade, she was going up to Shiloh Ridge for an intimate birthday party for Sammy. Apparently, her birthday was on Christmas Eve, but her family never celebrated it then. Her sister had passed away in December, and it was too hard for her parents to deal with much more than that.

Bear had planned a quiet hot chocolate bar with all of Sammy's favorite snacks, and he'd only invited a few people to come. Oakley felt honored to make the cut. If she really married Ranger, she and Sammy would basically be living in the same house, so Oakley needed time to get to know her and her son.

She rode with Brady out to garage five, where he said, "I'll go flip around and wait for you to come out."

"Okay." She got out of the cruiser and unlocked the garage door. The moment it opened, she knew something wasn't right.

Her heart ricocheted around inside her chest as she reached for the light switch. She'd poured over the proposal suggestions since the family gift exchange several days ago, even sending Ranger her favorite ones.

The distinct scent of chocolate hung in the air, and she distinctly remembered telling him there better be chocolate at any proposal he planned.

With the light on, she entered the garage slowly, peeking around the corner before fully committing to entering the space. "Oh, my."

A table had been set up in the garage, right in front of the car she and Ranger had decorated to perfection. She'd come out here yesterday afternoon before leaving work just to make sure all the lights still worked. They had. She was ready for tonight.

On the table, a bright white cloth had been spread, and at least a dozen chocolate desserts filled the space. Ranger emerged from the shadows between the two cars, wearing black pants instead of jeans, a pale blue polo instead of his usual plaid, and that sexy leather jacket that made Oakley's mouth turn to cotton. His cowboy hat perched on his head perfectly, and he hadn't traded out the boots for loafers.

He carried a single red rose, and Oakley reached for the wall to support herself.

"You gonna stay all the way over there?" he asked, smiling. The gesture slid off his face only a moment later, and she recognized his nerves.

Hers told her to move, so she did, entering the garage where the cars were and taking in the desserts again. "These look amazing," she said.

"I did not make a single one," he said. "Heidi Ackerman did, though, and she let me sample them." He came as close as the other side of the table.

Oakley looked up at him, her eyes wide.

"No one suggested I propose in garage five," he said. "Because they don't know about it. But I know about it, and I know the core of who you are resides here, with these cars. I want her. I love her." He took a shaky breath and came around the table.

Oakley turned with him, her eyes already filling with tears. He wanted her. Despite who she was and things she'd done, Ranger Glover wanted her.

"I love you, Oakley," he said, using the table to balance himself as he got on his knees. "Will you marry me?" He extended the rose toward her, and she took it.

She lifted it to her nose and smelled it, the scent of chocolate, grease, and roses now creating the basis of the best memory of her life. Better than winning Grand Championships. Better than multi-million-dollar signing bonuses. Better than a villa in Spain.

She'd hoped and prayed she could find her happily-ever-after in this tiny Texas town, but deep down, she'd never really believed it would happen.

Until the day Ranger had come to the car dealership and told her he wasn't interested in being her lunch date if she had another man taking her to dinner.

She looked past the rose to find Ranger now had a ring box held up toward her, and Oakley definitely saw the lights glinting on all those facets of the diamond.

She pulled in a breath, held it, and said, "Yes. Yes, I'll marry you." She laughed after, bounced on the balls of her feet while he stood, and let him slide the ring on her finger.

He kissed her then, and Oakley let the rose she held fall to the floor as she pushed her fingers through his hair. She'd never kissed her fiancé before, because she'd never had one before.

She told him this, and then kissed him again before suddenly pulling away. "Oh, my goodness. Brady's waiting outside." She was wondering why he hadn't come in.

"We have time," Ranger whispered. "I had him tell you a half an hour before you really need to go." He smiled at her in such a kind, loving way that Oakley couldn't be mad.

"Time enough to have a little dessert," she said, grinning up at him too.

"Exactly," he said, leaning down and kissing her again.

Chapter Twenty-Seven

Ranger sat next to Bear, a sigh pulling from this chest. "Well, she said yes."

"I knew she would." Bear grinned at him as Bishop leaned forward in his chair to see around his brother.

"When's the big day?" he asked.

Ranger cleared his throat, his tough questions for the day not quite done. With Oakley driving her racecar in the parade and Sammy orchestrating a lot of the lights for various vehicles, the Glovers were alone at the light parade.

"I actually wanted to talk to you both about that," Ranger said.

Bear pulled his attention from the street in front of him, where a group of jugglers tossed flashing bowling pins and lit, neon balls. "Shoot.

"Well, you're getting married on March sixteenth, right?"

"Right."

"At the ranch, right?"

"Most likely." Bear looked back to the curb and called, "Link, stay on the grass, bud." He looked at Ranger again. "Probably the ranch, yes."

Ranger looked at Bishop, hoping he wasn't about to blow everything wide open. He'd been doing it a lot lately, so maybe he didn't care. "I know you're renovating the blue barn to be an event hall of sorts. For Bear's wedding. I was thinking...I was hoping...I was—" He cleared his throat and told himself to spit it out.

"I'd like to marry Oakley the same day, in the blue barn with y'all."

Bear looked at Bishop. "We're renovating the blue barn into an event hall? For certain?"

"Yes," Bishop said slowly, his eyes not leaving Ranger's. "How did *you* know that?"

"Ward's my brother," Ranger said. "Oh, and so is Ace. It wasn't that hard."

"I live with Bear, and he didn't know." Bishop narrowed his eyes. "What did you do?"

"I may or may not have provided some data for Ward that he required," Ranger said, keeping things vague. "You don't need to know more than that."

"You've just told my brother about his wedding gift," Bishop said. "I think I need to know more than that."

"This is my wedding gift?" Bear asked.

"Yes," Bishop said, still not looking at him. "Which is why I didn't put it on the agenda for your ranch meetings, and no one knew about it except for me, Ace, Cactus, and Ward." He finally looked at Bear. "That barn is important to our ranch, as Ranger said. I wanted you and Sammy to have an amazing place to get married."

"You want an amazing place to get married too," Bear said.

"Of course," Bishop said.

"I do too," Ranger said. "And I don't want to wait. I don't think the barn will be ready much before the wedding, and I don't want you to be on your honeymoon while I get married. I just figured...we could do it on the same day. It could be two separate ceremonies."

"Let's talk to Sammy after the parade," Bear said. "I don't mind sharing, and I doubt she will either. But we should ask her."

"Sure," Ranger said, looking out into the street where the parade would take place.

The announcer started speaking at that moment, and Ranger was glad, because Bishop was still glaring holes in his face. "We're starting this year off with a roar," he said. "Our leader in the parade this year is none other than World Champion racecar driver, Oakley Hatch."

As if they'd timed it, the roar and growl of the racecar's engine filled the street. Everyone shrieked, laughed, and clapped, and all at once, the lights on Oakley's car burst to life.

Oohs and *ahs* filled the air now, and it was bright enough for Ranger to see the wonder on Lincoln's face as he turned back to Bear.

"Wow," Bear even said. "Look at that."

Oakley's engine rumbled as she inched down the street. Ranger couldn't see her, or really much of her car. They'd arranged the lights on her car according to her exact design, and it looked like a fireplace dripping with lights, stockings, and tinsel. The lights turned on and off according to a timer and made it look like the scene was moving. The stockings were blowing in the wind created by her forward movement, and the tinsel threw back reflections to the crowd.

"Now that's really putting some horsepower in your holiday," the announcer said, and Ranger could only grin, the pride and love filling him from bottom to top overflowing time and time again.

Oakley had wanted to become part of the Three Rivers community, and as she continued down the street, he couldn't imagine a single person who wouldn't want to talk to her about that amazing display and her racecar.

A COUPLE OF HOURS LATER, RANGER TURNED ONTO THE road that led up to the ranch. Finally. Oakley had been swamped after the parade, and it had taken Brady and his police badge to get people to leave her alone so they could leave.

She'd stowed the car back in garage five, given Brady a hug, and climbed into Ranger's truck. She'd been full of excitement and energy, and she'd been talking the whole way to the ranch.

She finally fell silent, and Ranger enjoyed that too. "Will you teach me to drive fast?" he asked.

Her eyes came to his, and she said, "Sure thing, Ranger."

"When do you want to call your parents?" he asked next.

"Tomorrow," she said with a yawn. She'd probably crash after such an adrenaline-filled night. She'd told him once that she often slept the whole day away after a Grand Prix.

"I'm coming to your place tomorrow, right?" he asked. "For breakfast and peace and quiet."

"Right." She smiled at him, and she looked sleepy and sexy in the little light coming from the moon.

He looked away, still one more question on his tongue. Maybe two or three. He wasn't sure.

"When do you want to get married?" he asked. "I mean, how much time do you need?"

"I don't know," she said. "I've never really planned a wedding before."

Ranger shifted in his seat and looked up at the sign announcing their arrival at Shiloh Ridge Ranch. "I had an idea, and I've already asked Bear about it. We need to talk to Sammy, but I don't see the point if you're not on-board."

"All right."

"He and Sammy are getting married on March sixteenth, in what will be the newly renovated event hall in the blue barn. I asked him if we could share the date and time with them. I figured...I don't know. No sense in making everyone dress up twice, and I really don't want to wait very long to have you in the east wing with me, and you said you wouldn't move in until we were—"

"Ranger," she said with a laugh. "Breathe."

He did, foolishness racing through him now. "Okay."

"March sixteenth," she said. "The blue barn." She actually sounded like she was considering it. "I think that's probably going to be just fine. If Sammy says yes, that is."

"We'll ask her tonight," Ranger said. "I'm pretty sure she's already here." He pulled to a stop in front of the homestead and got out of the truck. Oakley waited for him to open her door, and then she slid into his arms.

"How did the car look?" she asked. "Really, Ranger."

"It was stunning," he said. "I'm going to push out the question for the best part of the parade, and you'll see. You'll come in first."

She wrapped her arms around him. "I don't care when we get married, cowboy. I don't care where. I just want it to happen soon, and I just need you there."

He sure did like the way she held onto him as if she needed him. He closed his eyes and put this moment in his memory, hopefully for a good, long while. "I'll be there," he whispered. "I love you, Oakley."

"I love you too," she said.

With that, he kissed her, this time just as magical as the first time on her front porch, the second time under the Shiloh Ridge Ranch arch, and the kiss he'd gotten a few hours ago in garage five.

Way to put some horsepower in your holiday, he thought, and he couldn't wait to make Oakley a Glover.

Read on for the first couple of chapters of the next book in the Shiloh Ridge Ranch in Three Rivers series, **THE CONSTRUCTION OF CHEER, available now**.

Sneak Peek! The Construction of Cheer, Chapter One:

Bishop Glover looked in the mirror and adjusted his bow tie. He'd been praying for a solid month for two things: that the barn would be finished in time for today's weddings, and that the weather would be perfect.

The barn had literally been finished last night when Bishop himself had hung the mirror in the bride's room. As the project had commenced, he'd realized they'd need more than just a huge open space for dancing or eating and a kitchen.

They needed bathrooms. They needed a furnace room. They needed dressing rooms, especially if the barn was going to be used for weddings, which it obviously was.

His cousin had spilled the beans to his brother about the barn project, and Bishop had been annoyed in the beginning. As the construction got started and it outgrew his own vision for it, Bishop had been grateful Bear knew about the barn renovation.

He'd suggested Bishop contact Micah Walker, who'd designed and built the new mansion-like homestead for the family.

Bishop had, and Micah could see way beyond what he could.

So the barn now had bathrooms, dressing rooms, a kitchen, a mudroom, and a control room, where the music and lighting could be programmed or changed with a few taps and presses of a button.

There were two hot water heaters in the barn, an industrial kitchen they'd probably use several times a year, beautiful barn doors that sectioned off the back of the barn for the dressing rooms and bathrooms, and a hardwood floor throughout.

Bishop loved the barn with his whole soul. If he could put a bedroom in the loft, he'd live there.

As it was, the loft was just for show. There was no ladder to get up to it, and it sat above the kitchen and looked pretty with the new posts and pillars Bishop had carved by hand.

In the end, almost everyone—except the two groomsmen for today—who worked on the ranch had put in some labor on the blue barn, which Bishop had affectionately named True Blue.

He'd gone to his mother's and looked through the old photo albums she had, and together, they'd found several picture of his father and his uncle working on the barn. They'd built it with their daddy and a few cowboys who'd worked Shiloh Ridge Ranch at the time.

Bishop had taken the photos and gone to the

genealogical society in Three Rivers. He'd asked for the best way to enlarge them and frame them so the memories wouldn't be lost. A very nice woman there had helped him, and Bishop had hung those pictures last night too.

"Come on," someone said, pounding on his door. "We're going to be late."

"Coming," he yelled as he left the bathroom. He exited his suite to noise coming down the hallway from the living room. Until last week, he'd lived in the west wing of the mansion-slash-homestead, but he and his oldest brother, Bear, had switched places.

Bear was going to be married today, and his wife and step-son were coming to live on the ranch.

Bishop's suite had a large bedroom, a full bath, and a private living area. It was enough for him right now.

His cousin, Ranger, who was also getting married today, already lived in the east wing, and once he and his wife returned from their honeymoon, they'd live upstairs together too.

Bishop looked around at the chaos in the house and thought forward about twelve hours. All of this would be done. The brothers and sisters and cousins and aunts and uncles would all go home. The weddings would be over.

Bishop could order dinner, drive down to Three Rivers to get it, and come sit in a quiet house by himself.

Sort of.

His eyes caught on his only sister as she turned toward someone entering the kitchen. Arizona was coming to stay in the house with Bishop while the two newlywed couples were on their honeymoons, because her house needed to be sprayed for termites.

Mother was going to go stay with her sister-in-law in town, and she had plenty of sons to help get her there and back any time she wanted to come to the ranch.

"It's time to go," Cactus yelled, and he could have a loud voice when he wanted to. He'd really come out of his prickly shell in the past four or five months, though he still hadn't found a woman he wanted to go out with more than twice.

The men and women in the house started to move out, and Bishop joined the flow. They could get almost all the way to True Blue on a road, so most people loaded into vehicles and started rumbling down the gravel lane.

Some people walked.

Bishop caught up to Zona and asked, "Want a ride?"

"I'm going with Duke," she said, looking up at Bishop. "Do you want to ride with us?"

"Sure," Bishop said. He liked Duke Rhinehart just fine, though he knew there was something that had happened with him in the past. Bear didn't seem to mind him, and Bishop tried very hard to only make judgments based on his own personal experiences with someone.

He climbed in the back of Duke's extended cab truck, finding his younger brothers there too. "Howdy, fellas," he said. "You guys lookin' for more work?"

"No, sir," one of them drawled. "Our place keeps us plenty busy."

The other one nodded, his eyes round like Bishop

would force him to come work at Shiloh Ridge after they finished their chores on their own ranch.

"Maybe in the summer," Bishop said, pinning his grin in place. "If y'all have friends who need a job, send 'em up here. We always have more work than we can do ourselves."

"That so?" Duke asked, looking in the rear-view mirror. He'd been waiting for his turn, and he finally eased out onto the road.

"Yes," Bishop said, already tired and summer was still a month or two off.

"I might know some guys."

"We've got seven empty cowboy cabins," Bishop said. "I'm trying to get Bear and Ranger to fill them this year. They'll be busy with their new families, and I'm tired of working fifteen hours a day."

He loved Shiloh Ridge, and he didn't want to be anywhere else. He never had. He'd always seen himself working this generational land that his ancestors had cultivated and loved. He just wanted time to sleep too. Time to date. Time to watch TV. Was that so wrong?

A frown filled his face, and he looked out the window.

In a truck, getting to True Blue only took about five minutes, and Bishop got out with everyone else when they arrived. He noticed Duke coming around to Zona's side and helping her down as she was in a pretty dress the color of evening clouds. Sort of pink, but also sort of peachy, and maybe a little gold. The dress shimmered, and Bishop watched as Zona smiled up at Duke and laced her arm through his.

They made a cute couple, and they'd been dating since just before Christmas.

Bishop himself had been on many dates since Christmas, but nothing seemed to stick. Even with the women he really liked, he couldn't seem to make a relationship launch. Familiar frustration built within him, and he strode inside as a bit of a breeze picked up.

The Lord had heard his prayers about the weather, though he knew he wasn't the only one who'd been praying for such a blessing. The whole Glover family had been, and it certainly seemed like the rain would hold off for a few more hours.

Bishop slowed as he neared the barn. She'd gotten a fresh coat of blue paint, and she gleamed in the sunlight. The doors had been widened, and new ones fashioned and fitted on the tracks. They could lock, but right now, they'd been thrown wide open.

A tall vase of flowers and greenery stood sentinel on either side of the open doors, with a small podium next to one. People paused there to write their names in the two guest books, but Bishop didn't.

The scent of roses blew toward him from inside the barn, and he stepped from dirt to a wide rug that would help clean people's boots and shoes as they transitioned from outdoor to indoor space.

The hardwood stretched beyond that, and the huge serving window Micah had suggested in the kitchen had been rolled up. Trays and plates sat there, and people moved in and out as they got appetizers and snacks before the wedding began.

The altar was immediately to his left, with the rows of chairs filling what could also be a dance floor. The middle aisle ran straight back to another set of hand-planed and hand-stained barn doors. Through those sat the dressing rooms and bathrooms, and the brides and grooms would exit there, walk down the aisle, get married at the front, and be able to walk out the doorway where he stood easily.

It was a genius layout, really. Bishop had gotten them eighty percent of the way there.

"This place is incredible," Ace said, coming to a stop beside Bishop. The two cousins looked at one another and smiled. "I can't wait to get married here."

"Yeah? Are you gonna ask Bea?"

Ace's smile turned a bit mischievous. "You never know." He entered the barn, making a beeline for the kitchen window in the back corner, and Bishop shook his head. He knew what *you never know* meant.

It meant no.

Ace was currently dating Beatrice Gates, but he was really smitten with another woman.

Soft music played from the speakers high above the floor, and Bishop had installed those himself too. He could lean his head back and find them easily, though neither Ranger nor Bear had been able to spot more than one or two.

"Afternoon, Bishop."

He turned toward the male voice and found Pastor Summers. "Heya," he said, smiling and extending his hand to shake the pastor's. "Mrs. Summers. Good to see you." He shook her hand too.

"This is beautiful," she said, gazing around. She had blonde hair that had started to lose its color, and eyes the same as all the Glovers: blue. She had a kind soul, and Bishop had literally never seen the woman upset. "Are y'all renting it out?"

"I don't think so," Bishop said.

Her eyes came to his. "Our daughter would *love* to get married here. Don't you think, Curtis?"

"Hmm, probably," Pastor Summers said.

Mrs. Summers looked at Bishop again. "We need to talk some more."

"Okay," Bishop said, but he wasn't sure why she was talking to him. He was the youngest male in the family, and he literally had no say about how things were run on the ranch. Sure, sometimes Ranger and Bear sent emails or texts about big purchases or major projects, just to get feedback from everyone. In the end, though, they got to decide what happened at Shiloh Ridge.

"Excuse me," a woman said into the microphone. "It's time to take your seats, if you would, please. Our first bride will be coming down the aisle in only ten short minutes."

Bishop did what his cousin said to do, his seat decidedly up front. Both Bear and Ranger had opted for a wedding party in pictures only. Only the brides would be escorted down the aisle to meet their waiting groom. The wedding party would stand at the front for a moment, and then sit in the first couple of rows.

He got a fancy flower for his lapel too. He supposed that counted for something.

Bishop took his spot at the end of the row for his

family, his four older brothers and Zona already there. The only one missing was Bear.

And Daddy, Bishop thought, a momentary pang of sadness gonging against his heart. He'd only been eighteen years old when his father had died, and Bishop sometimes felt like he had no idea how to be a man because his daddy hadn't been there when he'd become one.

He swallowed against the emotions and looked to the other side of the aisle. Samantha Benton's family sat over there, but it was just her mother and a few friends. Her father and her son would be walking her down the aisle to Bear.

Sammy owned the mechanic shop in town, and all of her mechanics and their families had come. Bishop liked seeing them there, as they sure did feel like family for Sammy.

The music paused, and the very air itself seemed to pause. Then, a new song started, and the crowd got to its feet as Bear pushed open the barn doors at the back of the hall. He beamed out at the crowd, his face softening even more as he cocked his elbow for Mother to put her hand on.

They walked down the aisle together, and Bishop could not stop grinning. Once they'd reached the altar, Mother straightened Bear's tie and hugged him tight. His siblings surged forward, all of them seeming to step at the same time.

Bear chuckled as they did a group hug for him, and then they stepped back to their places, Cactus holding onto Mother now.

The music paused again, and Bishop spun toward the open doors. Sammy appeared, her dress simple and elegant. It hugged her close to the hip, and then flared into a traditional wedding dress shape. Her train was long, and her son helped her fan it out behind her.

Then Lincoln disappeared again, and when he returned, he held onto his grandfather, who limped and wobbled on his feet. He managed to get to Sammy, who secured her hand in his, a wide smile on her face.

Lincoln moved to her other side, and then the three of them marched down the aisle. Bishop reveled in the reverence and spirit in the barn, a sense of family and love so permeating he felt himself start to choke up a little.

Pastor Summers could really get going during some of his sermons, but today, he kept the ceremony simple and to the point. He spoke of love and forgiveness, and, "Most of all," he said. "Be willing to talk to one another. Don't be afraid to tell your partner how you feel. Most issues can be resolved through proper communication."

Bishop thought about his failed relationships. Maybe that was what he'd been doing wrong. Not saying what he should say.

"Bartholomew Stone Glover, do you take Samantha Eden Benton to be your lawfully wedded wife, to love, to cherish, and to weather life's storms with?"

"Yes, sir," Bear said, causing a few twitters among the crowd.

Pastor Summers smiled at him and switched his gaze to Sammy. "Samantha Eden Benton, do you give yourself to Bear, and taken him unto yourself, to be your lawfully wedded husband, to love, to cherish, and to weather life's storms with?"

"Yes," Sammy said.

"I now pronounce you man and wife," the pastor said, and Bear turned toward Sammy. He dipped her down as cheers erupted, and they kissed. Bear lifted her up, and they faced the crowd.

Bear stepped over to Mother and hugged her while Sammy separated from him and went to her mom. Once another round of congratulations had finished, Bear and Sammy took their places in the audience.

The music paused. Ranger appeared in the doorway, and he wore a darker suit, a darker cowboy hat, and plenty of joy on his face. Bishop loved his cousin almost as much as his brother, and he let himself get lost in the happiness pouring from him.

Ranger walked down the aisle himself, kissed his mother on the cheek, and took his spot at the altar.

His bride, Oakley Hatch, appeared in the doorway too, and she also did not have an escort. Bishop glanced at Ace, who frowned. "I thought her father was coming," Bishop whispered.

"Me too," Ace said, looking at Ward. He too wore a concerned look, and they all turned to look at Ranger.

Bishop wanted to race to the back of the barn and offer his arm to Oakley. *Should I?* he wondered.

He didn't feel like he shouldn't, so he nudged Ace. "Let's go. Get Ward." With that, he turned and went down the aisle on the outside of the chairs. He didn't care who saw him or what they thought. He was not letting Oakley walk down that aisle by herself.

She took the first step, and Bishop raised his hand. She caught sight of him coming toward her, and her eyes widened. Bishop arrived a moment later and offered his arm to her.

"Bishop," she said, her voice breaking.

"If you hate me for doing this, I'll go back to my seat," he whispered.

She shook her head, and then Ace crossed in front of them and took Oakley's other arm. Ward joined them, stepping behind Oakley and putting his hand on her shoulder.

Bishop looked up to the altar, where Ranger stood. He'd come forward a few steps and waited beside the first row of chairs.

All of the chairs were empty, because every Glover had followed Bishop. They foamed around Oakley now, who let out one sob and turned around.

Bishop looked at Ace, and they quickly stepped into the aisle to shield her from all the guests. Ward leaned down and said something to Oakley, and she nodded. He smiled at her, and Oakley handed her flowers to Zona and took a moment to wipe her eyes. Ida and Etta fretted over her for another few seconds, and then they nodded their approval.

Oakley took her flowers, took a giant breath that seemed to fill her whole body, and turned around.

Guilt tripped through Bishop. He should've stayed at his seat. He'd made her cry. "I'm sorry," he whispered.

"Don't be." She reached for him, and he and Ace took their positions on either side of her. The entire family walked down the aisle with Oakley, and they all gave her to Ranger. Really, they were giving Ranger to her, and Bishop actually thought it was a beautiful moment.

Another simple speech, and with less theatrics, Ranger kissed his new wife amidst the same loud cheering that Bear and Sammy had received.

Bishop drew in a deep breath and admired the men in his life he'd always looked up to. He sure did hope he could find someone as amazing as Sammy or Oakley, and he took a moment to close his eyes and offer up a simple prayer.

Thank you for showing me what true love is.

BISHOP GOT HIS QUIET SOLITUDE THAT EVENING. THE next day too, as it was the Sabbath, and everyone seemed exhausted from the previous day's events.

On Monday morning, Bishop had just set the coffee to brew when the doorbell rang. He whipped his attention that way, wondering who in the world would be out this way this early. Arizona hadn't gotten up yet, and if it was anyone else, they'd have just come in the house.

Bishop wasn't worried as he padded through the enormous kitchen, under the wide, arched doorway, and into the foyer. He pulled open the door to find a beautiful blonde woman standing there.

His mind said hello, but his voice stayed mute. He could only stare at her, taking her in piece by piece.

Pretty face, with plenty of personality in those vibrant blue eyes. She wore a black jacket over her shirt, which looked to be pink, red, and white plaid. She wore jeans and work boots, but the thing that caught Bishop's attention the most was the tool belt strapped around her waist.

His mouth turned dry.

She was an angel straight from heaven, crafted just for Bishop Glover.

"Good mornin'," she drawled, but he could tell instantly she wasn't from Texas. *Doesn't matter*, he thought. *It's a minor negative. Very minor.*

He still couldn't get his voice to work, and the woman slid her eyes down his chest, immediately bringing her gaze back to his. "Uh...I'm Montana Martin, and I'm wondering if you have any need for an extra hand with any construction projects. I have a certification in cabinetry, as well as a decade of experience with one of the biggest builders in San Antonio."

Bishop nodded, his vocal cords unknotting. Finally. "I could've used you three months ago," he said.

"Oh." Montana's face fell. "You're all caught up now?"

With the cabin remodels, the whole barn renovation, and the Ranch House set to get work done too, Bishop had hired multiple temporary workers to get the jobs done.

"We're never caught up," he said, curling his fingers over the top of the door and leaning into the frame. "I'm sure I can find something for you to do."

And if he couldn't, he'd invent something. Maybe a new chicken coop needed to be built. No matter what, he needed to keep Montana nearby so he could get to know her better.

Montana's face burst into a smile, and it dang near made Bishop groan. She was stunning, the morning light streaking toward her across the front porch. When it touched her, she'd light up like a flame, and Bishop really wanted to see that.

"Do you have a minute to talk?" he asked. "I don't have to be out on the ranch for a bit."

Montana swallowed and nodded, her fingers tightening around that sexy tool belt. "Do you live alone?"

"No, ma'am," he said. "My sister's here with me. I'll get her to come down." He was a proper gentleman, after all.

Montana relaxed, her hand releasing the tool belt, and she nodded. "Okay. I can stay for a few minutes. Could you, uh, maybe put on a shirt?"

Bishop's eyes widened. Horrified, he looked down at himself. Sure enough, his torso was bare, and a bomb of heat exploded through his body. Still, he thought he sounded pretty cool when he said, "Sure. C'mon in and help yourself to a cup of coffee while I get dressed."

Sneak Peek! The Construction of Cheer, Chapter Two:

Montana Martin entered the house after the tall, muscled man, realizing she hadn't gotten his name. She knew where she'd come though, and she knew the Glover family owned Shiloh Ridge. She didn't know all of their names, or even if they all lived here. She'd come to the first and biggest house on the ranch, assuming she'd get the owner.

She couldn't believe she'd made it through the front door. None of her other solicitations at other ranches had earned her more than a, "Sorry, we've got all the help we need," and a sympathetic smile.

Everyone in Texas sure was polite, she'd give them that.

She looked around the house, taking in the enormity of it. The ceiling here in the foyer stretched for two stories. The work on the banister leading up the double-wide stairs was custom and hand-made. Montana frowned at it, because she recognized the superior craftsmanship.

"Micah Walker," she muttered under her breath. The man had opened his custom home construction business at literally the same time Montana had. He had more money and more charisma, and his business had taken off while hers had whimpered in the darkness.

The only reason she'd survived for the past couple of years was because of her aunt and uncle's generosity and kindness. She'd had a job with a construction firm that had finished their subdivision three months ago, and Montana still hadn't found consistent full-time work.

The building boom in Three Rivers seemed to be slowing down a little, but she didn't want to leave town. She liked the stability she'd earned here, and she wanted to maintain some level of that for herself and her daughter.

Things had started to pick up in the past couple of months since she'd landed on a list in the Two Cents app, and Montana had been using that during some of her pitches.

What are you doing here? she wondered as she looked at the carved name above the doorway that led deeper into the house. Everything about this place screamed wealth, that was what she was doing there.

She needed a job, plain and simple.

It had taken her thirty-five minutes to get here from her aunt's house on the east side of town, and that was way too far to drive every day. Aurora was still in school, but Montana liked to be home when her daughter got off the bus.

She'd basically be able to work half-days with a commute as far as this one.

He's the first person who's let you in, she thought, quickly changing her internal dialog into a prayer. *Please, Lord, help this to work out. I need this job.*

"I said you could come in."

She turned toward the man, who now wore jeans instead of gym shorts, a black and white shirt with plenty of checkers on it, and a deliciously black cowboy hat. "I was jut taking in the beauty of this place," she said. "It can't be very old."

"A little over a year," he said, looking up at the ceiling and walls too.

"Micah Walker did it, didn't he?" Montana watched the man.

He smiled, which only made her want to roll her eyes. "He sure did." He met her gaze again. "Do you know Micah?"

"Doesn't everyone?" she asked, realizing too late how bitter she sounded.

He didn't seem to notice though. His smile stayed hitched in place, and he stared at her in a way that almost had her walking right back out the front door, job or not. He blinked, and Montana saw a hint of redness creep up his neck.

"Sorry," he said with a low chuckle. "I'm not properly caffeinated. Come in, come in." He turned and went into the kitchen, and Montana decided to follow him.

"I'm Bishop, by the way," he said. "I realize I never even told you that." He stood in the biggest kitchen Montana had ever seen. The house seemed to go on and on, and the massive dining table against the far wall intrigued her.

The living room held four couches and three more loveseats, a huge flatscreen TV, and even a couple of beanbags. She half-expected a little black dog to come trotting up to greet her, because she'd entered a fairytale where all dreams came true.

Her daughter really wanted a little black dog, and that would've been heaven for Aurora.

"Coffee?" Bishop appeared in front of her, a mug extended toward her. "I'll get the cream out. Sugar is on the counter there."

"Thanks," she said, taking the mug. She didn't know where to look next, and she took a sip of the coffee. It was mighty good too, even without sugar. She still stepped over to the counter and spooned in the good stuff. She sighed as she sat at the bar and watched Bishop doctor up a cup of coffee for himself.

He turned, his face already beaming, and walked over to her. "What's your schedule like?" he asked.

"I'm pretty open," she said, glancing at him. "I have a small job at the college to finish up, and then I'm all yours." She realized what she'd said and pressed her eyes closed.

"Hmm, I like the sound of that," Bishop said.

Montana's eyes flew open, and she faced him. "What?"

"Nothing," he said, lifting his cup to his mouth. He sipped and asked, "Where else have you worked? Do you have a general contractor's license? Business insurance? That kind of stuff?"

"Yes," Montana said. She went on to detail her latest job with Liberty Homes. "I do have a general contractor's license, and I'm a master carpenter." She watched his eyebrows go up. "I can do anything you need me to on your ranch, Bishop. Sir."

He burst out laughing. "You do not need to call me sir," he said. "And I'm—"

"Bishop," a woman called, and a moment later, she came running into the kitchen. "Have you seen that blasted lizard? Link says it's not in his room, and he swears it was last night when he went to bed."

"Haven't seen 'im," Bishop said, clearly unconcerned about the lizard. "Are you taking Link to school today?"

"Yes," the woman said, and Montana ducked her head as she realized she'd met this woman before—and not under good circumstances.

"My sister," Bishop said. "Arizona." His face lit up, and he got to his feet. "Hey, you guys both have state names." He looked from his sister to Montana and back.

Arizona finally noticed her, and Montana decided to simply stare back. If she was going to work here—and she hoped and prayed she was—she'd have to deal with the woman. If only she'd known she was a Glover.

"This is Montana," Bishop said, indicating her. "She's gonna work around the ranch for us."

"Us?" Montana asked at the same time Arizona scoffed and then started laughing.

"Right," she said as she moved into the kitchen and started pouring herself a cup of coffee. "I don't think so."

"No?" Bishop asked, clearly confused.

Arizona turned around and took a long drink of her black coffee, her eyes never leaving Montana. She finally ducked her head, because she couldn't withstand the loathing coming from Arizona.

"No," Arizona said. "She's not."

"Why not?" Bishop asked.

"I wasn't hitting on him," Montana said at the same time Arizona took a breath in.

"She hit on Duke right in front of me."

"No," Montana said again. "You just blew it all out of proportion."

"I did not," Arizona said. "You came right over to our table and asked him to dance as if I wasn't even there."

"I just wanted to ask him about a job." Montana flicked her eyes in Bishop's direction. She didn't need to be right here. She could let this go. "*He* asked me to dance. I said yes."

"Why would he do that?" Arizona asked, throwing her hands into the air. "It makes no sense."

Montana could see the situation from her point of view, and Arizona was right. Duke Rhinehart's behavior last week made no sense. "I don't know." She glanced at Bishop, who now wore confusion in the slant of his eyebrows. He seemed to be made of light on dark, and Montana sure did like the golden color of his skin, the way his hair was brown, yet also highlighted with blonde. He had light blue eyes the color of the flowers she'd had in her first wedding bouquet, and as she'd already seen him with his shirt off, she knew the man had muscles in all the right places.

His strong jaw reminded her of her brother's, though her feelings for Bishop weren't anything brotherly at all.

She looked away from him when she realized she even had feelings for him.

She didn't know if she should sit back down or leave. They hadn't agreed on a wage, nor had Bishop invited her back to his ranch so she could look at the projects they were doing. Montana clenched her jaw and held her ground.

"I apprenticed for Marion Thurgate," she said. "I don't know if you know him, but he's—"

"Only the best woodworker in the state," Bishop said, his charm and charisma returning in a single heartbeat.

Montana couldn't help the beam of sunshine that shone through her body too. She smiled at him. "I think so too. I worked with him for four years."

"Where are you from?" he asked.

"Alabama originally," she said. "But I've been in Texas for a while now. Fifteen or sixteen years."

"Alabama," Arizona said. "Fifteen. Sixteen. It doesn't matter." She glared at Montana and then Bishop. "You're not hiring her. What is she going to do anyway?"

"We've got cabins and the Ranch House," Bishop said easily. He barely looked at Arizona and her animosity toward Montana only seemed to bother the two of them.

"Bear will never approve another full-time carpenter," Arizona said.

"Bear's on his honeymoon," Bishop said coolly. He looked at Montana again. "What's your rate?"

"I—"

"You can't just hire her," Arizona said, a hint of desperation in her voice now.

Montana kept her head down, a healthy dose of embarrassment making her feel too hot. The barstool was way too hard. She should leave.

"I can," Bishop said.

"You don't own the ranch."

Montana looked up then. "You don't own the ranch?"

Arizona burst out laughing, and Bishop blinked a couple of times. "No," he said. "I never said I owned the ranch."

"Yeah, but you made me think you did." Montana got up, tired of these games already. She'd never survive out here. "Sorry to waste your time." She started for the foyer, saying, "I'm sorry, Arizona. I was not hitting on your boyfriend, and I apologize that you thought I was."

Her momma had taught her that it wasn't always easy to apologize, but always worth it. Not only that, but she could do so even if she didn't think she'd done anything wrong.

"Wait," Bishop said, jumping to his feet too. He followed her into the foyer, saying, "I have full authority to hire for my construction teams. I don't need to own the ranch to give you a job."

Montana took a deep breath and faced him. "What do you pay?"

"Tell me what you charge."

She folded her arms. "Depending on the project, of course, but I typically earn one-fifty per day if I'm working on a project you have going. If I'm designing and building custom pieces, it doubles."

"I can do that," he said without breathing or blinking.

Montana's eyebrows went up, but she didn't challenge him. No sense in that, when the man had agreed to her fees so readily. "My schedule is pretty crazy," she said.

"You just said it was wide open after this small job at the college."

"Yeah." Montana shifted her feet. "I may need to go back and forth a little. Don't worry, Mister Glover. I can get the whatever needs to be done, done. It just might not be during conventional work hours."

He cocked his head and studied her, and wow, Montana had the sudden urge to flirt with him.

"Explain that," he said.

She'd really rather not. She'd rather have her name signed in ink on a contract before she told him about Aurora. But he wasn't going to budge an inch, and the scent of Arizona's dislike of her hung heavy in the air too.

Before she could speak, Arizona called from the kitchen. "Stop flirting with her and come talk to me about this note Sammy left for Lincoln."

"I'm not flirting," Bishop called without removing his eyes from Montana's.

"We need to find that lizard too," Arizona said. "I'm not sleeping in this house with that thing on the loose."

"I'm hiring a construction team member," Bishop said, as if having two different conversations with his sister was normal.

Montana could not *believe* Arizona was his sister. What rotten luck.

"I am gonna need your number," Bishop said, a smile

gliding across his face. "I'll call you, and we'll work out the details of the contract. Okay?"

Montana nodded, reached into one of the pockets on her tool belt, and pulled out a business card. "That's my cell and my business number."

He took the card but didn't look at it. "You're going to have to tell me about your unconventional hours."

"All right."

"Maybe over dinner tonight?" He grinned at her and leaned closer. "Maybe I am flirting a little now."

Montana's eyes opened wider in surprise. It had been a while since a man had flirted with her, but she was glad she still recognized it. Of course, he'd come right out and *said* it, and Bishop Glover was unlike any man she'd ever met before.

"I have to ask my—" Thankfully, she managed to mute her voice before she could say "aunt." She wasn't twelve years old. She didn't need permission to go to dinner with a handsome cowboy.

"Assistant," she said, filling in the blank. "See what my schedule is."

"Oh, I see," he said, taking a step closer. "You'll have your people call my people, is that it?"

Montana had no idea how to respond. She looked at him, and he finally chuckled and shook his head. "You're a tough nut to crack, Montana. I like that."

He did? What exactly did he like?

"I'll call you later, okay? Check with your assistant so we can set something up."

"I knew you were asking her out," Arizona said,

appearing at his side. "Can you stop it already? I need help with that note. None of it makes sense." She gave a final glare to Montana and went back into the kitchen.

Montana turned and reached for the door, but Bishop jumped between her and it. He opened the door for her, and Montana's pulse spun cartwheels through her chest. "Okay, thanks," she said, finally getting her voice to work.

"See you soon," he said, and Montana walked away from the huge homestead, her blood running a little warmer in her veins and her head spinning a little bit.

As she drove away from Shiloh Ridge Ranch, she wasn't sure if she'd gotten a job or a date.

"Or both," she said to herself, seizing onto the idea of that and liking it very, very much.

Now she just had to wait for Bishop to call.

Read THE CONSTRUCTION OF CHEER now, available in Kindle Unlimited.

The Mechanics of Mistletoe (Book 1): Bear Glover can be a grizzly or a teddy, and he's always thought he'd be just fine working his generational family ranch and going back to the ancient homestead alone. But his crush on Samantha Benton won't go away. She's a genius with a wrench on Bear's tractors...and his heart. Can he tame his wild side and get the girl, or will he be left broken-hearted this Christmas season?

The Horsepower of the Holiday (Book 2): Ranger Glover has worked at Shiloh Ridge Ranch his entire life. The cowboys do everything from horseback there, but when he goes to town to trade in some trucks, somehow Oakley Hatch persuades him to take some ATVs back to the ranch. (Bear is NOT happy.)

She's a former race car driver who's got Ranger all revved up... Can he remember who he is and get Oakley to slow down enough to fall in love, or will there simply be too much horsepower in the holiday this year for a real relationship?

The Construction of Cheer (Book 3): Bishop Glover is the youngest brother, and he usually keeps his head down and gets the job done. When Montana Martin shows up at Shiloh Ridge Ranch looking for work, he finds himself inventing construction projects that need doing just to keep her coming around. (Again, Bear is NOT happy.) She wants to build her own construction firm, but she ends up carving a place for herself inside Bishop's heart. Can he convince her *he's* all she needs this Christmas season, or will her cheer rest solely on the success of her business?

The Secret of Santa (Book 4): He's a fun-loving cowboy with a heart of gold. She's the woman who keeps putting him on hold. Can Ace and Holly Ann make a relationship work this Christmas?

The Harmony of Holly (Book 5): He's as prickly as his name, but the new woman in town has caught his eye. Can Cactus shelve his temper and shed his cowboy hermit skin fast enough to make a relationship with Willa work?

The Chemistry of Christmas (Book 6): He's the black sheep of the family, and she's a chemist who understands formulas, not emotions. Can Preacher and Charlie take their quirks and turn them into a strong relationship this Christmas?

The Delivery of Decor (Book 7): When he falls, he falls hard and deep. She literally drives away from every relationship she's ever had. Can Ward somehow get Dot to stay this Christmas?

The Blessing of Babies (Book 8): Don't miss out on a single moment of the Glover family saga in this bridge story linking Ward and Judge's love stories!

The Glovers love God, country, dogs, horses, and family. Not necessarily in that order. ;)

Many of them are married now, with babies on the way, and there are lessons to be learned, forgiveness to be had and given, and new names coming to the family tree in southern Three Rivers!

The Networking of the Nativity (Book 9): He's had a crush on her for years. She doesn't want to date until her daughter is out of the house. Will June take a change on Judge when the success of his Christmas light display depends on her networking abilities?

The Wrangling of the Wreath (Book 10): He's been so busy trying to find Miss Right. She's been right in front of him the whole time. This Christmas, can Mister and Libby take their relationship out of the best friend zone?

The Hope of Her Heart (Book 11): She's the only Glover without a significant other. He's been searching for someone who can love him *and* his daughter. Can Etta and August make a meaningful connection this Christmas?

About Liz

Liz Isaacson writes inspirational romance, usually set in Texas, or Montana, or anywhere else horses and cowboys exist. She lives in Utah, where she writes full-time, drives her daughter to her acting classes, and eats a lot of peanut butter M&Ms while writing. Find her on her website at lizisaacson.com.

Made in the USA
Las Vegas, NV
23 October 2022

57998547R00226